SOMETHING TO WITCH ABOUT

A WICKED WITCHES OF THE MIDWEST MYSTERY BOOK FIVE

AMANDA M. LEE

WINCHESTERSHAW PUBLICATIONS

Copyright © 2014 by Amanda M. Lee

All rights reserved.

No part of this book may be reproduced in any form or by any electronic or mechanical means, including information storage and retrieval systems, without written permission from the author, except for the use of brief quotations in a book review.

❈ Created with Vellum

PROLOGUE

*I*t's happening again.

No matter how many times she'd told herself the previous time would be the last time, it never was. She never truly learned her lesson, and she hated herself for it.

She hated herself for taking it. And, even more, she hated herself for the love she still felt for him despite the way he treated her. Yes, the flashes of love were rare now, but they still ignited. Love doesn't disappear; it's misplaced until it can be discovered again.

The door of the house – more of a shack, really – flew open, causing the entire structure to shake.

She didn't see him, but she knew. She pictured his hateful glare even now. And his hands, those hands that had joined with hers five years before in front of a priest as they declared themselves to one another forever, would be clenched at his sides until he decided he was ready to hammer them into her body.

"Where are you?"

He was in the living room, leaving just one thin wall separating them as she worked on his dinner at the stove. She knew he was drunk, the telltale slur of his speech echoing through the house.

He was always drunk nowadays. That was the problem. Alcohol

turned her husband from the loving man she'd married into the monster she lived with today. That's what she told herself, anyway.

If he would just stop drinking … if he would just let go of the demon of alcohol … then things would be better. They would go back to the way things used to be. They would be happy again.

She'd talked to him about it, of course, but he refused to listen. He accused her of nagging. When she wasn't nagging, she was failing to perform the household duties to his expectations. There wasn't a crumb on the floor, a speck of dust on the shelves, yet she was a failure.

"Don't make me come looking for you!"

She sighed, wiping her hands with a nearby towel. She could flee out the back door, she told herself. She could run and hide in the woods behind the house. He would pass out eventually. He always did.

She could run and hide at a friend's home. They all knew. They'd tried to get her to leave him, offering her places to stay and support for the rough road ahead. She could spend the night elsewhere and return in the morning. It was the smartest thing to do, and yet she still wasn't sure.

He'd wake up with a hangover, sure, but he usually didn't beat her because he was feeling poorly. He saved that for when he was drunk – and he was invariably quick with an apology the next day, promising it wouldn't happen again.

It always did, though.

Her moment of indecision cost her. He was standing in the archway between the two rooms now, his icy blue eyes fixed on her drawn face. His face, which was no longer handsome or distinguished, was flushed from the whiskey she knew he'd been drinking down at Wayne's Tavern.

"What are you doing in here?"

"Cooking dinner," she said, being careful to keep the counter island between them. If she was quick, she'd be able to bolt out the back door. He wouldn't have the coordination to follow her once she hit the woods.

"Why didn't you come when I called you?"

"I didn't hear you," she lied, taking another step backward.

His eyes narrowed as he regarded her. "You didn't hear me? Bullshit!"

She bit her lower lip. "Why don't you have a seat at the table," she suggested. "I'll get you a cup of coffee and you can have some dinner. You'll feel better after some dinner."

She knew reasoning with him was a mistake but she still tried.

"I feel fine," he said. "I feel fabulous."

She wrung her hands, letting her eyes dart from him to the back door only a few feet away. She could make it. "I'm glad."

"Well, I felt fabulous until I came home and found you cooking this slop again," he said, striding to the island and flicking the handle of the pot so it tipped, spilling the soup into a puddle on the stove top. There was a loud crackle as liquid met open flame.

"I'm sorry," she said. "What would you like me to cook?"

"I don't want anything you're going to cook," he sneered. "You're a terrible cook – and a terrible wife. Ma told me you would be, but I didn't listen. I should've listened to her."

She wished she'd listened to her mother, too. Her mother had told her that marrying this man was a mistake – that he'd never amount to anything. She'd been blinded by love, though, and she'd thought that love would be enough to get them through.

She'd been wrong.

"If you don't want dinner, why don't you go and turn on a game or something," she said, keeping her voice even. If she cried, that only made him angrier. If she yelled, that fired him up further. The only way to fight him was with surrender, and a tactic she'd mastered these past few years.

"Don't tell me what to do!"

"I'm not telling you what to do," she replied. "I just thought … ."

"You don't think," he interrupted. "You never think. You're stupid."

She was stupid. Why hadn't she run when she'd first heard his voice? Why was she still here? She took another step toward the door. One more and she'd be able to escape.

He knew what she was doing. "Where do you think you're going?"

"Just out to the woodpile," she hedged. "I need to get some wood for the fireplace."

"That's a man's job," he said. "A man should do it."

"Then why don't you do it?" She practically exploded, knowing instantly that any chance of talking him out of the beating had evaporated.

His brow furrowed. "What are you saying? Are you saying I don't pull my weight around here? That I'm lazy?"

She hadn't said it, but she'd been thinking it. "No."

He staggered around the island, bumping into it twice as he closed the distance between them. "That's exactly what you were saying," he seethed. "You think you'd have anything if it weren't for me? You think you'd be able to cook your disgusting slop if I didn't put a roof over your head?"

He'd been unemployed for two months. She'd been living off the kindness of her friends and their gardens. That's why she'd been making soup so often. She didn't say that, though. "You're a good provider."

"Damn right," he agreed. "You're an awful wife, though."

He was practically on her now. She knew there was no escape.

"Please," she gasped, tears spilling down her cheeks. "Please don't hurt me."

"I'm not going to hurt you," he replied. "I'm just going to teach you a lesson. You obviously need one."

The realization came too late. This was going to be the last time he ever beat her after all.

ONE

"This was a terrible idea."

Sitting at the counter munching on a cookie, Thistle looked nonplussed as she rolled her eyes in my direction. "You're being dramatic."

I was being dramatic. That didn't mean this wasn't a terrible idea. "They're going to hate me."

"What's not to hate?" Thistle teased, checking out her newly blued hair in the mirror on the back wall.

"Why did you go back to the blue?" Clove asked from the other side of the counter, eyeing our cousin curiously.

"Because my mom told me that she didn't care what color my hair was as long as it wasn't blue again," Thistle replied. "Of course I had to dye it blue again. She was practically begging for it."

Of course.

"Twila is going to freak when she sees it," Clove said. "I hope that's the reaction you're going for."

"It is."

"Then I guess you'll be happy," Clove said, shrugging.

"I plan on it."

I love my cousins – I really do – but I might have to murder them both in their sleep if they don't shut up. "Can we focus on me?"

Thistle turned from her reflection and fixed me with a sympathetic smile. "It's going to be okay, Bay."

"How is it going to be okay?"

Thistle shrugged, smoothing down her crinkly, gray tank top. "It just is."

"You don't know that," I said.

"No," Thistle agreed. "I don't think freaking out about it is going to do any good, though."

Clove sighed, moving to my side. "Why don't you tell me what's got you so worked up."

"Well, for starters, Landon's family is going to be here any minute," I said.

"We know. We've been hearing about it for two weeks," Thistle complained. "It's getting tiresome."

I ignored her. "They're going to be staying here for a week," I said. "That's seven whole days."

"This is an inn," Thistle said. "Guests stay here all the time."

I shot her a withering look. "Yes, but these guests are … different."

"Why?"

"Because they're Landon's family," Clove answered. "She wants them to like her."

"That's not it," I scoffed. That's totally it. Mothers don't like me. They take one look at my wacky family and they run screaming in the other direction. There was no way this woman was going to like me. I just knew it.

"Bay's scared of Landon's mom," Thistle sang out. "I never thought I'd see the day."

I wanted to smack her – or drag her out into the backyard and make her eat dirt, at least – until she shut her mouth. I knew that wouldn't be a good first impression, though.

"I am not afraid of his mother," I said, choosing my words carefully. "I'm afraid that his mother – or any member of his family, for that matter – is going to figure out what we are."

"You think they're going to guess we're witches?" Thistle asked. "I don't see how. They know the town has been magically rebranded, and we can use that to explain away any accidents. As long as no one is casting any spells for the next seven days, you should be fine."

I scrunched up my nose. "And while I know that's not a problem for the three of us – and even our mothers – there is someone else in this family who is going to have a problem with it."

Thistle chuckled. "Aunt Tillie wouldn't risk exposure."

I tilted my head to the side. "Really?"

Thistle thought about it again. "We'll just have to keep a close eye on her."

"We always try to keep a close eye on her," Clove said. "How well has that worked for us in the past?"

"Well … ."

"Remember when she poisoned everyone at the senior center because she thought they were cheating at euchre?" I reminded her.

"Technically that just makes her a poor loser," Thistle replied. "As far as anyone knows she didn't use anything witchy to do that."

"What about when she cursed Eli Patton with a foot fungus that spread to his … um … private parts," Clove said. "He swears they turned green and almost fell off."

"That could've been a coincidence."

"How about the time she didn't like where the gazebo was downtown and she magically moved it so it was in the police station parking lot?" I asked.

"Hey, we convinced people that was a tornado," Thistle shot back. "Don't bring that up again."

"What are we talking about?"

I glanced up as Aunt Marnie entered the room. She seemed in a good mood, if her wide smile was any indication. She'd even touched up her roots the night before, so now her hair color more closely matched that of her daughter, Clove.

"Bay is scared of Landon's mother," Thistle said.

"I'm not afraid!"

Marnie patted my arm. "It will be fine, dear. The boy is besotted with you. His family will love you, too."

"What about Aunt Tillie?" I pressed.

"Well, they'll learn to tolerate her," Marnie said.

"Great," I grumbled.

"We've already warned her," Marnie said. "If she does anything … untoward … we've threatened to take her greenhouse away."

"They're out there doing construction right now," I argued, gesturing toward the back of the inn. "That's not a very good threat. She knows you won't stick to it."

"Besides," Thistle interjected. "You gave her that greenhouse to stop her from terrorizing the neighborhood when you took away her wine closet. You won't give in now and take it from her because that will just send her on another rampage – and no one wants that."

"We might take it away," Marnie argued.

"You won't," Clove said, reaching for a carrot stick from the hors d'oeuvres tray in front of her.

Marnie smacked her hand. "Those are for Landon's family."

"There's a whole plate of them," Clove protested. "I'm hungry."

"You'll live."

"I think Aunt Tillie is going to surprise us," Thistle said. "I think she's going to be an angel."

Suspicion niggled the back of my brain. "Since when are you Aunt Tillie's biggest fan? You're usually the one plotting against her."

"And look where that's gotten me," Thistle replied. "I don't want any more zits. I don't want any more pants that don't fit. I certainly don't want to smell like bacon again. I would like to make it through an entire week without her cursing me."

"So, you're going to be nice to her?" That didn't sound like Thistle at all.

"I'm going to kill her with kindness."

Yeah, that wouldn't last. "Well, great. Maybe if we all kill her with kindness she'll be on her best behavior."

"Or die." Thistle looked hopeful.

"She'd better be on her best behavior," Marnie said. "We had a long talk with her last night. We explained how important this was to you. She seemed to understand."

"It's not important to me," I sniffed. "I'm not nervous."

"Of course you're nervous," Marnie countered. "You're meeting your boyfriend's family. That's always nerve-wracking."

"I'm not nervous." I said the words but they were hollow, even to my own ears.

Thistle gave me a knowing look. "You should take a page out of my book," she said. "I wasn't nervous when I met Marcus' mother."

Marcus was Thistle's boyfriend. They'd been together for the past year. While Marcus hadn't always lived in Hemlock Cove, his mother had. "That's not fair," I said. "You've known Marcus' mother your entire life. It's not the same thing."

"It is, too."

"It is not."

"It is, too."

"It is not."

"What are you two arguing about?"

Great. My mother had arrived to make my mortification complete. "Nothing."

"Bay is worried about meeting Landon's family," Clove said.

"Of course she is," Mom said. "It's a big deal."

One look at her dreamy smile had my insides twisting. "I know what you're thinking."

Mom's face sobered. "No you don't."

"Yes, I do."

"Fine. What was I thinking?"

"You were thinking that meeting Landon's family means we're going to get married," I said. "Don't deny it. It's written all over your face."

"So?"

"So? So we've only been dating a couple of months," I cautioned. "It's too soon to think about anything like that."

"That's not the way I see it," Mom replied, her tone prim.

"How do you see it?" Thistle asked, clearly enjoying my agony.

"The way I see it, a man who is willing to introduce a woman he's been dating for only a few months to his family is a man with other things on his mind," she said.

Kill me now.

"As a mother, as her mother, I can't help but hope that those things will eventually lead to marriage," she said. "And grandchildren."

Did she just say grandchildren?

"Get that out of your head right now," I said. "That's so far down the road you're going to need Aunt Tillie's plow to find it."

My mom placed her hands on her hips and shook her blonde head testily. "I want grandchildren."

"You have Aunt Tillie," I said. "She's more trouble than any grandchild could ever be. Plus, if I know her, she's going to chase Landon's family out of here in twenty-four hours flat – and they'll probably take him with them when they go."

Mom pursed her lips. "Aunt Tillie has been warned to be on her best behavior. If she's not, there will be dire consequences."

"Is this like when you threatened to put her in a home if she didn't stop growing pot on the property?" Thistle asked. "Because that didn't work out so well. Now she just tells people she has glaucoma when she's holding."

Aunt Tillie's pot field was not only still intact, it was flourishing. Luckily for us, she'd erected a magical force field to keep it hidden. Unfortunately, it was so well hidden my mother and aunts couldn't find it and destroy it. That did bring up another worry, though.

"We've got to keep her out of that field while Landon's family is here," I said.

"She's already been warned," Mom said.

"And what was her response?" Clove asked, her curiosity evident.

Mom shrugged. "It doesn't matter."

"That good, huh?" Thistle chuckled.

"She said that since Landon was a narc that his family was probably full of narcs, too," Marnie said. "She's convinced they're all undercover and trying to bust her."

I dropped my head into my hands. "This is going to be a disaster."

Mom patted my back reassuringly. "You're always so dramatic. You were a dramatic child and now you're a dramatic adult. Things will be fine."

I wanted to believe her.

A flustered Twila, who was pushing into the kitchen from the dining room with an excited look on her face, interrupted us. "They're here."

Maybe I should sneak out the back door?

TWO

Mom eyed me suspiciously. "Don't even think about sneaking out of this house."

"I'm not."

"Good," she said. "Now, go and greet your guests."

I balked. "It's your inn."

"And they're your guests," Mom countered.

"It's your inn," I repeated.

Mom blew out a sigh. "Fine. We'll greet them." She focused on Thistle. "If she isn't out in that lobby in two minutes, I'm blaming you."

"What did I do?" Thistle protested.

"Nothing. Yet."

Mom flounced out of the room, Marnie and Thistle close on her heels. I could feel my heart hammering.

"She looks like she's going to pass out," Thistle said.

"She's not going to pass out," Clove argued, although she didn't look convinced. "You're not going to pass out, right?"

"I'm fine."

"Your face is really white," Thistle said. "Just take a deep breath."

"I said I was fine."

"Then why are you still in here?" Thistle prodded.

"I'm just … I don't want to seem too anxious. Mothers don't like anxious girls."

"Bay, I know I've teased you a lot about this," Thistle said. "I guess I didn't realize how much this was freaking you out. It's going to be fine. I swear it is."

"What if it's not?"

"Then I'll kill her and bury her under the greenhouse," Thistle replied cheerfully.

Clove patted my back. "We'll be there. We'll deflect as much as we can."

"We will," Thistle agreed.

I squared my shoulders. I could do this. They were right. I'd grown up with Aunt Tillie. Anything else should be easy. "Let's get this over with."

We found everyone congregated in the front foyer. Landon caught sight of me first and made a move toward me, stilling when he met my panicked eyes. His mouth tipped into an undisguised smirk. "There you are."

I plastered a smile on my face as I stepped into the room. "Hi."

"We were just going through introductions," Mom said. "We thought you would be out here sooner."

"I was just … I was just finishing up the vegetable tray," I said, knowing how lame it sounded.

"Of course," Mom said, watching me closely. "Well, don't just stand over there hiding. Come meet our guests."

I glanced at Thistle. "I'll trade you moms."

Thistle gave me a little shove. I moved closer to the group, trying hard to keep my breath from coming out in gasps.

For his part, Landon seemed more amused than anything else. I couldn't help but notice that his long, black hair was neatly brushed and tucked behind his ears, though. Since it was usually falling across his forehead and obscuring his electric blue eyes, I couldn't help but wonder if he was a little nervous, too. That thought warmed me.

"This is Bay," Landon said. "Bay, this is my family."

"It's nice to meet you all." I didn't get a chance to say anything else. Instead, I found my face pressed into the broad chest of Landon's father as he hugged me enthusiastically.

"You're a pretty little thing," he said.

He held me so tight I felt as though I was smothering. "Thanks."

"Earl, let the girl breathe," his wife admonished him.

Earl glanced down at me and shrugged apologetically. "Sorry."

"It's fine."

He looked like his son, I realized. Or, rather, Landon looked like his father. Earl's black hair was shot through with gray streaks, but they had the same strong jaw and flashing blue eyes.

A quick glance at his two brothers, who were watching the scene with undisguised glee, told me they took after their father, too.

Their mother was a different story. She was tiny. Like five feet tall tiny. Her auburn hair was short but perfectly coiffed. She was dressed in a simple gray pantsuit, with matching pumps and simple jewelry. While her husband's eyes were warm and inviting, her green orbs were decidedly wary.

"Mrs. Michaels," I said, sticking my hand out uncertainly. She didn't look like a hugger. Thank the Goddess.

"Call me Connie, dear."

"Connie," I said. "It's really nice to meet you. I've heard a lot about you." Actually, Landon hadn't said much about his family. I knew they were close, but he hadn't offered a lot of details.

One of his brothers pushed to the front. His black hair was cut very close to the scalp. "I'm Denny."

I wracked my brain. "You're the minister?"

"You seem surprised."

"You're not dressed like a minister," I explained. "It just took me by surprise."

Denny's eyes were twinkling. "How does a minister dress?"

"Umm … ."

"I think she meant you're not wearing one of those collars," Clove offered.

"That's a priest, moron," Thistle said, smacking the back of her head.

"Oh," Clove muttered. "Sorry."

"It's okay," Denny said. "I get that all the time."

My cheeks were burning. This was not a good start. "I'm really sorry."

"Don't worry about it," Denny said, patting my arm reassuringly. "It's fine."

Mom looked mortified. "They don't get out much," she said by way of apology. "They're ignorant sometimes."

"Well, when you're not raised around religion, those things happen," Connie said coolly.

Mom frowned but didn't offer further comment.

"This is my brother, Daryl," Landon said hurriedly, ushering the other man in the room forward. His hair was the same color as his brothers, but the length fell somewhere in between.

"It's nice to meet you."

"You, too."

The room lapsed into silence for a moment. There was still one other person in the room I'd yet to be introduced to. She was an elderly woman, her frame small and hunched. Her hair was platinum blonde, though, and her face was scrunched into a pronounced scowl.

Landon caught me looking in her direction. "This is Aunt Blanche," he said.

Her I had heard about. Apparently she was just like Aunt Tillie – without the magical aptitude. "It's nice to meet you."

"You keep saying that," Blanche said. "I can't help but think you don't mean it."

I bit the inside of my cheek. "No. I'm really excited to meet you."

"You need to learn to lie better."

Landon frowned. "I told you to be nice."

Blanche lifted her chin defiantly. "It's not my fault she's acting like a fool."

My mother straightened, clearing her throat. "I think she's just nervous."

Blanche fixed my mother with a disdainful look. "Is anyone in this place going to show me to my room? I need to get my things put away before they're all wrinkled and then I need my afternoon tea."

"You behave yourself," Connie warned. "Stop being rude."

"This is a place of business, isn't it?" Blanche pressed. "Since we're paying to stay in this … place, shouldn't we have the full services allotted?"

Thistle and I exchanged worried looks. Our mothers were nothing if not professional. If you said anything bad about the inn, though, you were in for a world of hurt. And, on several occasions, purposeful food poisoning.

Twila swallowed hard. "I can show you to your room."

Blanche looked her up and down, taking in her clown-red hair and eager expression. "Who gets drunk and cuts this family's hair?"

Connie's mouth dropped open in surprise while Thistle giggled madly. Landon had heard enough. He grabbed Blanche's arm and led her to the stairs. "What room is she in?"

Mom glanced down at the ledger. "Twelve." She handed over the room key.

"I'll take her upstairs," Landon said through gritted teeth. "Why doesn't everyone else get settled in the dining room?"

"Sure," Marnie said. "You don't need any help, do you?"

"No." Landon's voice was cold.

"Stop manhandling me," Blanche complained. "Treat your elder with some respect."

"I will," Landon replied. "When you've earned it."

Marnie led everyone into the dining room, ordering Thistle, Clove and me to take the assorted luggage upstairs before joining them. Once they were gone, Thistle couldn't stop her laughter.

"Does anyone else think that when Blanche and Aunt Tillie meet the world is going to cease spinning on its axis?"

The thought terrified me. "Where is Aunt Tillie?"

"I think she's outside bothering the construction crew," Clove said, hoisting two bags from the floor.

"Is Kenneth out there?" Kenneth's grandson owned the construction company that was building the greenhouse. He'd been "courting" Aunt Tillie for weeks. He seemed like a nice guy – or a glutton for punishment. I hadn't figured out which yet.

"I don't know," Thistle said. "She likes bothering them whether he's out there or not."

After depositing the bags in various rooms, the three of us made our way to the dining room. Connie, Earl, Denny and Daryl were all seated at the table – coffee and tea in front of them – as my mother and aunts plied them with baked goods and vegetables.

"This is a great inn," Earl said. "It's got an unusual name, though."

"We told them that," Thistle said, sitting at the far end of the table. "They don't get it."

"What's so bad about the name?" Twila asked, fixing her eyes on Thistle suddenly. "When did you dye your hair blue again?"

"You just noticed? I've been here all afternoon and my hair has been this color," Thistle replied. "I feel so neglected."

"You know I don't like that color."

"I know."

"You're just doing it to drive me crazy."

Earl cleared his throat nervously. "So, um, how did you settle on The Overlook for a name?"

"We're overlooking the bluff," Marnie explained, like it was the most natural thing in the world.

"They've never seen *The Shining*," Clove added. "They don't get it."

"I thought maybe you named it that on purpose because of this being a magic town," Earl said.

I froze. "What do you mean?" Had Landon told them?

Earl furrowed his brow. "I thought that Hemlock Cove rebranded itself as a witch town for tourists?"

Oh, that's what he meant. "Yeah," I said, sliding into one of the open seats at the table – one that was conveniently located several feet from Connie. What can I say? The woman makes me nervous.

"That's a great gimmick," Denny said. "From what Landon says, it's working out well for the town. Without an industrial base, these small towns have to survive any way they can."

"I wouldn't think you'd like magic," Thistle said.

"Why? Because I'm a minister?"

"Well, yeah."

"As long as you're not all sacrificing animals or worshiping Beelzebub, I think I'll be fine," he replied. "Besides, it's all pretend, right?"

"Right." Or not.

"I think it's sacrilegious," Connie said.

"It's not," Marnie said. "It's all good-natured fun."

"I don't think promoting evil is fun," Connie replied.

Uh-oh.

"We're not promoting evil," Mom said evenly. "Besides, who says witches are evil?"

Landon chose now to join the party. He slid into the seat next to me and grabbed a cookie.

"Is everything all right?" Earl asked.

"She's up there pouting," Landon replied. "I told her she couldn't come back down until she adjusted her attitude."

"She's fine," Mom said. "She was probably just tired from the trip."

"It was only two hours," Landon countered. "She's just mean sometimes."

"Hey, we've got Aunt Tillie," Thistle said. "We know all about mean."

"Yes, Landon told us you have an elderly aunt, too," Daryl said. "He said she's even more of a pill than Aunt Blanche. I can't wait to meet her."

"You're going to regret saying that," Thistle said.

"Don't talk about your aunt that way," Twila warned. "Has she seen your hair?"

"She doesn't care about my hair," Thistle replied.

"I take it the hair color is something new," Connie said. "It's really not your color, dear. It washes you out."

Thistle frowned. That was exactly the argument her mother had used when she'd first seen it the previous summer. The thing with Thistle is, though, if you don't like the present color all you have to do is wait. She changes it whenever the mood strikes.

"I think it looks nice," Daryl said, offering Thistle a warm smile. "It's eye-catching."

"She has a boyfriend," Clove said hurriedly, grunting when I kicked her under the table. "What? She does."

I shook my head. Clove was on the dry spell to end all dry spells. It didn't help that Marcus and Landon were constantly spending the night at the guesthouse we all shared on the edge of the property. Unfortunately, she has terrible taste in men. I could only hope she wouldn't set her sights on Landon's brother. That would just be all kinds of awkward.

Landon chuckled. "He knows."

"He knows?" I asked.

"I told him all about your family," Landon said.

I didn't know how to take that revelation so I decided to ignore it. "So, what are your plans while you're in town?"

"I don't know," Connie hedged. "What is there to do here?"

"Well, there's lots of shopping," Mom said. "It's spring, so none of the orchards are up and running yet. Still, there's horseback riding and walking trails."

Daryl laughed. "Mom isn't an outdoor kind of girl."

"Don't get fresh," Connie warned.

I glanced at the clock on the wall. Had it really only been twenty minutes? Had time ceased moving forward?

Luckily for us, a noise at the kitchen door drew everyone's attention. It was the construction foreman, Dirk.

"Is something wrong?" I asked. "Is Aunt Tillie bugging you?"

Dirk looked uncomfortable. "No. Well, yes, but we're used to that now. As long as she wears her hardhat I've given up arguing with her."

That was probably wise.

"Then what is it?" Marnie asked.

"Um, well, I don't know quite how to tell you this ... ."

"Just tell us," I said.

"We were digging with the backhoe and we found something," Dirk said.

"What?"

"A body."

All the air left my body in a whoosh. Crap.

THREE

The room erupted.

"Someone was murdered here?" Connie's voice was shrill.

"Cool," Daryl said.

"We should all pray," Denny said.

"Someone should call Chief Terry," Twila offered.

"I'll call him," Mom and Marnie said at the same time.

I glanced over at Landon. His face was grim. "What do you mean you found a body?"

"Well, it's not really a body," Dirk corrected. "It's more like bones."

"Bones?" Landon lifted an eyebrow.

"Yeah," Dirk said. "If I had to guess, I'd say the body has been there for a long time."

Landon got to his feet. "Call Chief Terry," he told my mother before turning to me. "You want to come with me?"

"We all want to come," Daryl said.

"It's a crime scene," Landon said. "You can't trample all over it."

"Hasn't the construction crew already handled that?" Daryl pressed.

"Just stay here until I know what's going on," Landon growled.

"Why do you get to go?" Daryl asked.

"Because I'm a FBI agent," Landon said.

"And why does she get to go?" Daryl pointed at me accusingly.

"Because I want her there," Landon said. "Now just stay here and eat your cookies."

I followed Landon out the back door wordlessly. My mind was a jumble. How could this be happening? Someone high up obviously hated me.

Landon must've read my mind because he reached over and linked his fingers with mine. "This could've happened to anyone."

"Really?"

Landon couldn't hide his laugh. "No. This would only happen to your family."

I blew out a sigh.

"Look at it this way, things couldn't have been going any worse in there," Landon said.

"I noticed."

Landon paused long enough to pull me to him. "It's going to be okay." He pressed a quick kiss to my forehead. "Things will settle down."

"We're going to look at a body," I reminded him.

"No, we're going to look at bones," Landon corrected.

"How is that different?"

"It means the body has been out here for a while," he said. "Trust me. Things could be worse."

I didn't know how. When we reached the construction site we found the workers standing around a big hole in the earth, looking down. We moved to the lip and saw the point of interest immediately. About ten feet down, a skull was staring back at us from the dirt.

Landon grimaced. "Yup. That's a dead person."

"Did you think Dirk was lying?"

"No," Landon shook his head. "I was hoping he was mistaken. That it was an animal or something."

I turned to Dirk. "I'm guessing this is going to put a halt to the greenhouse construction for a while."

"I figured."

I shrugged helplessly. "I guess we'll call you when you can come back."

"Wait," Landon said. "Chief Terry is going to want to get a statement about how it was discovered."

"I'll stay," Dirk said. "It's part of my job description."

"You have talk-to-the-cops-when-bones-are-found on your job description?" I was going for levity.

"Yeah," Dirk said, sighing. "I get all the cool jobs."

Dirk dismissed his crew and then headed up to the inn so my mother and aunts could stuff him with tea and cookies. Chief Terry arrived five minutes later.

"Yup, that's a dead body."

Cop humor is an acquired taste. "What's it doing down there?" I asked.

"I don't know," Chief Terry said. "I'm guessing it's been there a while, though."

"You're not going to go down there and look?"

"I've already called the state forensic team," Chief Terry replied. "The scene is compromised, but I'd rather do this by the book."

"You don't seem too concerned," I pointed out.

"It's obviously not a fresh body," he said.

"Does that somehow make it better?"

Chief Terry shrugged. "It makes it less dire."

"How?"

"He means that there's not a murderer running around the property," Landon supplied. "For that matter, we have no idea if this even is a murder."

I raised my eyebrows. "If it's not a murder, how did someone end up buried on the property?"

"Where is Aunt Tillie?" Landon asked, looking around the grounds.

That was a pretty good question. "I don't know. I thought she was out here."

"Was she out here when the body was discovered?" Landon asked.

I shrugged. "I have no idea."

"Why wasn't she inside?"

"I don't know," I said, resenting his tone. "It's not my day to watch her."

Landon's eyes softened. "That's not what I meant. It just seems to me that she would want to be out here if a body was found."

I realized what he was saying. So did Chief Terry. "Unless she already knew it was here," he said.

"No," I protested. "That's ridiculous."

Chief Terry patted my shoulder. "We're not saying she killed someone, Bay."

"Then what are you saying?"

"Just that … maybe … she knew it was out here," Chief Terry said.

"Absolutely not," I argued. "If she knew there was a body out here she never would've let them build the greenhouse here."

What? I know Aunt Tillie is capable of a lot of things. I just don't think she's capable of outright stupidity.

"She has a point," Landon said, running his hand through his hair. "If she knew this body was out here, she'd have come up with a reason to move the greenhouse someplace else."

"Well, it's nice to hear you all think I'm smart enough to hide a body."

I jumped when I heard her voice. You wouldn't think an eighty-five-year-old woman would be capable of sneaking up on you. In Aunt Tillie's case, you'd be wrong.

I turned around slowly, meeting four feet, eleven inches of furious aunt with my most placating smile. "There you are."

Aunt Tillie ignored me, instead fixing her angry eyes on Landon and Chief Terry. "If you two have something you want to ask me, then just ask me."

Chief Terry took an involuntary step backward. "No."

"Okay," Landon said. "Do you have any idea how this body got here?"

"No," Aunt Tillie said. "It probably got washed here by a flood or something."

"You live on a bluff," Landon pointed out.

"So?"

"So, bluffs don't flood."

"Are you a geologist now or something?" Aunt Tillie's hands were on her hips. "Are you trading in your narc badge for a geologist's hat?"

Landon pursed his lips. "No."

"Then you really don't know if this place floods or not, do you?"

Landon shifted his gaze to me. "How about you? Do you know if this piece of land floods?"

I shifted uncomfortably. "Not to my knowledge."

"Traitor," Aunt Tillie huffed.

Her attitude was worrisome. On any other day, she'd be interested in the body – interested in finding out who it was and how it got there. She was acting a little too blasé for my comfort level.

My attention was momentarily drawn from her, though, when I caught movement out of the corner of my eye. In his effort to keep distance between himself and Aunt Tillie, Chief Terry had stepped too close to the hole. The ground beneath him gave way, and he tumbled down the embankment, landing on top of the bones.

"Chief!"

I slid down into the hole, shifting loose dirt as I followed him.

"Sonuvabitch!" Chief Terry got to his feet gingerly, testing his ankles to make sure nothing was broken. He brushed dirt off himself irritably.

"So much for not contaminating the crime scene," Landon said, still standing where I'd left him seconds before.

"Way to help," I grumbled.

"It was a ten-foot drop into the dirt," Landon said. "I figured you'd be fine. Plus, I'm not done talking to Aunt Tillie."

"Well, I'm done talking to you," Aunt Tillie replied, turning on her heel and stalking toward the house.

"This isn't over," Landon said.

I couldn't see her retreating back, but I knew from Landon's scowl that he was at his limit. I helped brush Chief Terry's back off and then knelt down so I could get a better look at the skull.

"Don't touch that," Landon ordered.

"I'm not touching it."

Chief Terry crouched beside me. "Its definitely been here a while."

"How can you tell?"

"The bones," he said. "They're all bleached out."

"And that means?"

"It means they've been here for a while."

"How long is a while?"

Chief Terry shrugged. "I have no idea. I'm guessing at least ten years, though, probably more. Maybe a lot more."

Something was poking out of the dirt to my right. Without thinking, I pinched it with my fingers and tried to pull it out. I was concentrating so hard, I tumbled backward when my fingers slipped from it.

"I told you not to touch anything," Landon said.

"I just wanted to see," I said. Pulling my hand back sharply when I felt an odd tingling in the air.

"Give me your hand," Landon said to Chief Terry. "I'll pull you out. You, don't touch anything else."

I ignored him, keeping my focus on the ground next to the object I'd tried to free from the soil. I instinctively stood up, but I didn't move away. Something was happening. It was as though a mist was pooling a few inches above the ground – and it was getting bigger by the second.

Landon grunted behind me as he pulled Chief Terry out of the hole. I remained where I was, staring at the mist, while they talked gibberish a few feet above.

"How long will it take the state boys to get here?"

"I don't know. It shouldn't be long, though."

"I guess we should tape off the construction site," Landon said.

"Do they have anything here that will work?"

"I don't know."

The mist was taking shape now – and the shape was human. I couldn't make out any features, but the white cloud looked like a detached shadow.

"Bay."

Landon was trying to get my attention. I couldn't force myself to face him, though. I couldn't force myself to do anything but stand there.

"Holy crap," Chief Terry said. "What is that?"

"Get her out," Landon said. "Get her out."

"Bay," Chief Terry said. "Bay, get over here."

I remained rooted to my spot.

Landon's voice was desperate. "Bay, look at me. Bay!"

The mist was moving now, standing – for lack of a better term. Once I was face-to-face with it, I realized that it was taller than me by at least six inches. And, while I couldn't put a face with the entity – or a name – it felt decidedly male.

"Bay!"

The entity moved fast, like a flash of lightning, pushing through me and forcing me against the hard wall of the excavation. I lost my footing, ice water suddenly slogging through my veins, and slumped to the ground.

I could hear screaming – only it wasn't Landon or Chief Terry. It was a memory. Someone else's. I screwed my eyes shut to force the memory out. I didn't want to see this. It wasn't my hell, after all. It was someone else's hell.

Oh, Goddess, stop the screaming.

FOUR

"Bay, look at me."

I wrenched my eyes open and found Landon's worried face inches from mine.

"There you are." He ran his hands behind my neck, forcing my head up so I could meet his gaze evenly. He searched my face for an answer that I couldn't give. At least not now.

"What … ?"

Landon glanced at Chief Terry. He was back in the hole, kneeling beside me, his face equally drawn. "We're not sure what happened," Chief Terry said. "We thought you might be able to tell us that."

"I don't … I … ." Memories were rushing through my mind. Some were my own, consisting of the minutes before the entity struck. Others, though, belonged to someone else. I shuddered.

Landon pulled me to him, wrapping his arms around me. I shivered when I felt the warmth of his body. It was a sunny, spring day. Why was I so cold? "You scared the life out of me," he said, rubbing my back.

I sucked in a deep breath. "I don't know what happened."

"Something ran through you," Landon said. "It looked like … ."

"It looked like a ghost," Chief Terry interjected.

"That wasn't a ghost," I said, my voice shaky. "That was something else."

"What?"

I shook my head, trying to dislodge the echoing screams from my mind. "I don't know."

"Would your mother or aunts know?" Chief Terry asked.

"I don't know," I admitted. "I've never seen anything like that before."

Landon pulled away so he could look at me again. "Can you stand up?"

"Yeah."

Landon kept his hand wrapped around my wrist as he got to his feet and then carefully pulled me up beside him. Once I was standing, he wrapped his arm around my waist to offer support.

I glanced up. "Um, how are we going to get out of here?"

Landon rubbed his jaw. "I don't know. I wasn't thinking about that when I jumped in here."

"Oh, well, good," I said. "With your family and my family inside, I think we can just live out here now. We'll build the bedroom over there."

Landon barked out a laugh. "I don't suppose you have your phone on you?"

I felt for the pocket of my jeans, handing him the phone wordlessly. Landon paused before dialing.

"What are you waiting for?" Chief Terry asked.

"I'm trying to decide who to call," Landon admitted.

"Call Thistle," I suggested. "Tell her to keep it quiet."

"Do you think Thistle has the strength to pull me and Chief Terry out of here?"

I bit my lip. "No."

Landon sighed. "I guess I'm going to have to call my father and brothers."

"How long will it take them to get here?" Chief Terry asked.

"They're at the inn," I said.

Chief Terry's eyebrows shot up. "Your family is staying at the inn?"

"Yeah," Landon said, punching a number into the phone.

"Oh, this will end well," Chief Terry said, not bothering to hide his sarcasm.

AN HOUR LATER, I was showered, changed and hiding in the big kitchen at The Overlook again. Landon and I returned to the guesthouse long enough to get cleaned up. He'd watched me carefully after the incident, but he hadn't brought it up again. I couldn't decide whether he was giving me time or whether he really didn't want to know what new evil I'd managed to dig up.

"Hey, what's going on?" Thistle had slipped into the kitchen while I was lost in thought.

"What's going on out there?" I asked, inclining my head in the direction of the dining room.

"Not a lot," Thistle said. "Connie is making fun of the centerpiece, Earl is looking through the books in the library, Daryl and Denny are playing pool in the game room, and Blanche is bitching about everything."

"Oh, well, good."

"What's up with you?"

I glanced around, making sure we were alone, and then I told her what occurred in the hole, leaving out the part about the screaming dream. I still wasn't sure what to make of that.

"Holy crap."

"Yeah."

"What do you think it was?"

I shook my head, absentmindedly stirring the sauce on the stove to give myself something to do with my hands. "I don't know."

"And you're sure it wasn't a ghost?"

I can actually see ghosts. It's my "gift." All of the Winchester witches have one. My mothers are all accomplished kitchen witches, and Clove and Thistle have varying degrees of precognitive and postcognitive recognition. Unfortunately, I was the one who inherited the ability to see and hear ghosts from Aunt Tillie. It had deemed me the weird-girl-with-invisible-friends when I was a child. Yeah, I'm still a little bitter.

"No, it wasn't a ghost. This was something else."

Thistle shrugged. "Maybe, whatever it is, it's gone now."

"Maybe." Or maybe we were about to be haunted by something wholly terrible. I rubbed my head worriedly. "This couldn't have happened at a worse time."

"Look at it this way," Thistle said. "It's a distraction."

"There's something else," I hedged.

"What?"

"Aunt Tillie."

"What about her? She might actually be able to help in a situation like this."

"There's something going on," I admitted. "She wasn't out there when the bones were discovered or, at least if she was, she disappeared afterward and then reappeared when I was out there with Landon and Chief Terry."

"So? The woman is like an evil cat," Thistle said. "She slinks around wherever she wants to. We should get her a bell."

"I know," I said. "She said that the body had probably been washed there by a flood, though. And she didn't seem interested in it at all."

Thistle stilled. "That doesn't sound like her."

"No, it doesn't."

"You don't think ... ?"

"I don't know what to think."

I heard footsteps on the stairs and pressed a finger to my lips to quiet Thistle. There were two sets of stairs in the inn. The front set led up to the guest bedrooms. The back set led to the family living quarters, which were only accessible through the back of the house. While The Overlook was technically a modified Victorian, the family quarters at the back were still strictly off limits to guests and only accessible through the kitchen, which no guests dared enter.

I glanced at the stairs, not surprised to find Aunt Tillie standing there. She didn't look thrilled to see us. "I heard you fell into the hole."

"Chief Terry fell into the hole," I corrected. "I jumped in to make sure he was all right."

Aunt Tillie snorted. "He's out there flirting with your mothers," she replied. "He seems fine."

I motioned to the door that led to the dining room and Thistle took the hint. She positioned herself next to it so she could hear if someone approached. Aunt Tillie watched her warily. "What's going on?"

"Something happened out in the hole," I said.

"Terry fell in," Aunt Tillie said. "You already told me."

"Something else happened."

Aunt Tillie's face was blank. "What?"

I told her about the white shadow and pooling mist. I told her about it rushing through me. I didn't tell her about the screaming, though. I wanted to wait.

"Crap."

That wasn't the response I was expecting. Aunt Tillie is cool under pressure. The big things never get to her. It's the little things that send her careening off a cliff. This wasn't good.

"Crap? All you can say is crap?"

"What is it?" Thistle asked.

"It's a poltergeist," Aunt Tillie replied, glancing over her shoulder worriedly. "You set loose a poltergeist."

"I didn't set it loose," I argued. "I was just standing there."

"Well, someone set it loose."

"You know who it is, don't you?" Thistle asked, her gaze fixed on Aunt Tillie.

Aunt Tillie averted her eyes. "I have no idea what you're talking about."

"You're lying," Thistle challenged. "I can tell. You know who was buried out there."

Aunt Tillie pointed a gnarled finger in Thistle's direction. "Don't call me a liar."

"Oh, god," I moaned. "You do know who was out there. Who is it?"

"I told you, I don't know who it is."

"And you're lying," Thistle pressed. So much for killing her with kindness.

"Watch yourself, girl," Aunt Tillie said. "I promised to be on my best behavior, but I'm not going to tolerate any of your sass."

I grabbed Aunt Tillie's threatening finger, forcing her to focus on me. "You have to tell us what's going on."

"I don't know what's going on."

"Dammit!"

"Don't swear," Aunt Tillie warned. "And stay out of this."

"Aunt Tillie, the police are going to find out," I said. "There's a forensic team out there right now collecting the body."

"Well, good for them," she sniffed. "A whole yard full of narcs. It must be my lucky day."

I sucked in a calming breath. "This is going to blow up in your face if you don't tell us what's going on."

"I don't know what's going on," Aunt Tillie replied. "I'm old. I'm senile. I can't help that."

Aunt Tillie only used her age as a crutch when she was hiding something. When she's wreaking havoc, though, you'd swear she was thirty-five.

"Is that going to be your defense in court?" Thistle challenged. "If so, you might want to work on your befuddlement before it gets to a jury."

Aunt Tillie glared at Thistle. "You're pushing your luck."

Thistle met my gaze and I shook my head. "We can't," I said. "Landon's family is out there."

Thistle clenched her jaw. "This is going to blow up, whether you want it to or not."

Aunt Tillie brushed past her and pushed opened the swinging door between the kitchen and dining room. We all froze when we saw Landon standing on the other side eyeing us. "Ladies."

Aunt Tillie regarded him coldly. "Were you eavesdropping?"

"I was just coming to get you," Landon replied. "Your company is required for some pre-dinner drinks."

Aunt Tillie smiled widely, although I could still see the worry reflected in her brown eyes. "Good. I could use some hooch."

"I think we all could," Thistle grumbled.

I watched the two of them leave before focusing on Landon. "Were you eavesdropping?"

Landon ignored the question and held out his hand. "Let's get something to drink."

FIVE

"As usual, this looks wonderful, ladies."

Chief Terry had agreed to join us for dinner. Not only was he a fan of the Winchester cooking gene, he was also a fan of the constant attention my mother and aunts showered upon him every time he visited. Each one of them was determined to snag him – and he was comfortable with all effort exerted during the attempts.

"Yes, it looks great," Earl agreed. "What is this?"

"It's a braised pork loin," Twila said. "We brine it and soak it for two days. It makes the meat really tender."

Daryl forked a piece of meat into his mouth, groaning with appreciation. "I think I just died and went to heaven."

Mom basked in the compliment. "There's fresh bread, too."

"You baked this yourself?" Denny asked, grabbing a roll and breaking it apart. "Oh, it's still warm."

Landon watched his brothers, amusement flitting across his face. "Mom isn't a big cook," he said. "This is a real treat for everyone."

Connie bristled. "I can cook," she argued. "I just choose not to."

Landon rolled his eyes. "You can't cook."

Earl rubbed his wife's shoulders. "You're a wonderful cook, honey."

"Don't placate me."

"I need more wine," Aunt Tillie announced.

She was sitting at the head of the table to my left, while Landon's thigh was pressed snugly against mine on the right. He wasn't saying it, but I had a feeling he was still shaken by this afternoon's activities.

"You don't need any more wine," Mom replied. "You've had enough."

"I made the wine," Aunt Tillie countered. "I can drink as much of it as I want."

Earl looked impressed. "You make your own wine, too? Wow."

"I make the wine," Aunt Tillie stressed. "Me."

"She makes great wine," Kenneth said. I wasn't sure when he'd arrived at the inn, but he was now firmly entrenched in the seat next to Aunt Tillie. "Everything she does is great."

"And who are you?" Blanche asked from the far end of the table. It was the first time she'd spoken since dinner began.

"I'm Kenneth."

"He's Aunt Tillie's ... friend," Clove supplied.

"Her boyfriend," Thistle teased.

"Listen, sass mouth, eat your dinner and shut up," Aunt Tillie ordered.

Thistle glowered but said nothing. For their part, Daryl and Denny seemed amused by the dinner theater.

I rubbed my forehead ruefully. "I could use some more wine."

Landon grabbed the bottle from the center of the table, pulling the cork with his teeth, and poured fresh glasses for both of us.

"So, tell us about the body," Daryl said.

"It wasn't a body," Chief Terry said. "It was bones. Old bones."

"And how did the three of you fall in the hole?" Denny asked.

"The ground gave way," Chief Terry replied, purposely evasive. "It was an accident."

"And you don't have to be out there now?" Connie asked, frowning as she watched Marnie and Mom add food to his plate.

"The state forensic team will take the bones and do the autopsy," Chief Terry shrugged. "I won't have anything to do until I have more information."

"And you don't have to do anything with this case?" Connie turned to Landon.

"I'm on vacation this week," Landon replied. "Besides, this isn't really a case for the FBI."

"How do you know?"

"Because, even if the individual was murdered, it happened a long time ago," Landon explained. "It's not really a pressing matter."

"So, tell me about yourself, Kenneth," Blanche broke in.

I shifted my shoulders so I could see her. She eyed Kenneth as though he was the blue ribbon pie at the county fair. Uh-oh.

"I own a construction company," Kenneth replied. "My grandson runs it now, but it's still my company."

"That must be exciting," Blanche said, her voice breathy.

I shot Landon a questioning look. He shrugged in response. He was clearly at a loss.

"Not really," Kenneth said. "It's a way to pay the bills, though."

"And you make good money doing it?" Blanche pressed.

Aunt Tillie swallowed the rest of her wine and shoved her glass in my direction. "Fill it."

"Mom said no more wine."

"I'm an adult. I say when I've had enough."

I glanced at Mom for permission. She looked torn. Landon filled Aunt Tillie's glass, ignoring Mom's accusatory stare.

"And this is why I like him," Aunt Tillie said.

"You didn't like me a couple of hours ago," Landon reminded her.

"That's because you were in narc mode," Aunt Tillie said.

"Ah."

"So, Landon says you two own a magic shop," Denny said, trying to turn the conversation to a safer topic by focusing on Thistle and Clove. "It's called Hypnotic, right? That must be cool."

"It is," Clove said. "You should stop by."

"Do you have devil-worshipping stuff in there?" Connie asked pointedly.

"Um, no."

Thistle frowned. "There's no devil in the craft."

"And what craft are you referring to?" Connie asked.

"Witchcraft."

I pinched the bridge of my nose. "I think what Thistle is saying is that their shop is really full of incense and candles."

"That's not what I was saying," Thistle countered.

"That's not what she was saying," Aunt Tillie agreed.

"Drink your wine," I growled.

"So, Kenneth, what happened to your wife?" Blanche asked.

Oh, good Goddess.

"She died."

"A long time ago?"

"A good number of years." Kenneth seemed confused by Blanche's questions. Aunt Tillie understood what was going on, though.

"Why do you care?" Aunt Tillie asked, her tone cool.

"Who says I care?" Blanche said.

"Drink your wine," Earl instructed Blanche.

"So, Bay, you run the local newspaper," Denny said, clearly desperate now. "That must be exciting."

"It has its moments," I said. "That's how I met your brother."

"Oh, yeah?" Denny said. "Landon never really told us how you met."

I bit the inside of my cheek. Landon had been undercover when we met. It made sense he wouldn't have told his family the specifics of the case. "Um, yeah."

Landon shifted next to me. "I can't talk about my cases."

"She seems to know about it," Daryl pointed out.

"She was there when the drug dealers hit the fan," Aunt Tillie said. "We all were."

"Drink your wine," Mom commanded.

Connie puckered her lips. "I'm sorry, I don't understand what kind of FBI case involves all of you."

"I'm sorry," I muttered so only Landon could hear me.

He squeezed my hand under the table. "They just happened to stumble on a crime scene."

"You mean we solved the case for you," Aunt Tillie said.

Landon leveled an angry gaze on Aunt Tillie. "You solved the case for me?"

I put my hand on Aunt Tillie's arm. "Drink your wine."

"You wouldn't have survived if it weren't for us," Aunt Tillie said, ignoring my comment.

"You're the reason I got shot," Landon practically exploded.

"You were shot!" Connie was on her feet, her face ashen.

Uh-oh.

"You didn't tell your mother you were shot?" Marnie was flabbergasted. "You should always tell your mother when you're shot."

"Shut up, Mom," Clove said, tugging the arm of her mother's shirt.

"Son, I can't believe you didn't tell us you were shot," Earl said. "Why wouldn't you tell us?"

"I didn't want to worry you," Landon said, patting his chest. "See, I'm fine. Everything turned out fine."

"But these people, you told these people," Connie said. "You told these people and not your own family."

"He didn't tell them," Chief Terry supplied. I think he was trying to help. "They were there when it happened."

"You were there?" Connie's voice was shrill.

"We weren't," Twila offered. "Just Bay and Aunt Tillie."

Connie took in a deep breath, clearly trying to calm herself. "And why were you there?"

"We were looking for murderers," Aunt Tillie replied. "We knew they were hanging out in the corn maze, so that's where we went. We're law-abiding citizens and we were there to solve a crime."

"If you don't shut your mouth, I'm going to drown you in that wine," I threatened.

"Why were you in a corn maze?" Connie asked her son.

"Because I had to be," Landon said, sighing. "I can't talk about this."

"Everyone at the table already seems to know," Connie pointed out.

"That was an accident, nothing more."

Connie let Earl pull her back down to a sitting position. Her face was murderous, though. "Is she the reason you got shot?"

Connie didn't identify which "she" she was referring to, but I knew it was me. "Mrs. Michaels … ."

Connie held up a hand, stopping me mid-sentence. "I am talking to my son."

Landon's jaw clenched. "Will you not do this now? Please?"

"I want to know if she's the reason you got shot," Connie pressed. "Is that … woman the reason my boy almost died?"

My heart sank.

"Connie," Earl warned.

"Mom," Landon growled.

"I need more wine," Aunt Tillie announced.

"Yes," I said, my voice small. "It was my fault."

Landon stiffened next to me. "It wasn't your fault."

"Then whose fault was it?"

Landon ran his hand down the back of my head. "It was an accident."

Chief Terry focused on Connie. "Ma'am, I was there that night. Nothing that happened was on purpose. Things just kind of … spiraled out of control."

"And yet she's still to blame, isn't she?" Connie said. "If she hadn't been there, my son wouldn't have been shot."

"Don't you blame her," Aunt Tillie said. "He was the one undercover with a bunch of meth heads he couldn't control."

Connie fanned herself. "Oh, God help me."

"Connie, maybe you should go and lie down," Earl prodded.

"Don't handle me!"

"Don't you yell at my dinner table!" Aunt Tillie was on her feet.

"Don't you yell at my niece," Blanche countered. "She has a right to be upset. Your niece got her son shot."

"Oh, she did not," Aunt Tillie scoffed. "He got himself shot."

I stared down at my plate, recrimination washing over me. Landon wrapped his arm around my shoulders and pressed his lips to the side of my head. "It wasn't your fault."

I knew he meant it but, the truth was, if we hadn't been in the corn maze that night things would've turned out differently. I opened my mouth to argue but Landon slapped his hand over my mouth. "No!"

Everyone at the table hushed when they heard the tone of his voice.

"I'm not dealing with this," Landon said. "I should've told you I was shot. That's on me. Bay is not the reason I was shot, and I'm not going to listen to this anymore."

"But ... ."

Landon pointed the index finger of his free hand at his mother, keeping the other hand fixed firmly over my mouth. "I said 'no.'"

The table lapsed into silence. After a full minute, Landon finally pulled his hand from my mouth.

I had lost my appetite, so I pushed the food around my plate to keep my hands busy. Finally, I felt Aunt Tillie's eyes on me so I focused on her. I was surprised when she reached over and patted my hand. "You've had a really crummy day, haven't you?"

"I've had better," I agreed.

"Drink some wine. You'll feel better."

I wanted to argue, but Landon was already filling my glass.

The silence was shattered by the sound of breaking dishes in the other room.

"What was that?" Connie asked.

"Is anyone else in the house?" Landon asked.

I shook my head. Chief Terry and Landon were already at the door, though, so he didn't see the gesture.

Chief Terry pulled his gun while Landon pushed open the door. "What the hell?"

I moved to Landon's side and peered in the room. Every dish that we'd left on the counter had been smashed – and yet the room was empty. Chief Terry and Landon moved to the back of the house, searching to make sure it was empty.

I knew what it was, though. I turned my head so I could see Aunt Tillie. She was focused on me. "There's no one here," I said.

"It must have been a small earthquake," Aunt Tillie replied.

"Yeah, that's what it must have been."

Something told me the white shadow from the hole was to blame. Could my life get any worse?

SIX

"Well, that was an ... eventful dinner," Landon said as we walked back to the guesthouse alone two hours later.

"If you mean that was hell, I totally agree."

Landon sighed. He looked whipped. "Bay, I'm sorry for what my mother said to you."

"You mean the truth?"

Landon stopped in the middle of the trail. "No."

I kept walking, even as Landon stayed behind. His eyes bored a hole into my back. I could practically feel his anger. Finally, I stilled, too, but I couldn't meet his gaze.

"Come here."

I finally met his blue eyes but didn't do as ordered.

"Come here," he said again.

I remained several paces ahead of him.

Landon growled as he closed the distance between us, wrapping his arm around my wrist. "It wasn't the truth."

"If I'm not the reason you got shot, who is?"

Landon shrugged. "Fate?"

"You don't believe in fate," I said.

"I never said that."

His answer surprised me. "You believe in fate? You?"

"I believe that things happen for a reason," he said. "I believe that you were out in that corn maze for a reason. If you weren't there … if Aunt Tillie wasn't there … things might've been different."

"Yeah. You might not have been shot."

"No," Landon agreed. "I might not have been. Have you ever considered, though, that I might have been shot and bled to death in that corn maze because you weren't there?"

I placed my tongue in my cheek, considering. That thought hadn't occurred to me.

"That's what I thought," Landon said. "Bay, we can't go back and change what happened. I was shot. You were there. I'm fine now. You're fine now. Things worked out the way they were supposed to."

"Still … ."

"Still, nothing," Landon said. "I don't want to hear about this again. What happened wasn't your fault."

"Tell that to your mother," I grumbled.

"I should've told them what happened," Landon conceded. "I can't go back in time and fix that either."

"Why didn't you? Tell them, I mean."

"You know why," he said. "My mother is a little … high strung."

"Is that what we're calling it?"

"She's just protective," Landon explained. "She's not a bad person."

"I didn't say she was a bad person." Never attack a man's mother.

"I know."

"She just doesn't like me."

Landon barked out a laugh. "She doesn't know you."

"She knows that she doesn't like me."

"My mother has never liked any woman I've dated."

"How many women have you dated?"

Landon shook his head. "That's a trap, missy, and I'm not falling into it."

"Fine," I said, opting for a different tactic. "How many women has she met?"

Landon rolled his head, cracking his neck. "A few."

A few? That was disheartening. "And why didn't she like them?"

"She's never liked anyone that any of us have dated," Landon said. "Not one."

I felt better – if only marginally. "Not one?"

"Not one."

Landon rubbed his thumb over the inside of my wrist. "Bay, she'll come around."

What if she doesn't? I didn't voice my concerns, though. "Okay."

Landon pulled me to him, pressing his lips to mine gently. "I promise this will all work out."

I sank into him, letting his warmth wash over me. I was still filled with doubts, but his presence was enough to push them away for the time being.

We stood, wrapped together and let the night sounds engulf us. It was only spring, but the crickets were already in full throat. Aunt Tillie said crickets were signs of luck. I was choosing to believe that little nugget of wisdom – or maybe I just needed some shred of hope to cling to.

Landon seemed reluctant to break the moment but, finally, he took a step back. "I do have something I want to talk to you about, though."

"I knew this was coming."

Landon kept his arms on my shoulders, seemingly unwilling to let me move too far away. "What was that thing in the hole?"

I wasn't sure how to answer. Landon was growing accustomed to our witchy ways, but there were times skittishness took hold of him. I was fearful this would be one of those times.

"Aunt Tillie says it's a poltergeist."

Landon frowned. "Like the movie?"

I shrugged. "I guess. I've never seen one before."

"So you honestly didn't know what it was?"

I shook my head, my blonde hair brushing against my shoulders. "I had no idea. Why? Did you think I was lying to you?"

"No, not lying. I thought maybe you didn't want to tell me in front of Chief Terry."

"Is that different from lying?"

Landon chuckled. "I guess not. I thought there was a chance that you just didn't want to say until we were alone."

"And you would've been okay with that?" That didn't sound like the Landon I knew.

Landon moved a hand from my shoulder to my neck, rubbing small circles in the tender spot behind my ear with his thumb as he thought about his answer. "I don't want you lying to me," he clarified. "I also understand that you can't always tell me exactly what's going on when someone else is around."

"Chief Terry knows about us," I reminded him.

"I know," Landon said, exhaling heavily. "That doesn't mean you tell him everything."

"And you think I tell you everything?"

"I hope so."

I considered the statement. "I want to tell you everything," I admitted. "Well, not everything. I don't think you need to know when I have cramps."

Landon's chest shook with silent laughter. "No. I don't need to know that." He paused momentarily. "Then tell me what you, Thistle and Aunt Tillie were talking about in the kitchen."

This was a test – and I knew it. "Weren't you eavesdropping?"

"Are you going to be angry if I was?"

"No."

"Really?" Landon didn't look convinced.

"Really."

"Yes, I was eavesdropping," he admitted. "I didn't come in until halfway through the conversation, though."

"Well, you didn't miss much," I replied.

"So Aunt Tillie won't admit she knows who the body belongs to?"

"No."

"But you think she does?"

"So does Thistle."

Landon pressed his body closer to mine, allowing me to rest the side of my head against his shoulder. He swayed back and forth slowly, thinking. Finally he spoke. "Who do you think it is?"

"I have no idea."

"And she doesn't have any husbands she's failed to mention, right?"

I laughed, despite myself. "No."

"What about your Uncle Calvin? He died of natural causes, right?"

"Yes," I replied. "And Aunt Tillie would never hurt Uncle Calvin. He was the love of her life."

"Then why did she turn him into that wind monster?"

I pulled back slightly, my mind wandering to the incident in question. A few months ago, when a crazed drug runner from Canada had taken us all hostage, Aunt Tillie called upon vengeance to protect us. That vengeance had taken the form of my long-dead Uncle Calvin, a man I had no memories of and knew only from photos.

"That wasn't Uncle Calvin," I said.

"You said it looked like him," Landon prodded.

"My Uncle Calvin didn't have a mean bone in his body," I explained. "He was ... an angel."

"I would think he'd have to be the devil to marry Aunt Tillie."

"He loved her," I said. "Sometimes ... sometimes people are different."

"Aunt Tillie was different?" Landon looked doubtful.

"I don't know," I said, laughing softly. "I wasn't alive back then. I've only known her as she is now. My mom says that they were really sweet together, that he doted on her."

"And what about her?"

"From what I can tell, she doted on him, too," I said. "She was lost when he died."

"I understand that. I still don't understand about the wind monster, though."

"That wasn't really Uncle Calvin," I said. "That was ... her."

"Her?"

"Her rage."

Landon was dumbfounded. "I don't understand."

"Aunt Tillie was the one who gave the spell form," I answered. "She's the one who gave form to her anger – and it was her anger that fueled the spell."

"And she made it look like him?"

"She did."

Landon rubbed his hand across my back thoughtfully. "Why did she make it look like him?"

I shrugged. "Because that's what she's angry about."

"I thought she loved him?"

"She did," I replied. "She does. It's just that … she's angry he died."

Landon clucked understandingly. "So, when she's angry, it's his face she sees."

"Exactly."

Landon was quiet for a few seconds. "If it's not Calvin, who is it then?"

"I don't know," I admitted. "I just don't know."

Even though it was spring, the night air was growing cold. It was still too early for the rare balmy night a lower Northern Michigan evening could offer.

Landon pressed a kiss to my forehead. "Let's go inside."

"Okay."

"You owe me some righteous sex," he said, opting to break the serious mood.

"Excuse me?"

"Did you sit through that dinner?" Landon said, chuckling. "I need someone to console me."

I pulled away, fixing him with a pointed stare. "What if I need consoling?"

Landon pinched my rear. "I think we can console each other."

I squealed as he chased me back to the guesthouse. Things were looking up.

SEVEN

"Let's eat breakfast here." Landon was standing at the counter in the guesthouse's small kitchen, drinking a cup of a coffee, his hair still wet from the morning shower. "We have to go up there."

"No, we don't," I argued. "We could spend the whole day in bed. You always want to do that. I'll do whatever dirty things you want."

It was the next morning. We were both showered and dressed, and yet I was dragging my feet. I so did not want to see Landon's mother.

Landon narrowed his eyes, considering my offer. "They would just come down here looking for us."

That sounded like the opposite of fun. "Fine."

Thistle breezed into the kitchen. The guesthouse is really like a small ranch house, everything on one floor, except for a dark and dank basement where the furnace and water heater hummed and bubbled. Thistle, Clove and I each had our own bedroom, all situated around a spacious living room and smaller kitchen. "What's up, kids?"

Landon poured her a cup of coffee and slid it across the counter. "Bay is trying to entice me to stay here all day by offering sex."

"Isn't that what the two of you were doing last night?"

I shot her the finger. "We were consoling each other."

"For what?"

"Were you at the same dinner we were last night?"

Thistle nodded. "Yeah, your mother is a piece of work, Landon."

"Don't attack his mother," I warned.

Landon rolled his eyes. "Please. If I wasn't here, you two would be knee-deep in insults about my mother."

"That's not true," I lied.

Landon raised his eyebrows. "Really?"

I bit my lip. "Clove would be here, too."

"That's what I thought."

Thistle sipped from her mug of coffee thoughtfully. "We're in a little bit of trouble here."

Landon glanced at her. "Explain."

"We have a dead body on the property," Thistle said. "A dead body I have a sneaking suspicion that Aunt Tillie knows a heck of a lot more about than she's telling."

"We figured that, too," Landon said.

"That's not the big problem, though."

"It's not?" I asked.

"We both know Aunt Tillie didn't kill someone and bury the body on the property," Thistle said.

Did we both know that? Because I wasn't so sure.

"The poltergeist is the real problem," Thistle continued.

"And that's what broke the dishes?" Landon asked.

"Well, they didn't just break themselves," Thistle said.

"I don't know a lot about poltergeists," I admitted.

"Me either," Thistle replied. "We have some books at the store, though. I'm going to do some research today."

"That sounds like a good idea."

"We have to be careful, though," Thistle cautioned. "If the poltergeist keeps visiting the inn, we're going to have to come up with an excuse to explain it."

Crap. She had a point.

"You mean Aunt Tillie saying it's an earthquake isn't going to work forever?" Landon asked, his grin wide.

I ignored him. "What do you have in mind?"

Thistle shrugged. "I have no idea. We have to come up with something, though."

I glanced at my watch. "We have fifteen minutes to make it up to breakfast. Where's Clove?"

Thistle furrowed her brow. "I have no idea."

"I'm right here," Clove said, popping out of the bathroom.

That was weird; I hadn't heard her enter the bathroom – which was located on the same side of the guesthouse as my bedroom. "Where have you been?"

"Getting ready."

"But … ."

"Let's go," Landon said. "The faster we get down there, the faster this will be over with."

I sighed. I guess I couldn't put it off any longer.

"**ISN'T THIS** NICE?" Twila said, placing a serving bowl of scrambled eggs at the center of the dining room table. "Everyone in one room … eating again … with no yelling."

This table is like the seventh circle of hell, I swear.

"It's great," I agreed, forking eggs onto my toast. "It's totally great."

"It is," Landon agreed, digging into a stack of blueberry pancakes.

I glanced at Connie to gauge her reaction, but her face was fixed on the dry toast and fruit she'd insisted upon. For the record, my mother and aunts are not fans of dry toast and fruit for breakfast.

"These are wonderful," Earl said, dishing a bite of pancakes into his mouth. "I've never had pancakes this good."

"It's just Bisquick," Connie said. "Let's not elect them Aunt Jemima or anything."

Marnie frowned. "We do not use Bisquick."

"These are from scratch?" Daryl asked.

"We make everything from scratch," Mom replied, her tone clipped. "We don't take shortcuts."

"Bisquick," Twila grumbled, staring down at her plate.

I rolled my neck. This was deteriorating quickly. "So, what does everyone have planned for the day?"

Earl grasped for the lifeline I threw. "I thought we would take a tour of the town."

"That sounds fun."

"I'm hoping so," Earl said, casting a forlorn look at his wife. "I certainly hope so."

The table lapsed into silence.

"I'm going to do some gardening," Aunt Tillie announced.

"No, you're not," Mom countered.

"Don't tell me what I can and can't do," Aunt Tillie warned.

I knew exactly what gardening she was referring to. "Why don't you read a book or something?"

"Are you trying to be funny?"

Not today. "I was just offering a suggestion."

Landon narrowed his eyes. "What kind of crop are you gardening?" He knew all about the pot field, although I'm sure, right now, he wished he didn't.

Aunt Tillie sniffed. "Flowers, not a crop."

"Really?"

"Really."

"Something smells good."

Chief Terry sauntered into the room, a wide smile on his face.

Mom, Marnie and Twila jumped to their feet simultaneously. "Sit here."

Chief Terry looked uncertain.

Mom nudged Marnie with her hip. "Sit here. Let us get you a plate."

Chief Terry took the proffered chair, pretending he didn't notice as my mother and her sisters scrambled to claim the chair next to him. Mom, as usual, won the battle. "Pancakes?"

"Sounds good."

"Bacon?" Marnie offered, shoving the plate in front of his nose.

"Um, yeah."

Twila didn't want to be left out. "Fruit?"

Chief Terry looked like the last thing he wanted was fruit. Of course, he would never be rude. "I love fruit."

The only sound for the next few minutes consisted of the noises made when cutlery meets plates. I glanced at Landon, but he was fixated on his breakfast.

"Breathe, boy," Aunt Tillie said. "You're acting like you haven't eaten in days."

Landon swallowed. "I didn't get to finish my dinner last night."

"Or you worked up an appetite," Aunt Tillie suggested, her eyes twinkling.

I wanted to pinch her, but I refrained.

"Where did you sleep last night?" Connie asked.

Landon furrowed his brow. "I slept at the guesthouse."

"With ... her?"

"Her? You mean Bay? Yes, I slept with her last night." Landon didn't appear to be embarrassed by the implications.

I was another story. "He slept on the couch." Why did I say that?

Landon rolled his eyes.

"He didn't sleep on the couch," Aunt Tillie scoffed.

"I didn't sleep on the couch," Landon agreed, shoveling another forkful of pancakes into his mouth.

I risked a glance at Connie, my stomach roiling when I saw "the look." I decided to change the subject. "What did you find out about the bones?"

Chief Terry glanced up from his well-stocked plate. "Well, the good news is the forensic team says they've been there for more than forty years – probably closer to fifty."

"How is that good news?" Denny asked.

"That means that Bay, Clove and Thistle can be ruled out as suspects," Landon answered.

Since when were we suspects?

"Are we sure?" Connie asked, her gaze pointed in my direction.

This woman was never going to like me.

"We're sure," Chief Terry replied.

AMANDA M. LEE

"What else do you know?" Landon asked, squeezing my knee under the table.

"Not much," Chief Terry admitted. "There was no overt trauma to the bones."

"So, he died of natural causes," Aunt Tillie said. "That's a relief."

I shifted a sideways glance in her direction, which she steadfastly ignored.

"We can't rule out foul play," Chief Terry replied. "Just because there's no obvious trauma to the bones, that doesn't mean that he wasn't murdered."

"He?"

"We have ascertained that the bones are those of a male," Chief Terry confirmed, slipping into cop-speak.

My mind flashed to the poltergeist. No, that didn't surprise me. It also hadn't escaped my attention that Aunt Tillie had referred to the body as a male before Chief Terry confirmed it. "What happens now?"

"Now? Now we wait," Chief Terry said. "I need more information."

"So we still don't know who it is," Mom mused.

"Actually, I have an idea on that," Chief Terry replied, shifting a nervous glance in Aunt Tillie's direction.

Her face was immovable. "Do tell."

Uh-oh.

"I went through the files," Chief Terry said. "I found one missing person who fits the parameters."

"Who?" Twila asked.

"Floyd Gunderson."

No one spoke. One glance at Aunt Tillie, though, and I knew. I knew that the body did belong to Floyd Gunderson. I had a hundred questions, though, none of which she was about to answer. "I thought Floyd Gunderson ran away."

"That was the working theory," Chief Terry said.

"Who is Floyd Gunderson?" Landon asked.

"Mrs. Gunderson's husband."

Landon rolled his eyes in mock surprise. "Really?"

"I'm sorry," I said. "Floyd Gunderson was … ."

"A drunk," Aunt Tillie supplied.

Chief Terry regarded Aunt Tillie, his face unreadable. "What do you know about Floyd Gunderson?"

Aunt Tillie averted her gaze. "I know he was a drunk."

"Mrs. Gunderson," Landon said, his mind busy. "She's the woman who owns the bakery, right? That's his wife."

"Yes."

"She seems like a nice lady," Landon said.

"She is," I replied.

"Her husband was a drunk, though?"

"I never met her husband," I said. "He was gone before I was born."

"And good riddance," Aunt Tillie huffed.

Landon fixed Aunt Tillie with a hard look. "I guess the question is, how did he end up in your back yard?"

Aunt Tillie's face was serene. "I have no idea."

Crap.

EIGHT

"This is a beautiful town," Earl said.

We'd managed to finish an uncomfortable breakfast, and now everyone was gathered in downtown Hemlock Cove for a day of sightseeing. In other words: My life sucked.

"It is," Landon agreed.

Since space in vehicles was at a premium, I snagged a ride with Clove and Thistle – where I'd unloaded twenty-four hours of misery and fear during a ten-minute ride. Aunt Blanche opted to remain at the inn, a fact that infuriated Aunt Tillie but made my life easier.

"It seems small," Connie sniffed.

Landon frowned. "I think you mean quaint."

"No, I mean small."

I blew out a sigh. I needed a break. "I have to stop at The Whistler."

Landon regarded me suspiciously. "I thought you took the week off?"

"I did," I said. "We still have only three employees. I have to make sure the layout is set."

He obviously wanted to argue but he reined in the impulse. "Fine. Why don't I go with you?"

"I thought you were going to spend time with us?" Connie interjected.

Landon clenched his fists, shooting me a hard stare. "I am. I just thought I would go to the newspaper with Bay to make sure she was fast."

"Does she need help doing her job?"

A muscle ticked in Landon's jaw. "No."

"Then why would she need you?"

"I didn't say she needed me."

I held up my hand. "I just need to stop in," I said. "Brian will probably be there."

Landon frowned. He hated Brian.

"I'll stop in, check the layout, and then I'll catch up with you," I said.

"We'd like to see the newspaper," Denny said.

I had no doubt he was speaking the truth. One look at Connie, though, told me she'd rather have Aunt Tillie remove her toenails with pliers than spend one more minute with me.

"Any time you want to see the newspaper, you're more than welcome," I offered.

Connie forced a smile. "After we've seen the rest of the town, maybe."

That's what I figured. "Sure."

Landon gave me a quick kiss. "You have thirty minutes," he warned.

"Thirty minutes," I said.

"I'll come looking for you."

Thirty minutes. I needed thirty days. I waved at Landon's family and trudged down the street. I could only hope that Brian Kelly – The Whistler's owner – could dream up some new article for me to focus on in those thirty minutes.

I wasn't holding my breath.

Edith, the resident ghost at The Whistler, greeted me the second I walked through the door. "Where have you been?"

Edith and I had been traversing a rocky chasm as far as our relationship during the past few weeks. In a nutshell: I'd found out she was a racist and she was still bitter about it.

"I'm off this week." I wanted to retain my anger but, the truth was, I preferred Edith's company to Connie's right now.

"Why?"

"Landon's family is in town."

Edith mulled over my answer. "He's introducing you to his mother? That's a big deal."

"She hates me," I admitted.

"You're probably exaggerating," Edith replied, floating a few inches above the floor, her severe bun ever present. "She's probably just nervous."

"She thinks I got Landon shot."

"Didn't you?"

Edith annoys me just as much as Landon's mother. "I guess."

Edith let out a long-suffering sigh. "She's a horrible person."

"You don't even know her."

"No," Edith acknowledged. "I know I'm sick of you being mad at me, though, so I'm willing to take a side."

I tried to fight the smile playing at the corner of my lips. "Thanks."

"You're welcome."

"Anything going on here?"

"Brian is plotting against you. Again."

I tried to muster some righteous indignation but, unfortunately, Brian had been plotting against me since he came to town. His grandfather, William, had left the newspaper to Brian with the stipulation that I remain editor. If Brian tried to change that – if he tried to sell the paper – the will stopped him in his tracks.

I'd tried to like Brian. No, really I had. He was just so ... full of himself. He'd been living at The Overlook since he came to town. Since my mother and aunts were so mean to him, though, he'd stopped eating meals there unless he was desperate. I rarely saw him at The Overlook these days.

"Who is he plotting with now?"

"That Sam guy."

I froze. Sam Cornell was not just some guy. He was more than that ... so much more than that.

"What is Sam doing here?"

"Plotting against you."

Edith was prone to histrionics. While I didn't trust Sam, I also didn't trust Edith to gauge the situation correctly. She'd freaked out over nothing before – and I knew she would do it again. "How do you know?"

Edith hedged. "I don't know ... I just know."

Oh, well, good. "Where are they?"

"In Brian's office."

I squared my shoulders, pointing myself toward the hallway. I didn't want to deal with this, but I didn't want to ignore it either. I paused outside Brian's office door, my hand raised, and then considered my options.

I'd been suspicious of Sam since he'd arrived in Hemlock Cove. He seemed too ... eager. He was interested in the Winchester family – and the real history surrounding the witches who lived in this town.

Yes, people know we're witches. Most of them, though, pretend they don't know the awful truth. The town's new "history" made that easy.

Sam Cornell wasn't one of those who pretended they didn't see. In fact, before leaving town a few weeks ago, he'd informed me that he knew exactly what my family was: Real witches.

I still remembered his face, his words, his matter-of-fact pronouncement. I'd feigned shock and surprise, but the truth was his interest concerned me.

I stepped back from the door. What was I going to do? If he confronted me in front of Brian, things could get ugly. I had to approach him when I was alone.

I fled, finding solace – and Edith – in my office.

"I don't blame you," she said. "He's creepy."

I paced the small space, wondering what to do. I didn't have a lot of options. I could try to hide here or face Landon's mother. I had twenty minutes left; there was no way I was giving that up.

I sat at my desk and booted up my laptop. They wouldn't even know I was here, I told myself. It's not as though my car was in the parking lot.

I lost myself in the mundane activities of my daily work life, forgetting for a few minutes that I wasn't alone in the building. I felt the presence at the door before I saw him.

"Sam."

"Bay."

"Is there something I can do to help you?" I kept my gaze trained on my laptop screen.

Sam didn't move to enter the office, instead resting his frame against the archway. "I thought you were off this week."

"I had a few things I wanted to check on."

"Me?"

Not even. "I didn't know you were in town," I replied honestly.

"You knew I bought the Dandridge, though."

The Dandridge was the local lighthouse. The previous owner was running a human-trafficking ring from the hidden cove on the property. Sam swooped in to buy the property in the aftermath. I was still a little bitter.

"I did," I agreed. "I just didn't know you were back in town."

"I told you I would be back."

"You did." I focused on my computer. This situation was uncomfortable, to say the least.

"I thought you might want to talk."

That was the last thing I wanted. No, talking was bad. "Nope."

Sam sighed. "I know I took you by surprise when I told you what I knew. That wasn't my intention. You have to know that."

I ignored him.

"I didn't mean for it to come out like that," Sam admitted. "I was just ... I just wanted you to know."

"Know what?" I faked confusion.

"Know that you're a witch."

The statement was simple – and yet it took my breath away. "I think you might need to seek psychiatric help."

"Don't ... don't do that," Sam warned.

I forced my eyes to meet his. "You're delusional. I think this town is getting to you. Hemlock Cove isn't a real witch haven."

Sam swallowed his upper lip with his lower. "You're not ready yet."

"Ready for what?"

"To tell the truth."

"I've told you the only truth I have."

Sam nodded stiffly. "Fine."

"Great."

"Good."

"Is there anything else you wanted?"

Sam shook his head. "No. Hide. Do what comes naturally."

I ignored his pointed remarks. "Can you close the door when you leave?"

NINE

Rejoining Landon's family at Hypnotic was a relief. Yeah, I know, I never thought I'd say that either – even if it was only internally.

"So, how's it going?"

Landon, sitting on the couch, leaned his head back against the top of the backrest and stared at the ceiling. "How do you think?"

"That bad, huh?"

We'd kept our voices low. His family was perusing Hypnotic's laden shelves, although they looked bored more than anything else.

Landon turned to me, his blue eyes tired. "Have you ever wished you were an orphan?"

"Not really," I said, plopping down on the couch next to him. "I've wished I was the last woman standing in the Winchester line from time to time, though."

Landon chuckled, running his hand up my back. "How were things at the paper?"

I debated how to answer the question. I'd told Landon about Sam's accusations minutes after he leveled them, but he'd dismissed my concerns. I wasn't sure now was the right time.

"What?" Landon pressed.

"N-nothing."

"Oh, God, what?"

"Sam was there," I admitted.

Landon scowled. "I thought he left town?"

"I told you he bought the Dandridge," I reminded him.

"I didn't think that meant he'd be back," Landon replied. "I thought that meant he'd be running it from afar."

"Apparently not."

Landon sighed. "Well, good. We certainly didn't have enough to deal with."

I leaned my head against Landon's shoulder, following his gaze as he zeroed in on his mother. Clove was standing next to her, fidgeting nervously. "It's just a candle."

"It's shaped like a skull," Connie replied, her face full of disdain. "Where did you even find someone to make these?"

"I made them," Thistle replied stiffly.

Connie glanced in her direction. "Figures."

Landon exhaled deeply. "Mom."

Connie shot Landon an impatient glance. "What?"

"The candles are great," Landon said. "Thistle works hard on them. She's very talented."

"How do you know?"

Landon kept his gaze even. "Because she makes them at the guesthouse. I've seen her. You wouldn't believe how much work goes into them."

Connie pursed her lips. "It sounds like you spend a lot of time at this ... guesthouse."

"I do," Landon said, nodding. "Every night I can manage I'm there with them."

"That sounds nice," Earl interjected. "Happy."

"It's home," Landon said, no hint of guile in his voice.

"Her home is your home?" Connie asked.

"No," Landon said.

My heart plummeted – although I couldn't figure out exactly why. His words hurt, though.

"She's home," Landon added, nodding in my direction.

My heart soared. Crap, I'm such a girl.

I met Thistle's gaze. She knew. "Landon is part of our family," she said. "An important part."

"So is Tillie," Connie countered.

Thistle scowled. "Aunt Tillie is ... well, she's difficult."

"I've noticed," Connie replied.

Thistle was at her wits' end. "So is Blanche."

Connie frowned. "She's old."

"So is Aunt Tillie," Clove said.

"She's mean."

"So is Aunt Blanche," Denny interjected. "She's just as mean as Aunt Tillie – if not meaner."

"That's completely untrue," Connie said. "Blanche is family."

"And Tillie is their family," Daryl said. "All the umbrage you take when people talk badly about Aunt Blanche? That's the same umbrage they take when someone talks about Aunt Tillie. Family is family."

"There's a difference," Connie sniffed.

"Only because you know Aunt Blanche," Landon said.

Connie focused on Landon. "I think you're mistaken."

"I think you're mistaken," Landon argued.

"I agree," Earl said, picking up one of the skull candles. "And I think this is a great candle. Wrap it up. I love it."

Thistle took the candle from him and walked behind the counter. Earl pulled his wallet from his pocket. "How much?"

"It's on the house," Thistle said.

"That doesn't seem fair."

Thistle glanced at me. "You're family."

Landon nestled his head against mine. "See? This is working out great."

One look at his mother told me otherwise. As easygoing as Earl, Daryl and Denny were, Connie and Aunt Blanche were a whole other story. "Yeah."

Landon squeezed my knee. "You don't seem convinced?"

"I'm ... leery."

Landon laughed. "I don't blame you."

"Your mother just seems to hate me."

"It's not like your family loves me," Landon replied.

"Oh, please," I scoffed. "My family thinks you're the bee's knees. They treat you like a king."

"Aunt Tillie would curse me if she had the chance," Landon said.

"She's had the chance," I argued. "She thinks you're a narc, but she still likes you."

"How can you be sure?"

"She hasn't made your … manly bits … shrivel and die," I pointed out.

Landon shuddered. "Can she do that?"

"She says she can."

"I guess I should be thankful for small favors."

"You should."

Landon shifted his head so his lips met my temple. "It's getting better."

"Your mother hates me," I repeated.

"She doesn't hate you."

I rolled my eyes. "Have you looked at that woman?"

Landon watched his mother as she poked around the store. "She's just … not sure."

"Not sure I'm going to corrupt you, you mean," I said, keeping my voice low.

"Baby, I want you to corrupt me every chance you get." He was going for charming.

I pinched his arm. "You have a dirty mind."

"I'm fine with that."

"Your mother isn't."

"I don't care what she thinks."

I didn't believe him, even though I wanted to. "Whatever."

Landon met my gaze. "If your mother didn't like me, would you care?"

I considered the question. "Probably not."

"Well, I don't care either."

How could he not care? "She's your mother."

"And you're my girlfriend."

I had a feeling girlfriend didn't trump mother. "She's your mother," I repeated.

"And you're my girlfriend."

I fought the urge to kiss him senseless. I didn't think his mother would appreciate the show of affection. "You're too cute for your own good."

Landon smirked. "I know."

"I'm hungry," Denny announced.

I sighed, forcing my gaze from Landon's handsome face. "What are you in the mood for?"

"What are they cooking up at the inn?" Daryl asked, clearly excited at the prospect of a home-cooked meal.

"We can eat in town for a change," Connie said.

Thistle exchanged a knowing look with me. "We have everything. Is there something you're hankering for?"

Thistle had laid down the gauntlet. Connie wasn't going to back down now. "I love French food."

"The diner has some great fries," Thistle replied, her tone dry.

"That's not French."

"They're French fries," Thistle countered.

"We're open to suggestion," Earl said hurriedly. "What's good?"

Thistle wrinkled her nose. "The Thai is great."

"I love Thai food," Daryl said. "You do, too, Mom."

"Only if it's prepared correctly."

Earl sighed. "Connie."

"The Thai is great here," Landon said. "You'll like it."

"You've eaten it?" Connie asked.

"I've eaten lunch here more times than I can count," Landon replied. "We've had Thai numerous times."

Connie scowled. "You eat lunch here? In this devil store?"

"I do."

"Here?"

"Mom, we're trying desperately to appease you," Landon said, never moving his head from mine. "If you don't want Thai, what else do you want?"

"French."

"You want fries? Great. The diner has great fries. I've had those, too – on numerous occasions."

"Fries are not French."

"You're killing me," Landon muttered.

This could turn into World War III if I didn't do something about it. "How about Middle Eastern?"

Connie wrinkled her nose. "That's terrorist food."

Landon sighed dramatically. "We're trying to give you the choice here, Mom. If you don't make one in the next thirty seconds, I'm going to side with Bay and order the terrorist food. It's really good."

"I would like a sandwich," Connie sniffed. "Something simple."

"Great."

"Turkey, no mayo, whole grain bread."

"Great."

I took the opportunity to get to my feet, escape in reach. I grabbed the writing pad from the counter and took everyone's orders, flashing Connie a placating smile as I moved toward the door. "I'll go down to the deli."

"I'll go with you," Landon said.

"Oh, no," I replied. "You should stay here with your family. They'll miss you if you're gone."

Landon scowled. "What about you? Will you miss me?"

I will. Not as much as I will hate his mother's reaction to his absence, though. "I will. You should spend time with your family, though. I get to see you all the time."

"I hate you," Landon grumbled.

"I know."

I waved at Thistle and Clove as I exited Hypnotic, finally breathing a sigh of relief as the spring air filled my lungs. If I was lucky, I could milk this food run for a good half hour. I planned on being lucky.

I kept my pace slow as I meandered down the street. The deli was only three stores away. I had to make this count.

My attention was diverted by a figure – a familiar one – rushing down the sidewalk across the street. Instinctively, I darted under a nearby awning and watched.

Aunt Tillie seemed oblivious to the world. She wasn't looking around, obviously not caring who saw her. She darted into the bakery – the Gunderson bakery – without a backward glance.

What the hell?

TEN

What is she doing?

Aunt Tillie rarely comes to town. In fact, my mother and aunts try to dissuade her from the idea whenever she mentions it. Most of the townspeople either don't trust her, which is richly earned, or they outright fear her, which she encourages.

It couldn't be a coincidence that she was going into the Gunderson bakery. Not now.

I knew it!

I was across the street and crouching beneath the open window on the far side of the bakery in less than a minute. Gunderson's Fresh Baked Goods – one of three bakeries in town – was located on a coveted corner lot. That meant that while the front of the store was completely visible from Main Street, the side wall was brick, boasting only three small windows. In other words, I wouldn't be able to look in without being seen, but I could eavesdrop in the shadow of the building.

What? She's lying and I want to know what's going on. Aunt Tillie deserves it. Just don't tell her I said that.

Luckily for me, Hemlock Cove doesn't have a lot of street traffic. I could easily hear what was going on inside of the bakery.

"Get out!"

"Tillie, you can't just kick my customers out."

"Watch me."

I heard the bell over the front door jangle and a moment later saw the two Davis boys run down the sidewalk, doughnuts clutched in their hands.

"Run! She's going to turn us into frogs," one of them screeched as they raced down the street.

Aunt Tillie has a way with kids.

I pressed my back to the wall and settled in to listen.

"Something happened," Aunt Tillie announced.

"Yeah, you chased my customers out," Mrs. Gunderson replied. "I'll have you know they hadn't paid for those doughnuts yet."

"I think you can survive without the seventy cents."

Silence.

"Don't you want to know why I'm here?" Aunt Tillie asked.

"Not really," Mrs. Gunderson replied. "Since I haven't talked to you in years, I'm figuring that nothing you have to tell me now is good."

"Well, you're right on that front," Aunt Tillie said.

Mrs. Gunderson sighed. "Fine. What happened?"

"We're having a greenhouse built out on the property."

"I heard. Congratulations? I'm not sure what to say."

"That's not the news," Aunt Tillie said, her tone harsh. "The news is, while they were out there, they unearthed a body."

The announcement must have knocked Mrs. Gunderson for a loop, because it was met with absolute silence.

"Aren't you going to say anything?" Aunt Tillie asked.

"I don't know what to say."

"Well, that's not going to do us any good," Aunt Tillie said. "Terry was out at the inn for breakfast. He's already figured out it's Floyd."

"How?"

"Well, he hasn't a hundred percent figured it out," Aunt Tillie conceded.

"What, exactly, has he figured out?"

"He knows the body has been there more than forty years, and he knows that Floyd is missing."

"That doesn't mean he knows it's Floyd," Mrs. Gunderson pointed out.

"It's only a matter of time," Aunt Tillie replied. "You know that. You're just being difficult."

"What are we going to do?"

"I don't know," Aunt Tillie replied. "Bay and Thistle are already suspicious of me. They know that I know something, although they haven't figured out what yet."

"And when they do figure it out?"

"Maybe they won't," Aunt Tillie suggested.

"Those girls aren't going to give up," Mrs. Gunderson said. "They've got too much of you in them."

"We have one good thing going for us," Aunt Tillie said. "The body is just bones. They might not be able to figure out how he died."

"What if they do?"

"We'll cross that bridge when we get to it."

"Can't you just … you know … poof it away?" Mrs. Gunderson sounded desperate.

"If I could do that I would've done it fifty years ago," Aunt Tillie said. "I'm not omnipotent."

"This is a nightmare."

Holy crap! What had she done?

"What are you doing?"

I froze when I heard the voice, forcing my gaze up to meet Landon's quizzical expression. He was standing on the street corner, his family behind him, and he didn't look happy.

"I … um … I … ."

"What are you all doing out here?"

Uh-oh. Aunt Tillie had obviously left the shop. I couldn't see her yet, but the Michaels family had all turned their attention to the front of the store.

"What are you doing?" Landon asked her, placing his hands on his narrow hips in a show of defiance.

"Shopping."

"You didn't buy anything."

"I placed an order." Aunt Tillie appeared on the street in front of Landon, swiveling around when she felt my presence. Her eyes narrowed dangerously. "What are you doing?"

I straightened up instinctively. "I thought I saw a penny. I was going to pick it up for luck."

"Really?"

Landon remained silent, but his eyes were busy as he glanced between us.

"What are you doing?" I turned the question around on her.

"Shopping."

"Why would you be here? It's baking day at the inn. Mom and Twila will be elbow-deep in dough all day."

"Are you calling me a liar?"

"No," I said hurriedly. "I just … I'm confused."

"I still don't understand what you're doing," Aunt Tillie said.

"I was getting lunch for everyone," I replied.

"This everyone?" Aunt Tillie asked, gesturing at the Michaels family.

"Yes."

"We decided we wanted to eat at the diner," Daryl offered. I think he was trying to be helpful. "Landon thought we would be able to catch up with you. That's when we saw you … well, I'm not exactly sure what you were doing."

"I was picking up a penny," I replied, sticking to my lie.

Landon was at his limit. "Why don't we all get lunch?"

"I'm not hungry," Aunt Tillie said.

"Sure you are," Landon countered.

"I think I'd know whether I'm hungry," she replied.

Landon pursed his lips. "Well then, you can just grace us with your wonderful presence. That will be fun, too."

"That sounds nice," Earl enthused.

"Yes," Denny agreed.

Aunt Tillie glared at Landon before shooting me a pointed scowl. "What do you think about this?"

I think I lost my appetite. "I think it sounds like a great idea," I said, trying to tamp down my worry. "I think a nice lunch with everyone sounds just ... fantastic."

"You never were very bright," Aunt Tillie said.

"Let's go," Landon said.

Ten minutes later we were settled around a rectangular table at the diner. Our orders had been placed, and the handful of diners in the restaurant were busy staring at Aunt Tillie – a fact that wasn't lost on Connie.

"Why is everyone staring?"

"The town loves new people," I lied.

Connie's eyes sharpened. "It seems like something else."

"She doesn't think you're very smart either," Aunt Tillie said.

"Drink your iced tea," I growled.

Landon leaned back in his chair, his body feigning relaxation – even though his eyes were curious. He obviously had questions he wanted to ask, but now clearly wasn't the time.

Earl cleared his throat. "So, um, I bet you know a lot about Hemlock Cove's history, Mrs. Winchester."

Aunt Tillie rolled her eyes. "Now I see where he got his conversation skills," she said, inclining her head toward Landon.

"Be nice," I hissed. I plastered a wide smile on my face as I regarded Earl. "What did you want to know?"

"How did the rebranding come about?"

"Oh, that's a great story," Annabelle Lafferty, the owner of the diner, said, interrupting with a conspiratorial grin. She'd been eavesdropping between the table and the counter since we placed our orders. I was actually glad she was filling the conversation gap, though. It gave me time to think.

"Why don't you tell them, Annabelle," I suggested.

"Okay." Annabelle pulled a chair up and launched into her story, embellishing with each sentence. I'd heard her tell it to tourists so

AMANDA M. LEE

many times I could almost recite it myself. "It all started with Selene Ravenstalk."

I tuned the rest of the story out and focused on Aunt Tillie. "I didn't even know you were close with Mrs. Gunderson," I said, keeping my voice low.

"What makes you think I am?"

I bit the inside of my mouth. "I saw you go into the bakery."

"No, you didn't."

"Yes, I did."

"No, you didn't."

Goddess, I totally hate this game. She used to play it when we were little – telling us we hadn't really seen something when we knew we had. It worked until we were about nine and realized what she was doing. That didn't stop her from dusting it off from time to time to annoy us, though.

Landon shot an occasional smile down to the other end of the table, pretending he was interested in Annabelle's colorful tale. His attention was focused on us, though. I had no doubt.

"You drive me crazy," I muttered.

I jumped when I felt someone move in closer on my right side. I glanced over and saw Melody Davis – the older sister of the fleeing Davis boys – staring at Aunt Tillie intently.

"Do you need something, sweetie?" I asked.

"That's her, isn't it?" She was breathing hard.

"That's her." I knew she was talking about Aunt Tillie. All the kids in town were fascinated with – and terrified of – the reigning Winchester matriarch.

"Is everything they say about her true?"

I tucked a strand of hair behind my ear. "Yes."

"Does she really have a pet scorpion?"

"Yes."

"Does she really hang out with ghosts?"

"Yes."

"Does she really have dog paws for feet?"

That was a new one. "I don't know," I said, smiling. "She won't take her shoes off when I'm in the room. She's must be hiding them from me."

Melody nodded in agreement and then looked over at Landon, smiling shyly. "Who is he?"

"He's Landon," I said. "He's with the FBI."

Landon smiled for Melody's benefit, gracing her with a heartfelt grin. "And who are you?"

Melody's face was red, so I answered for her. "This is the fabulous Melody Davis. She's the reigning Little Miss Hemlock, if memory serves."

Melody's shiny brown hair shook as she giggled. "How did you know that?"

"I put the story in the newspaper when you won," I reminded her.

"Oh, yeah."

"We're in the presence of a real-life beauty queen," Landon raised his eyebrows. "I'm honored."

Melody glanced back at me. "Is he your boyfriend?"

"Last time I checked," I said, smiling tightly. I didn't tell her I was worried that Aunt Tillie's latest drama would chase him right out of my life.

Melody didn't seem satisfied with the answer. "Are you her boyfriend?"

Landon smirked. "I am."

"And you're a policeman?"

It was a gross understatement, but Landon nodded anyway. "I am."

"Are you here to arrest her?" Melody asked.

Landon furrowed his brow. "Who?"

Melody cupped her hand over her mouth and whispered in Landon's ear. I couldn't hear what she said, but the furtive looks she kept darting at Aunt Tillie were a dead giveaway.

"I'm not here to arrest her, no," Landon said. "I'm just here to have lunch."

"With your girlfriend," Melody clarified.

"With my girlfriend."

Melody bit her lower lip. "Is she going to curse me?"

I realized that every face at the table was now focused on us. Crap. "No."

"Yes," Aunt Tillie grumbled.

Melody's eyes widened, panic evident.

I pinched Aunt Tillie's arm viciously. "Don't tell her that." I turned back to Melody. "She won't hurt you."

"No," Aunt Tillie agreed, rubbing her arm. "I might hurt you, though."

"Drink your iced tea," I ordered.

"Is something going on?" Connie asked.

"No," Aunt Tillie and I said in unison.

I was pretty sure no one at the table believed us – including me. Why can't I have a normal family? Just one day in my life. That's all I'm asking.

ELEVEN

"Are you sure you don't want to ride back with us?" Landon asked.

We were standing outside of Hypnotic, one of the worst lunches in recent memory only minutes past. The rest of the Michaels family was sitting in Landon's Explorer, watching us.

I felt like the bug on the windshield they were looking through.

Aunt Tillie had disappeared before the bill came – not that I blamed her, or expected anything different. Heck, I was fighting the urge to flee now.

"I'm sure."

Landon ran his hands down my shoulders. "Do you want me to stay with you? I can give the keys to one of my brothers and catch a ride with Thistle and you."

"That should go over well," I grumbled.

Landon sighed. "This couldn't have come at a worse time. That doesn't mean it's the end of the world. We don't even know who the body belongs to yet."

I hadn't told him what I'd overheard in the bakery. "No."

"Are you going to tell me what they were talking about?" Landon's question was pointed.

"Yeah." I didn't hesitate with my answer. "Not here, though."

Landon glanced at his family. "All right. I'm guessing you want to stay here and talk about it with Clove and Thistle."

He knew me too well. "Does that make you mad?"

Landon pressed a quick kiss to my forehead. "No."

"Really?"

He shook his head. "No. I'm not angry that you tell them stuff. I'm angry when you lie to me."

"I know."

"This situation is ... it's totally screwed up."

"Welcome to life with the Winchester witches," I mumbled.

Landon lifted my chin with his thumb. "I happen to like the Winchester witches – most of the time."

"Even Aunt Tillie?"

"Yes."

"You're not a very good liar."

"I'm not lying."

I blew out a frustrated sigh. "I'm so mad at her right now."

"I know."

"I'm going to throttle her."

"She'll just curse you again," Landon warned.

"Mom made her promise not to do that when your family is in town," I replied. "Once they're gone, though, it's going to be open season."

Landon snorted. "Do you really think that my family staying at the inn is going to stop her?"

"No."

Landon brushed his lips against mine softly and then pulled away. "Don't do anything crazy with the two of them," he ordered.

"I won't."

"I mean it. Oh, and if she's going to curse you anyway, can you see if she'll make you smell like bacon again?"

"No!"

"And taste, I liked it when you tasted like bacon," Landon said, his gaze distant as he remembered. "That was the best few days of my life."

Men.

I watched him drive away and then slipped inside Hypnotic. I tossed the bag of sandwiches and chips I'd carried from the diner onto the counter and threw myself on the couch dramatically. "My life sucks."

"I just saw you making out with Landon in front of the store," Thistle countered. "It can't suck that bad."

"We weren't making out," I shot back. "His family was watching us from his SUV."

Thistle smirked. "Kinky."

"I like his family," Clove said.

Thistle rolled her eyes. "You like his mother?"

"I think she's just a little nervous," Clove replied. "We're hard to take if you're an outsider."

"It doesn't help that the police are crawling all over the inn because a body was discovered," Thistle added.

Speaking of that .... "Guess who joined us for lunch?"

"Who?"

"Aunt Tillie."

Clove scrunched up her face. "Aunt Tillie? How?"

"Well, when I left to get lunch, I saw her going into the Gunderson bakery," I explained.

Thistle, who was organizing incense behind the counter, stilled. "What?"

"Yeah. She went into the Gunderson bakery."

"Why?"

"She wouldn't say."

"What did she say?" Clove asked.

"Well, she told Landon she was placing an order," I said. "When she saw me, though, she denied even being in the bakery."

"Wait, where were you?" Thistle asked.

"I was crouching down by one of those side windows and eavesdropping."

Thistle laughed. "Is that where Landon found you?"

"Yes."

"And then Aunt Tillie found you?" Clove asked.

"Yes."

Thistle sucked in a breath. "Did she know what you were doing?"

"She didn't say," I said. "She couldn't really, not with Landon's family standing there and watching us as though we were circus freaks performing acts of great debauchery for public consumption."

"There's a reason Aunt Tillie says you're dramatic," Thistle said.

"Forget that," Clove interjected. "What did you hear while you were eavesdropping?"

"I heard Aunt Tillie tell Mrs. Gunderson that the body hadn't been identified yet – but that it would be identified as Floyd eventually."

"You're kidding!" Thistle exploded. "She admitted she knew who it was?"

"She didn't know anyone was listening."

"Did she say anything else?" Clove pressed.

"She said that the cops probably wouldn't be able to figure out how he died because he's just bones now," I replied.

Thistle thought about it a second. "She didn't admit to killing him, though. That's got to mean something."

"It just means that she didn't admit it," I said, "not that she didn't do it."

"Maybe Mrs. Gunderson did it and Aunt Tillie covered for her?" Clove suggested.

"That doesn't sound like Aunt Tillie," Thistle countered.

Actually, it did. "Wait a second," I said. "Aunt Tillie might've done something like that. She's loyal."

"She's loyal to family – kind of," Thistle said. "Why would she be loyal to Mrs. Gunderson?"

"Maybe they're friends," Clove said.

"I've never seen them together," I said. "Have either of you?"

"No."

"Maybe they used to be friends," Thistle mused. "Maybe something happened that ended the friendship."

"Like murder and hiding a body?" I asked.

"Maybe," Thistle said.

"We don't know that, though," Clove cautioned. "Maybe we should just ask her."

"It's not like she's going to tell us," Thistle scoffed. "She's going to keep lying. They could have her in handcuffs, in the backseat of a cop car, and she'll still lie."

More than twenty years of living with the woman told me that was true. "So, what do we do?"

"We could do a truth spell," Clove suggested.

Thistle's eyebrows jerked up. "You want to cast a truth spell on her now?"

Clove shrugged. "Why not?"

"Because Landon's family is here," I reminded her. "That has disaster written all over it."

"We don't do it when they're around," Clove said. "We do it when it's just us."

"Do you really think she's just going to sit there and let us cast a spell on her?" Somehow I had my doubts.

Clove's mouth dropped open. "Um, no, duh! We'll do the potion one."

I'd forgotten about the potion spell. Still, there were a few problems with that scenario, too. "How are we going to get her to drink it?"

"We'll put it in her wine," Clove replied.

"How do we guarantee no one else drinks the wine?" Thistle asked.

"We put it in her secret stash, the one she has in her bedroom," Clove said.

Huh. Clove wasn't usually the devious one. She'd put some thought into this. "When did you think of this plan?"

"Last night when you and Landon were rattling headboards and I had nothing better to do than listen," Clove said.

Clove's dry spell was making her bitter. "Sorry."

Clove waved off the apology. "Don't worry about it. I'm just jealous."

"Landon has two brothers here," Thistle interjected.

I shook my head vehemently. "No."

"I'm not saying she try and corrupt the priest."

"I think he's a minister," Clove said.

"What's the difference?"

"How should I know?"

"Daryl looks like he could be fun," Thistle continued. "He seems like a nice guy."

I didn't want to dissuade Clove, but the idea of the two of us dating brothers gave me the heebie-jeebies. "Let's find her someone else."

"Fine," Thistle conceded. "Tourist season is almost here. She can have the pick of the litter."

Thistle's words reminded me of Melody's question. "Oh, and Melody Davis stopped by the table at lunch today, too."

"She's cute," Clove said. "Her brothers are monsters, though."

"Well, she asked me if the rumor that Aunt Tillie has dog paws for feet is true."

Thistle laughed. "What did you tell her?"

"I told her I've never seen her feet."

"That's so funny … ." Thistle cocked her head to the side. "You know, come to think of it, I've never seen her feet."

"That's not possible," Clove said.

"Have you ever seen her feet?" I asked.

Clove furrowed her brow, concentrating. "No. But that doesn't mean that she's got dog paws down there."

"It doesn't mean she doesn't," Thistle said. "Maybe she's part Bigfoot?"

Clove shuddered. She's afraid of Bigfoot.

Aw, man, now I was going to have nightmares.

I jumped when a candle fell off one of the shelves on the far wall. Thistle was behind the counter. I was still on the couch. Clove was closest, but she was still a good eight feet away.

"What was that?"

Clove moved over and picked up the candle. "I don't know. Maybe someone from Landon's family moved it and left it too close to the edge of the shelf. It looks fine." She put the candle back on the shelf and moved back to the books she'd been dusting.

The candle fell to the floor again.

I sat up straighter on the couch.

Clove moved back toward the candle and picked it up. "That is so weird."

"Maybe it's warped on the bottom," Thistle suggested. "Let me see it." She moved to Clove and took the candle, tipping it over so she could study the bottom. "It looks smooth."

The incense bags she'd been packing on the counter jumped, tossing a mixture of sticks and cones into the air, some dropping to the floor.

I got to my feet slowly.

"What is that?" Thistle asked.

"I don't know." I glanced around the store, but nothing jumped out at me.

"Is it a ghost?" Clove asked.

I was the only one who could see ghosts, but if they were around me long enough and I was talking to one my cousins could eventually hear them.

"There's nothing here."

I felt something against my back and whipped around, a clump of hair sticking to my lip.

"What?" Clove hissed.

"Something touched me."

"Touched you? Like in a naughty way?"

"Don't be gross."

Thistle jerked. "I felt something behind me."

Clove grabbed Thistle's arm. "What do we do?"

"How should I know?"

A sterling silver photo frame – the one behind the counter showing the three of us standing in front of one of the gardens at The Overlook – toppled over.

"It's got to be the poltergeist from yesterday," I said. "It followed me here."

"Well, take it out," Clove said, her voice shrill.

"It's not like I can put it on a leash," I grunted.

"It has to be Floyd," Thistle said. "He's obviously angry about … something."

"Like being murdered and buried at the inn?"

"Yeah, that."

"Let's get out of here," I said.

"What about the mess?" Clove asked.

"Maybe it will leave when we do," I suggested.

"Maybe he can clean it up when we're gone," Thistle suggested before moving behind the counter and grabbing her and Clove's purses.

"We definitely need to dose Aunt Tillie with the truth potion," I said. "We have to find out what's going on here."

Another candle tipped and rolled across a shelf, finally dropping to the floor with a solid *thunk*.

"It better work," Thistle said. "If this keeps up, Clove won't ever come back to the shop."

TWELVE

"Let's spend the day in bed."

Landon's body was pressed to mine, the covers tugged over both of our heads. The alarm had sounded two minutes earlier, but neither of us had made a move to start the day.

"We promised your family we would take them to the spring festival," I said.

"Isn't it running all week? We can take them tomorrow."

I kissed his jaw lightly and then shoved the covers aside. "That's not going to work. Your mother will come down here – and she's going to hate our housekeeping skills. We can't hide here."

"Can't you put a spell on the door so it won't open?"

"I could," I said. "We're doing a different spell today, though."

I'd filled Landon in on everything when we got back to the guesthouse last night. His family had opted to drive to a neighboring town for dinner – which was a relief – so we hadn't gotten a chance to catch up until late in the evening.

"And you think this truth spell is going to work?" Landon was getting more comfortable around the world of magic, but he still seemed confused about how things worked. I'd been in the world since birth and I still didn't fully understand it.

"Do you have any other ideas?"

"Can't you just ask the ... poltergeist?"

"He doesn't talk. He just breaks things."

"You talk to ghosts, though."

"A poltergeist isn't a ghost," I said. "They're different."

Landon ran his fingers up my arm, thinking. "How?"

"A ghost is a lost soul looking for rest," I explained. "A poltergeist is ... well, it's a whole lot of rage. It doesn't want rest, it wants revenge."

Landon leaned up, resting his weight on his elbow. "If he wants revenge, why isn't he going after the person who killed him? Why is he going after you?"

"What makes you think he's going after me?"

"Because he attacked you in the hole."

"I was the only one there."

"You were also at Hypnotic," he pointed out.

"So were Clove and Thistle."

"You're the common denominator."

He had a point. "We don't know that he hasn't been anywhere else," I said. "He could be going after Mrs. Gunderson, too."

"Why isn't he going after Aunt Tillie?"

"Maybe Aunt Tillie didn't do anything to him."

"Do you really think that?"

"I want to."

Landon kissed my arm. "Okay. Let's shower and get this day started."

"You want to shower together?"

Landon's blue eyes were full of faux innocence. "What? It will be faster."

"WE'RE LATE," Thistle complained to Clove.

We were parked in front of Hypnotic. I'd caught a ride with the two of them while Landon played chauffeur for his family.

"Like ten minutes."

"We're going to have to bleach that shower to get it clean," Thistle said.

"Stop."

"Leave her alone," Clove said. "You're just jealous because Marcus has been so busy getting the festival ready."

Thistle wrinkled her nose. "Shut up."

"Do you want me to go in the store with you?" I asked.

Thistle shook her head. "No. That will look suspicious. We'll go in, clean things up, and go from there."

"Besides," Clove added. "If you don't go in the store, maybe Floyd won't come and visit either."

I understood their wariness. "I have to spend the day with Landon's family."

"It won't be so bad," Clove said. "The festival will be busy."

That was a bonus. I climbed out of the car, joining Landon on the sidewalk. "Well, here it is."

Connie's eyes were flat. "It's big."

"We don't do small here," I admitted.

"I think it's neat," Denny said. "Look at all the people. There's a carnival, too. That's great."

"They have horses," Daryl said, pointing. "Can we ride them?"

"Sure," I said. "I know the guy running it. He'll get you guys saddled up right away."

"Is he an ex-boyfriend?" Connie asked.

That was a weird question. "No. He's actually Thistle's boyfriend."

"Someone dates her?"

I clenched my hands at my sides. "What is that supposed to mean?"

"Her hair is blue," Connie sniffed.

"And her heart is big," Landon interjected. "Thistle is a good person – most of the time."

"Her name is Thistle," Connie said.

I was really starting to dislike this woman. "She didn't pick her name."

"No, a woman named Twila did."

AMANDA M. LEE

That did it. Landon gripped my arm. "Why don't you guys look around? We're going to go … over there."

Earl patted Landon's shoulder. "That sounds like a good idea." He tugged on his wife's arm. "Why don't we have a talk over here?"

Landon dragged me to the pie booth. "I know you're angry. She doesn't mean what she says."

"She sounded like she meant it."

"She's … out of her element."

She's evil is what she is – and a whole other level of evil from Aunt Tillie. Huh, how frightening is that?

I rubbed my forehead tiredly. "I'm sorry."

"Don't apologize," Landon admonished. "I'm going to talk to her."

"Don't. That's just going to make her hate me more."

"She doesn't hate you."

"She certainly doesn't like me."

Landon slung an arm around my shoulders. "I guess it's good that I do then, huh?"

If he wasn't so cute I swear I'd kick him in the shins and lock his mother in one of the kissing booths when no one was looking. "So, what do you want to do? You want to go on a ride with your brothers?"

Landon looked torn. "I don't want to leave you here with Mom. Why don't you come with us?"

A ride sounded nice, but something else caught my attention. "I'll be fine. I'll just stay away from your mother."

Landon eyed me, his face unreadable. "Are you sure?"

"Yeah," I said, forcing. "Just find Marcus. He'll hook you up."

Landon dropped a small kiss on my mouth. "Don't do anything stupid."

"That seems like a broad order," I teased.

Landon grinned. "Just be good."

"I'm always good."

"Be better than that."

Once he was gone I searched the crowd for the face I'd glimpsed. I found Mrs. Gunderson under one of the tents where the buffet would be set up in the next hour. That's the direction I headed.

Mrs. Gunderson jumped when she found me standing next to her. "Bay, dear, you gave me a fright."

"I'm sorry."

"Are you looking for something to eat? The food won't be here for a while."

"I'm looking for you."

She stiffened, but she didn't meet my gaze. "Oh, do you need to place an order or something?"

I shook my head. I didn't have a lot of time, so I decided that playing games was out of the question. "I heard you and Aunt Tillie yesterday."

Mrs. Gunderson crumpled the pile of napkins she'd been holding. "I don't know what you mean."

"Your husband's body was buried at The Overlook," I said. "I'm kind of curious how that happened."

"My husband was having an affair and left town," Mrs. Gunderson said. "It was sad. It was hurtful. I got over it a long time ago, though."

She was tough. I wasn't going to let up, though. "Mrs. Gunderson, I know that the body found at the inn was Floyd."

"Floyd left town before you were born. You don't know anything."

I softened my tone. "I would like to understand."

"You mean your cop boyfriend would like to understand," Mrs. Gunderson corrected.

"Landon isn't a cop," I replied. "He's also on vacation. He's not involved in this."

"Wasn't he with you when the bones were discovered?"

I pinched the bridge of my nose. She'd obviously found out more information after Aunt Tillie left yesterday. "His family is staying at the inn. He was there as my boyfriend, not in his capacity with the FBI."

"Does that mean he's not going to investigate a murder if it falls into his lap?"

"Are you saying Floyd was murdered?"

Mrs. Gunderson's jaw tightened. "I'm saying my husband left town almost fifty years ago. If that is his body, I have no idea how it got there."

"With all due respect, I know you're lying."

Mrs. Gunderson finally faced me, her features a mask of anger and fear. "You should be careful what you say. I'm not a liar. I'll sue you if one word of your … conjecture makes it into the pages of The Whistler."

"I don't print gossip, Mrs. Gunderson," I replied. "It just so happens, I'm on vacation this week, too."

"Then it would seem you have nothing else to do here."

"That doesn't mean I won't find out what's going on."

"Why do you care?"

"Because Aunt Tillie is family," I replied. "She's clearly hiding something. The problem is, I don't know if she's protecting you or herself."

"Tillie doesn't protect anyone but herself," Mrs. Gunderson said, swallowing hard. She wanted me to believe the words but, I didn't.

"Fine."

"Good."

I moved away from her, turning to find a bench or something to rest on. I needed to think. Instead, I found Landon standing about twenty feet away, watching me. Crap.

I walked to him stiffly. "I thought you were going for a ride."

"I thought you were going to stay out of trouble."

"What makes you think I wasn't?"

"Because that's the woman from the bakery yesterday," Landon replied. "Mrs. Gunderson, right?"

Don't lie. "Right."

"And what were you two talking about?"

"She says her husband ran away with another woman almost fifty years ago," I said.

"Do you believe her?"

"Not even close."

"What else did she say?"

"She said that if Aunt Tillie is protecting someone, it's herself."

The corners of Landon's mouth tipped down. "Do you believe that?"

Not even close. "No. She said the words but there's something else going on."

"Do you think she killed her husband?"

I shrugged. "I have no idea."

"If he was having an affair maybe she freaked out and killed him," Landon suggested.

"I've known her a long time," I said. "She's never seemed violent."

"Infidelity can make people lose their minds."

"So, I guess you better never cheat on me," I said, going for levity.

Landon smirked. "Honey, you're more than I can handle. Trust me."

I rolled my eyes. "I thought you were going riding with your brothers?"

"I decided to wait for you."

"You mean you didn't trust me," I corrected.

"I trust you," Landon replied. "I trust you to find trouble even when you're not looking for it."

Fairly certain that was an insult, I turned to look at the crowd, which was growing by the minute. "I'm not going to fight with you."

"Good, because I'm not going to fight with you either."

I took a few steps back in the direction of the fair. "You know, I was thinking we could maybe go into one of the kissing booths before it gets too busy."

"I thought a kissing booth was so someone could pay to kiss a politician or something?"

"It is," I said. "The mayor will be in there all day. He likes it. It's empty for now, though."

Landon smirked. "Are you trying to get me to do something lewd in public?"

"Do I have to try?"

"Nope."

I scampered ahead, Landon close on my heels. Suddenly, his hands were gripping my shoulders and yanking me backward. Man, he was anxious for a kiss.

The sign – the one that said "Monster X-ing" standing next to the trail we were walking down – toppled over, hitting the trail with a loud clang.

"What the hell?"

Landon wrapped his arm around my chest, pressing his body into mine. "Why did that sign just fall?"

I didn't answer, but I had an idea.

"Was that the ... ?" Landon glanced around, lowering his voice. "Was that that thing?"

"I don't know."

I didn't know. I just had a feeling.

THIRTEEN

Landon was shaken.

"It was probably just an accident," I said. "That sign is new. It probably wasn't anchored correctly."

Landon looked dubious. "Right."

"Don't freak out."

"I'm not freaking out."

That was good. Only one of us could freak out at a time. "I need to sit down."

"I'm going to sit down with you."

We found a bench and settled. Landon pulled my hand into his, his thumb rubbing a trail of circles over my knuckles.

"Oh, hi," Marnie said, greeting us with wide eyes. "I'm so glad I found you."

"What's wrong? I thought you guys weren't coming until later."

"We weren't," Marnie said, tightening her jaw. "Unfortunately, Aunt Blanche decided that she had to come now and we were her ride."

"Why?" Landon asked.

"She found out Kenneth was going to be here."

Uh-oh.

Landon tilted his head to the side. "I don't understand."

"I think she likes Kenneth," Marnie said.

"He must have a magic penis or something," I mused.

Marnie snorted. "I was wondering that myself."

Landon pinched me, the worry from a few minutes earlier passing. "What's a magic penis?"

"What?"

"I think he's asking if he has one," Marnie said.

My cheeks burned under their scrutiny. "You two are sick."

"Anyway," Marnie said, "Aunt Blanche is here."

Landon sighed. "I'll find my parents."

"Aunt Tillie is here, too."

The world was coming to an end. "Aunt Tillie is at the festival?"

"She is now," Marnie replied.

"Why? She never comes to these things. She says they're full of people perpetuating stereotypes and acting like idiots."

"She came when she found out Blanche was coming," Marnie replied.

"Ah."

Landon groaned. "This is going to get ugly, isn't it?"

"You have no idea."

"I need to find my parents."

"I'll try to head off Aunt Tillie," I said.

Landon gripped my hand. "Maybe you should come with me."

I knew what he was worried about. "I'll stay away from any signs."

Landon seemed unsure.

"No sign would dare attack with Aunt Tillie present."

"You were attacked by a sign?" Marnie asked.

I pointed to the fallen sign, which Marcus was planting back into the ground. "It fell over."

"It almost hit her," Landon said.

Marnie shifted her gaze between the two of us. "It sounds like an accident."

She didn't know about the poltergeist, I reminded myself – at least not everything about the poltergeist. "It was nothing." I dropped a kiss on the corner of Landon's mouth. "I'll catch up with you in a few minutes."

"You'd better."

I followed Marnie through the crowd, finally finding Mom and Aunt Tillie next to the flower booth. Yeah, we have a lot of booths at these things.

"Aunt Tillie," I greeted her. "I can't believe you're here!"

"Have you seen Kenneth?"

"No."

"Have you seen that viper, Blanche?"

"No." I was thankful on that front. Blanche had spent more time holed up in her room than anyplace else since arriving at the inn. I had no idea what she was doing up there – but ritual human sacrifice wasn't out of the question.

"I'm going to make all of her hair fall out," Aunt Tillie warned.

"No, you're not," Mom shot back. "You are going to behave yourself. You're in enough trouble."

I narrowed my eyes. What did that mean? Did Mom know something about the body?

Marnie swore under her breath. I followed her gaze, inhaling sharply when I saw what had caught her attention.

"Let's look over here, Aunt Tillie," I said hurriedly.

Aunt Tillie slapped my hand away, scowling out at the dance floor where Kenneth was pushing Blanche around while wearing a wide smile. Who starts dancing this early? They were the only couple out there.

"I'm going to make her teeth fall out, too," Aunt Tillie said.

"No, you're not," Mom said.

"You're right. They're probably dentures, anyway. I'm going to make her smell like a pile of compost."

Well, that should be fun. "Aunt Tillie, let's go for a walk or something."

I was hoping to distract her, but I also wanted to tell her about my conversation with Mrs. Gunderson. I didn't get a chance to press the issue, though, because Chief Terry was standing in front of us.

"Is something wrong, Terry?" Mom asked. "Why don't you come over here and let me give you a hug? You look like you need one."

"Me, too," Marnie piped up, sneering at Mom.

Chief Terry shifted uncomfortably. "I don't want to do this."

"You don't want to do what?" Marnie asked.

I knew. Oh, crap.

"I need to talk to Tillie."

"About what?" Aunt Tillie barked.

"The body has been identified."

Crap.

"Oh, that," Aunt Tillie said. "So, you know it's Floyd Gunderson and now you think I killed him, don't you?"

Double crap.

"**Let's just** have a seat here."

Chief Terry was all nerves and worry. Mom and Marnie were so angry about Aunt Tillie being hauled in for questioning I was sure their protests were still echoing in his head. In the end, I'd volunteered to go to the police station with Aunt Tillie, appeasing them only slightly..

So, here we were. Chief Terry, Aunt Tillie and me – and a whole lot of anger and recrimination.

"Your office is small," Aunt Tillie said, wrinkling her nose. "It smells, too."

"It doesn't smell," I said, turning to Chief Terry. "It doesn't."

"It smells like lies and false accusations," Aunt Tillie said. "It smells like narcs."

Great. This was going to go well. I decided to try to exert some control. "You identified the body?"

"We did," Chief Terry said. "We matched dental records."

"And it was Floyd Gunderson?"

"Yes."

Silence. I glanced at Aunt Tillie. "I think he wants to know how you knew it was Floyd Gunderson," I prodded.

"He told me."

"No, he didn't."

"Yes, he did."

"When?"

"The other day at the inn," Aunt Tillie replied. "He said it was Floyd Gunderson."

"No," Chief Terry said. "I said that Floyd was the only one to go missing that far back."

"It's not my fault you weren't clear," Aunt Tillie shot back.

The door to the chief's office opened as Landon let himself in. He propped himself against the back wall, nodding at Chief Terry, but remaining silent. The unspoken message was clear: Landon was here; he just wasn't here in an official capacity. Yet.

Chief Terry cleared his throat. "Tillie, you must know how Floyd Gunderson's body ended up on your property."

"Why? You don't know. How should I know?"

"I don't live there."

"Neither did Floyd," Aunt Tillie pointed out. "Maybe he got drunk – he was always drunk – and fell in a hole or something."

"That sounds … unlikely," Chief Terry said.

"Well then, Sherlock, why don't you tell me what sounds likely."

Chief Terry shifted uncomfortably. "I don't know what sounds likely."

"Then I guess we're done here." Aunt Tillie pushed to her feet.

"Sit down," I ordered.

"You're walking on thin ice here."

"Aunt Tillie, I talked to Mrs. Gunderson earlier."

"Why would you do that?"

"You know why."

Aunt Tillie settled back in the chair. "I'm sure I don't."

"She told me that if Floyd was on the property, she had no idea why."

"I'm sure she doesn't."

"That means you must know something about it," I pressed.

"I don't."

"What about Margaret Little?" Chief Terry broke in.

To anyone else, Aunt Tillie probably looked calm. I knew her, though. There was a subtle shift.

"What about her?" Aunt Tillie asked.

Yeah, what about Margaret Little? All I knew about her was that she was widowed, she peddled pewter unicorns, and she was often mean and condescending.

Chief Terry sighed. "Margaret Little was rumored to be having an affair with Floyd Gunderson."

Eww. "Who told you that?"

"It's one of those town-gossip things that has survived a few decades of rewrites," Chief Terry admitted.

I focused on Aunt Tillie. "Is it true?"

"You'll have to ask her that."

If we're ever kidnapped and tortured by terrorists, I want Aunt Tillie with me.

"So, you don't know whether Margaret Little was having an affair with Floyd?" Chief Terry asked.

"I was a happily married woman," Aunt Tillie said. "I didn't go in for things like that. I have morals."

I ran my tongue over my teeth. "Did Mrs. Gunderson kill Floyd because he was sleeping with Mrs. Little?"

"I have no idea," Aunt Tillie said. "Although, to be fair, Floyd was so drunk I don't think he could get it up. It probably just laid there and flopped around."

That was a nice visual. "You know that, but you don't know whether Mrs. Little was having an affair with Floyd?"

"I don't like gossip."

Of course.

"Tillie, this doesn't look good for you," Chief Terry said. "Floyd was supposed to have left town. He didn't have a job. He was known to be a … royal SOB … but somehow he ended up dead in your back yard."

"He probably got drunk and fell in a hole."

"Do you have a lot of holes that people can fall into and die?"

"Do you know how Floyd died?" Aunt Tillie asked.

Chief Terry gritted his teeth. "No. Without any flesh, his cause of death is pretty much impossible to ascertain."

"So you don't even know he was murdered," Aunt Tillie said. "That sounds like shoddy police work to me."

She had a point. Not about the shoddy police work, mind you, but about Chief Terry's certainty that Floyd had been murdered.

"If Floyd died of natural causes, how did he end up buried?" Chief Terry asked.

Well, there was that.

"You'll have to ask him," Aunt Tillie said. "Are we done here?"

Chief Terry sent a helpless look in my direction.

"Aunt Tillie, you need to tell us what you know," I said.

"What I know? I know that Floyd Gunderson was a drunk. I don't know how he ended up on our property. That's what I know."

I met Chief's Terry's eyes and shrugged wordlessly.

"Is that all?" Aunt Tillie asked.

"That's all."

This day sucks.

FOURTEEN

"I can't believe I let you drag me up here," Landon said.

We'd entered the inn through the back door and were now hiding in the family living quarters before facing my family and, ultimately, his.

"I wanted to stay in bed as much as you did," I reminded him. "It's not an option for us. We have, what, five days and a breakfast left? Suck it up."

"You know what?" Landon said, looking around the room carefully to make sure we were alone. "The next time we take a vacation, we're going somewhere alone. It's going to be just the two of us and no clothes. That's it. I'm putting my foot down."

I laughed. "That sounds good to me."

Landon framed my face with his hands, resting his forehead against mine. "I want this week to be over."

"You want to go back to work?"

"I want to go back to … sanity."

"Since when do you equate my family with sanity?"

"Since your family met my family and life exploded," Landon replied.

"At least we didn't all have dinner together last night," I offered. "That's something."

"Yeah, that was fun," Landon agreed. "My family sat at one table. Your family sat at another. Aunt Tillie kept whispering threats between the two. I want to relive that night for the rest of my life."

My shoulders shook with silent laughter. "She's got a lot on her mind right now."

"She's awesome in police interrogations, by the way."

"She's ... something."

Landon laced his fingers through mine. "Let's go eat some brunch."

"You're looking forward to brunch with both our families?"

"No," Landon said, shaking his head. "However, my family wants to spend the rest of the day in Traverse City."

That sounded like a horrible trip. "I can't go."

Landon smirked. "I wasn't planning on taking you."

I couldn't hide my frown – or the small, disappointed tug at my heart.

"Not that I don't want you with me," Landon said, reading my expression. "I just think it will be good to get to spend some time with my mother while you handle your family."

He had a point.

"Handling my family might take more than an afternoon."

"I thought you guys were going to spell Aunt Tillie?"

"We are," I replied.

"Well, this afternoon seems like a good time. The inn will be empty. Get some truth out of her and maybe we can salvage this week."

I hated it when he was pragmatic.

"Fine."

Landon gave me a short, sweet kiss. "It's going to be a good afternoon."

I sent him a thumbs-up. "It's going to be great."

No one was in the kitchen, so we continued through, following the noise into the dining room.

"Tell me what's wrong, baby doll." Kenneth stood next to Aunt Tillie's chair, his face wrought with confusion.

Great.

Thistle glanced up when we entered. "Welcome to hell."

"I'm very excited to be here," I deadpanned.

"No you're not," Clove said, sliding into the chair next to Thistle. "This has been going on for ten minutes."

I glanced at Kenneth. "Good morning, Kenneth."

"Tillie is mad at me – and she won't tell me why."

"It's because you danced with me," Blanche supplied. She was sitting at the far end of the table, dressed as though she were headed to Sunday Mass or the Kentucky Derby, and smiling as if she'd just won the lottery. "She's upset because you like me more."

Kenneth looked confused. "I don't understand."

"Women live longer than men," Landon replied, patting Kenneth on the shoulder. "You're a big prize, my man."

"My heart belongs to one woman," Kenneth said. "One beautiful and amazing woman."

"Me," Blanche said, her smile wide.

Aunt Tillie scowled. "Not that I care where Kenneth's heart belongs, but you're no match for me."

"You're not even an opponent," Blanche said. "You're mean and bitter. Men don't like mean and bitter."

"It takes one to know one," Aunt Tillie shot back.

"I'm so confused," Kenneth said.

"Sit down," Mom ordered, pushing Kenneth into the seat next to Aunt Tillie. "Eat your breakfast."

"My love is upset."

"She's always upset," Thistle said. "Get used to that."

"I'll show you upset," Aunt Tillie warned.

"How can he like her more than me?" Blanche looked scandalized.

"Kill me now," Landon muttered.

I squeezed his hand. "You and me both, honey."

Landon pinched my rear. "I like it when you call me honey."

"Having sex in front of people is frowned upon," Aunt Tillie announced. "It's immoral."

"Who's having sex?" Landon asked, pulling me behind him to the other side of the table.

"You two will be in a few minutes," Aunt Tillie replied.

"I wish," Landon said, settling into his chair. "Bay is too much of a prude, though."

Thistle snorted. Connie frowned. Earl smiled. Mom swatted Landon with a dishtowel.

The sound of a throat clearing at the door drew everyone's attention. Chief Terry stood there, hat in hand, looking uncertain.

"Hey," I greeted him. "Have a seat."

Chief Terry looked in the direction of my mother and aunts. They met his look with a triple dose of consternation.

"There's a seat open down by Blanche," Mom said.

I was stunned. For as long as I could remember, my mother and aunts had been fighting for Chief Terry's affections. For them to join together – united by anger over him pulling Aunt Tillie in for questioning – well, it was a big deal.

Landon shot Chief Terry a sympathetic look. "There's a chair right here," he said, patting the empty spot beside him.

Chief Terry slid into the chair. He was lost. "I'm sorry about yesterday."

"What happened yesterday?" Connie asked.

"He accused me of murder," Aunt Tillie replied.

"Why didn't you lock her up?" Blanche asked.

"Because I didn't do it," Aunt Tillie replied, snidely.

"Of course she didn't," Kenneth interjected. "My love would never hurt anyone."

I was starting to wonder if cataracts were rendering him blind where Aunt Tillie was concerned.

"I bet there are hundreds of bodies buried on the property," Blanche said. "She's got a mean streak."

Look who's talking?

"Eat your breakfast, Aunt Blanche," Landon ordered.

"I'm done."

"Then shut your mouth."

"Landon!" Connie's face was pinched. "Don't talk to your aunt that way."

"She's being obnoxious," he replied. "On purpose."

"She's always obnoxious," Daryl said. "It's part of her charm."

"That's how we feel about Aunt Tillie," Clove said, shooting Daryl a flirtatious smile.

Crap on toast.

"They're a lot alike," Daryl agreed, fixing her with an equally flirty smile.

"I may cry soon," I admitted to Landon.

"Will you think less of me, as a man I mean, if I join you?"

He's too cute for words sometimes.

"Are you two in heat or something?" Aunt Tillie flicked my ear.

"Eat your breakfast," Mom ordered. "You're in enough trouble."

"Yeah," Thistle teased.

"Don't press me, girl."

Thistle visibly blanched. She'd stayed out of Aunt Tillie's line of fire for a whole week now. She wasn't keen on stepping back into danger.

"I think everyone is being unfair," Chief Terry announced.

"How so?" Mom asked, her frame stiff.

"I had to question Tillie," he replied. "You know I had to."

"She's innocent," Twila said. "She would never hurt anyone."

"She's awful," Blanche said. "She's a terrible person."

"Don't you talk about her that way," Kenneth warned. "You're being mean."

Had he even met Aunt Tillie?

"Don't listen to her, Kenneth," Aunt Tillie admonished. "She's going to get what's coming to her."

Landon glanced at me. I couldn't answer his silent question, so I merely shrugged in response.

"You eat your breakfast," Mom warned. "I'm not telling you again."

"You're not the boss of me," Aunt Tillie grumbled.

"I think I'm being persecuted," Chief Terry admitted.

"I always think that," Clove said.

"There are answers to be found in prayer," Denny offered.

Aunt Tillie snorted. "I pray that this breakfast is over. Are we done yet?"

"I'm going to lock you in your room all day," Marnie warned.

That sounded like a great idea. Clove had slipped the truth potion in Aunt Tillie's wine stash this morning while Thistle distracted her and we were ready to put our Truth Plan into action.

"Don't threaten her," Kenneth said, pointing at Marnie angrily. "She's had a rough couple of days."

"How?" Thistle asked.

"The cops are harassing her," Kenneth replied. "The fuzz is trying to force her into a confession for a crime she didn't commit."

"The fuzz?" Landon asked.

"You know what I mean."

"I'm not sure I do."

I wasn't joking about the crying.

"I think we should go shopping," Connie announced. "I'm ready to leave."

"I'm always ready to leave," Thistle said.

"I want to stay here," Blanche said.

"You're not staying here," Landon said. "We're going to Traverse City as a family. One big, happy family."

"You're not the boss of me."

"Listen to your nephew," Aunt Tillie warned. "There's nothing but heartache for you here. In fact, if you want to stay in Traverse, I'm not going to argue."

"Eat your breakfast," I said.

"Don't push me."

"I'm not pushing you."

"Why is everyone ignoring me?" Chief Terry asked, his face drained of color. "This is all wrong."

"They'll get over it," Clove said. "Trust me."

Landon exhaled so deeply his bangs fluttered on his forehead. "I think I've died and gone to hell."

I was right there with him.

FIFTEEN

"So, we're just going to wait for her to drink the wine?" Thistle asked. "That's the plan?"

We were standing in front of The Overlook, waving as Landon pulled away, his entire family crowded inside his Explorer. The minute they left the parking lot we all exhaled deeply.

"Thank the Goddess."

"You didn't answer my question," Thistle said.

"We can't make her drink it," I said. "If we try to force the situation, that's just going to make her realize something is up."

"Which we definitely don't want," Clove said.

"Exactly."

"What if she doesn't drink it?"

"She'll drink it."

"What if she doesn't?"

"Then we'll have to think of something else," I admitted. "Let's hope for the best. We're due to beat her at something."

"History seems to tell us exactly the opposite," Thistle replied.

She had a point.

"Look at it this way," I said. "Landon's family is gone all day. That means Mom will relax the rules on Aunt Tillie for a couple of hours.

Aunt Tillie had a rough day yesterday – and that breakfast was straight out of the seventh circle of hell – she's going to need a drink."

"So, what then? We're just going to hang around here all day asking her questions until she finally answers one truthfully?" Thistle looked nonplussed. "That sounds like a terrific way to spend the day."

"Isn't the store open today?" I asked.

Thistle shook her head. "No. The festival is going on and that will soak up all the business. We don't have to open today."

"Well, that means you guys are on Aunt Tillie duty today," I said.

"What are you doing?" Thistle asked.

"I'm going into town," I replied. "I'm going to have a talk with Mrs. Little."

"Are you going to ask her if she was sleeping with Floyd Gunderson?" Thistle asked.

"Do you have a better idea?"

"No."

"I can't stay at the inn today," Clove announced.

Thistle cocked her head to the side. "Why?"

"I have a few errands to run," Clove said, dropping her eyes evasively.

"What errands?" Thistle asked.

I was suspicious, too. "Yeah, what errands?"

"I'm going out to the Dragonfly, if you must know," Clove replied. "Not that it's any of your business."

The Dragonfly was a new inn on the other side of town. It was nearing completion, and the grand opening was quickly approaching. It also happened to be jointly owned by all three of our fathers. They'd spent years away from town, returning only a few months ago to open their own competing business.

Aunt Tillie was still ticked off, although recent upheavals had disrupted her revenge plans.

"Why are you going out there?" I asked.

"Um, to see my dad," Clove said. "That's allowed, right?"

"How is he doing?" Thistle asked. "You know, after the whole Karen thing and all."

Uncle Warren was still recovering from his own emotional turmoil since his engagement abruptly ended when it was revealed his intended was actually trafficking children along Lake Michigan.

He was understandably upset.

"He's doing okay," Clove said. "I just thought I would take him some baked goods and spend a few hours with him."

"That sounds like a good idea," I said. "Thistle can follow Aunt Tillie alone. By the time you get back tonight, hopefully she'll be in a chatty mood."

"Yeah, Thistle can follow Aunt Tillie all day," Thistle grumbled. "Thistle can do it."

"Stop pouting," I said, flicking her wrist. "You'll be fine."

"I didn't say I wouldn't be fine," Thistle countered. "Of course I'll be fine."

"She's afraid of her," Clove said. "I don't blame her."

"I am not afraid of her."

I furrowed my brow as I regarded her. I was afraid of Aunt Tillie and I wasn't even the one following her. I pushed the thought out of my mind, though. I had my own scary quest for the day.

PEWTER POWER IS one of Hemlock Cove's most popular stores. Since Main Street is full of all things kitschy, that's saying something.

It creeps me out.

Don't get me wrong; I'm not averse to pewter. It's just the abundance of unicorns that freaks me out. I'm still not sure what unicorns have to do with the Hemlock Cove rebranding, but I stopped asking the question out loud years ago.

Mrs. Little was sitting in her favorite rocking chair and flipping through last week's edition of The Whistler. She glanced up when I entered, her face flashing surprise before shifting to uneven blankness.

"Bay, this is a surprise."

Mrs. Little is, well, little. She's about five feet of fire and judgment wrapped in some really tacky floral patterns. Her auburn hair, which refuses to tip over into gray, is always pulled back in a severe bun, and her flat, gray eyes are often wary.

She makes me nervous.

"Mrs. Little, how are you?"

"Well, I'm not dead yet," she replied. "I'm counting that as a win."

I could see that. "That's good then."

Mrs. Little continued to rock, watching me edge around the store nervously but refusing to ease the tension by engaging in further mindless chitchat.

"Bay, you're showing three of the four signs of being a shoplifter," she said. I guess she couldn't take the silence either.

"Which ones?" I asked.

"You won't make eye contact. You're touching everything but buying nothing. Oh, and you keep looking at the door, like you're making sure you'll be able to make it through it quickly when the time comes."

"I'm not shoplifting."

"I know," Mrs. Little replied. "You're not the type. Now, if it was Thistle, I would be worried."

"Thistle wouldn't shoplift either," I said. "She's not a big unicorn fan."

"I guess. Do you want to tell me what's going on?"

"I … uh … I'm not really sure how to broach this with you," I admitted.

"Well, why don't you just ask me what you want to ask me. We'll take it from there."

Okay. That sounded reasonable. "Did you know that the construction crew out at The Overlook discovered the remains of a body the other day?"

"The town is small, Bay," Mrs. Little replied, never taking her eyes off me. "Everyone knows."

"Did you know the body was identified as Floyd Gunderson?"

Mrs. Little's face remained passive. "I heard that also."

She wasn't going to volunteer anything. Crap.

AMANDA M. LEE

"I heard that … perhaps … you might have some inside information about Mr. Gunderson," I hedged.

"Let me guess. You heard I was having an affair with Floyd and you came to find out if it was true," Mrs. Little said, her tone clipped. "You're hoping that I killed him, which would exonerate Tillie, and make your life a whole lot easier right now."

She was good. "Actually, that's only half true," I said. "I was hoping that you would be able to tell me that Floyd actually died in some terrible accident and you guys all buried him in some misguided attempt to protect one another."

Mrs. Little raised a perfectly manicured eyebrow. "I did have an affair with Floyd."

I waited.

"I did not, however, kill him," Mrs. Little continued. "I was under the assumption, like everyone else in town, that Floyd left of his own volition."

"Aunt Tillie says he was a drunk," I said. "If you forgive my … skepticism, I can't see you with a drunk."

"I was having troubles of my own at the time," Mrs. Little conceded. "My husband and I were always fighting. We were having money trouble, you see. You probably don't remember, because this Hemlock Cove is very different from what the town was before, but when the industrial base fell there were a lot of people in this town struggling."

I sat down in the open chair across from her. "Was Floyd having trouble?"

"Floyd was always having trouble," Mrs. Little said. "You should know, Floyd and I went to high school together and we had a past – even then."

"You dated in high school?"

"We did."

"But you didn't get married after graduation?"

Mrs. Little smiled. It was a small expression, full of woe and regret, but there was something else there, too.

"I'm sure, for someone your age, the ways of the world back when

I was young seem foreign," she said. "You probably think that women of my day had only one option: high school and then marriage."

She wasn't wrong.

"I wanted to go to college," she said. "It wasn't an option for me, though. I'm not sure I ever truly got over that."

"So, you married Mr. Little?"

"I don't want you to think that I didn't love Bob," she said. "I loved him with my whole heart. I still love him – and he's been gone a long time now."

I kept my lips pressed firmly shut. I wanted to ask her why, if she loved her husband so much, she fell into bed with a drunk. I didn't, though.

"Bob and I always wanted children," Mrs. Little said. "We couldn't have them, though. He always blamed me and I, well, I always blamed him. I have no idea what the truth was – or whether it was a truth for either of us."

"So you slept with Floyd to see whether you could get pregnant?"

Mrs. Little shook her head emphatically. "I slept with Floyd because he was as lost as I was."

"Was he unhappy? Was his marriage to Mrs. Gunderson unhappy?"

"His marriage to Ginny was plagued with difficulties," Mrs. Little said. "Their marriage was happy for a time, though. I would never pretend that Floyd didn't love Ginny. That wouldn't be fair to either of them."

"So, what happened?"

"A mistake."

"I guess I don't understand," I said. "Didn't you think it was suspicious when Floyd disappeared?"

"Honestly? No," Mrs. Little replied. "I was too relieved. Floyd taking himself out of the equation made it easier for me."

"How so?"

"It just was," Mrs. Little said. "The specifics aren't important. What's important is that Bob and I were happy again when he was gone. We found happiness."

"What about Mrs. Gunderson?"

"Let's just say everyone was a lot happier after Floyd left town and leave it at that."

SIXTEEN

I left Pewter Power with some answers – and even more questions. Instead of going back to The Overlook, though, I headed to The Whistler. There was someone else in town who might have some answers.

I found Edith in the employee lounge – really just a small kitchenette – watching television. Since she spent most of her days locked in the building (even though she had the freedom to roam anywhere in town) I left the small television on the counter switched on for her entertainment.

She was a big fan of *General Hospital* and was watching it now.

"I can't believe they recast Jason," she said, not bothering to glance up. "This guy looks too young."

"At least he has more than one facial expression," I offered.

"I liked his one facial expression," Edith countered.

"I know you did."

I sat down in one of the chairs. "Where's Brian?"

"He left a few hours ago," Edith said.

"Where to?"

"Maybe he's at the festival. I'm not sure."

"Has he been up to anything?"

AMANDA M. LEE

"Just spending a lot of time with that Sam guy," Edith said.

"Sam has been around?" That was worrisome.

"He stopped in a few times," Edith said. "He tried to talk to me."

"He did?"

"He can see me."

"I know. He told me."

Edith finally wrenched her eyes from the television. "He told you? When?"

"Before he left town," I said. "He ambushed me at the inn and told me that not only could he see ghosts, he also knew we were witches."

Edith doesn't breathe, but I swear she sucked in a breath to steady her nerves. "What does that mean?"

"It means I'm avoiding him," I replied.

"That doesn't sound very mature."

"I'm fine with that."

"What does Landon say?" Edith asked. She was privy to all the gossip in my life – and she thrived on it. She was a busybody when she was alive. Since I'm her only form of entertainment in death – other than the television -- she straddles a line bordering on obsession from time to time.

"He said he would beat him up if I wanted him to."

"I like him."

"He's likeable," I agreed.

"Speaking of, isn't his entire family staying at the inn this week?"

"Yup."

"Why aren't you with him?"

"They went to Traverse City for the day," I said.

"He didn't ask you to go with him?"

"I think he knew I needed a break."

"From him?"

"No, from his mother. Oh, and his great aunt."

"He's got a great aunt, too? Is she anything like Tillie?" Edith has a tortured past with Aunt Tillie. Actually, that's putting it mildly. She hates her.

"If you can believe this, she's worse."

"I don't believe it."

I didn't blame her.

"So, why would you need a break?" Edith asked.

"Oh, well, let's see," I said. "Between the bones uncovered by the construction crew, Landon's aunt hitting on Aunt Tillie's boyfriend, his mother pretty much hating my guts and Chief Terry hauling Aunt Tillie in for questioning regarding a fifty-year-old murder, I guess you could say I just needed a day to myself."

Surprising a ghost isn't easy. Edith's raised eyebrows were a dead giveaway that I'd managed just that, though.

"You found bones at the inn?"

Oh, right, I'd gotten off track. "Yeah, that's actually why I'm here. I thought you might know something about the victim."

"Why? Who is it?"

"His name was Floyd Gunderson," I said. "I figured, since you were around back then you might know who he was. I mean, I know you died long before he disappeared, but you were privy to all the news from those days."

I glanced at Edith, who was sitting as still as possible. Since she was a ghost, I'm not sure how impressive that was.

"What's wrong?"

"The bones belong to Floyd?"

"You knew him?"

"Sort of."

"Do you want to elaborate on that?"

"Do they know how he died?" Edith asked.

"No. Edith, what's going on? You look white as a … ghost."

"Floyd was my brother."

"How? You have a different last name."

"He wasn't my full brother," Edith corrected. "After my father died, my mother married another man – and they had a child together."

"Floyd?"

"Floyd."

"How old would Floyd be now?"

Edith did the math in her head. "I think he would be about eighty."

That made sense. "Were you close with him?"

"Not really," Edith said. "We weren't enemies or anything. Floyd was just a different type of person."

"How much older than him were you?"

"About ten years," Edith said.

"I guess that's a big difference when you're that age."

"I was a little bitter about my mother getting remarried," Edith admitted. "I didn't take it well."

"Did you die before Floyd disappeared?"

"The year before," Edith said. "I heard the people in the paper's offices talking about Floyd disappearing when it happened. It didn't really surprise me."

"He didn't disappear, though," I said. "He ended up dead in Aunt Tillie's back yard."

"Well, the good news is that your mother and aunts would've been small children then," Edith said.

"How is that good news?"

"They can't be arrested for being accomplices."

Thank the Goddess for small favors.

"Edith, did you know Mrs. Gunderson?"

"Ginny? Yeah. She was a nice woman. I never understood what she saw in Floyd. She was so happy on their wedding day. I knew it wouldn't end well, though."

"Would she be capable of killing your brother?"

"I seriously doubt it."

"What about Mrs. Little?"

"Margaret Little? Why would you ask that?"

"Because apparently she was having an affair with Floyd," I replied.

"Really? I guess that makes sense."

"Because they dated in high school?"

"Yeah." Edith seemed lost in thought. "You know, I guess Floyd being dead makes a weird sort of sense."

"How?"

"If what you're saying about Margaret is true, I bet she killed him to cover up the baby?"

I jerked my head up. "What baby?"

"She was pregnant in late 1966," Edith said. "There was a birth announcement in the paper. I remember seeing it. I was happy for her."

"She said she couldn't have a baby," I said. "She doesn't have a child."

"No," Edith said. "She lost the baby at birth. It was some sort of tragedy, I guess. A stillbirth. William was talking about it in the newsroom when it happened. I think everyone in town rallied behind her when they found out. I always assumed the baby was Bob's."

"From everything I've heard about Floyd, it sounds like he was kind of … lost," I said.

"You mean the drinking?"

"Yeah."

"He had some demons," Edith said. "I always hoped he'd outgrow them."

"I don't think he did."

"No," Edith agreed. "I don't think so either."

"So, basically, I have two options," I said. "Either Mrs. Little – or even Mr. Little – killed Floyd to hide the paternity of the baby. Or, Mrs. Gunderson found out about the affair and killed him herself."

"I guess," Edith said, not seeming particularly perturbed by either prospect.

"That still doesn't explain how the body ended up on our property."

"No," Edith said. "I guess you'll have to ask your Aunt Tillie about that."

Great.

SEVENTEEN

Chief Terry was my next stop. He was sitting behind his desk, staring off into space, when I walked into his office.

"What are you doing here?" he asked. "Did your mother send you to ban me from the inn? Am I the new devil in town?"

"They're just upset," I said. "They'll get over it."

"Your mother didn't send you?"

"I'm fairly certain Mom is enjoying an afternoon of freedom right now," I said. "Landon's family is in Traverse City."

"Yeah, things seem tense out there."

"They've been better."

"So, your mother didn't send you?" Chief Terry looked disappointed.

"If it's any consolation, I haven't seen her since breakfast," I said. "Once Landon left, I headed straight to town."

"Why?"

"I wanted to talk to Mrs. Little." There was no point in lying.

Chief Terry shifted forward in his seat, resting his elbows on his desk. "What did she say?"

"She admitted having an affair with Floyd," I said.

"I'm not surprised she was having the affair," Chief Terry said. "I am surprised she admitted it."

"She claims she hit a rough spot with Mr. Little and the affair was a mistake," I said. "She also said she didn't kill him. She said she assumed like everyone else that he'd run away."

"She probably did."

"Except she also told me she couldn't have children," I added.

"She doesn't have any children."

"No, but she was pregnant in 1966," I said. "Edith told me."

"Edith? The ghost at the paper?" Chief Terry was aware of my ability. "Wasn't she Floyd's half-sister?"

"Yeah. I just found that out."

"Edith died before Floyd disappeared, if memory serves," Chief Terry said. "How could she know about a pregnancy?"

"She said there was an announcement in the paper," I explained. "She said it was a stillbirth."

"How could she know that?"

"She heard that at the paper, too," I said. "I guess it was a big deal when it happened."

Chief Terry rubbed his jaw, considering. "How come I never heard about this?"

"You would've been a child then," I said. "That's probably not something parents talked about with their kids in those days."

"Or any day."

"No."

"This is a mess," Chief Terry said. "Floyd could've knocked up Margaret, which means that Margaret, Bob and Ginny are all prime suspects in a suspicious death."

"Except you don't know how he died," I reminded him. "He really could've gotten drunk and fallen in a hole."

"No, I don't," Chief Terry said. "I do know that he was found buried on your property, though. He didn't fall in a hole. And, given the timeline, the only people who could've buried him out there were Tillie or Calvin."

The thought had never occurred to me. "Uncle Calvin?"

Chief Terry nodded grimly. "I didn't want to say anything in front of your mother or aunts, but burying a body isn't an easy task. I think your aunt is capable of anything she puts her mind to, but burying Floyd is a big deal."

"What if she and Mrs. Gunderson buried him?"

"It's possible."

"Or she could've done it with Uncle Calvin's help," I supplied.

"I don't want you to jump to any conclusions," Chief Terry said. "From everything I've heard about Calvin, though, he wouldn't hesitate to do whatever Tillie asked of him."

"Even cover up a murder?"

"Yes."

"What if he murdered him?"

"In this whole hodgepodge of motives and hidden truths, the only one I can't assign a reasonable explanation for murder is Calvin," Chief Terry said. "If he was involved, I think it was just tangentially."

"Which means Aunt Tillie was involved directly."

"We don't know that," Chief Terry cautioned. "That woman is … unpredictable. That doesn't mean I think she's a murderer."

"What do you think?"

"I think she's capable of covering up a murder," Chief Terry said. "I'm also worried she's capable of protecting a friend if it comes to that."

That was a nice way of looking at things. I'd just never known her to have any friends.

"Well, we're hoping to have some answers from her tonight," I offered.

"How are you going to manage that?" Chief Terry asked, doubt clouding his features.

"We slipped a truth potion in her private stash," I said. "Once she drinks it, she'll have no choice but to tell us the truth."

"What if she doesn't drink it?"

"Then we'll have to figure something else out," I said. "I'm confident she'll drink it, though."

"Isn't that risky with Landon's family out there?"

"They're gone for the day," I said, leaning back in the chair. "Their excursion couldn't have come at a better time."

Chief Terry chuckled. "It seems like everyone is ready to kill each other out there."

"His mother hates me."

His mouth tipped into a frown. "Why do you say that?"

"Because she does. You should see the way she looks at me. If she could pick anyone for her son, I would be the person standing behind her."

"Bay, let me tell you something," Chief Terry said, his voice stern. "I've known you your whole life. You make the world a better place just by being in it. Landon sees that. I see it in his eyes.

"That's not to say you don't frustrate the hell out of him," he added. "That's a special gift where the Winchester women are concerned. You're all capable of driving men to distraction."

"That's what I'm worried about."

"When I first met Landon, I wasn't sure about him," Chief Terry admitted. "I'm sure now."

"When you first met him, he was undercover with a bunch of meth heads," I reminded him.

"I knew who he was and what he was doing," Chief Terry replied. "He informed me of his presence and case when he came to town. He didn't want any misunderstandings."

"Well, at least he told you," I laughed, my mind rushing back to the day I'd met Landon. I definitely hadn't been so sure of him back then. "I thought he was a dirtbag."

"When he first came to town, I thought he was kind of full of himself," Chief Terry said. "FBI agents have a reputation for thinking they're above everyone else. That's what I thought he was like."

"He's not like that," I countered.

"You know, when I realized he was interested in you I warned him to stay away," Chief Terry admitted. "That's how unsure of him I was."

"You did?"

"What? You've been my favorite since you were little," he replied. "I didn't want just anyone stealing your heart."

I laughed. "He's not just anyone."

"I know," Chief Terry said. "That's also why I know he won't let his mother's unwarranted judgments get in the way. The boy is ... well ... he's a good man. And that's all that matters."

He was right.

I got to my feet and moved toward the door. "I'll tell you what we find out."

"I hope it all works out."

I paused before leaving. "You want to know something?"

"Always."

"You were always my favorite, too."

Chief Terry couldn't hide the blush creeping up his cheeks. "Tell your mother that."

"She already knows," I said. "I'll remind her, though."

EIGHTEEN

"Good morning, sleepy head." Landon snuggled his face into my neck, spooning me from behind. "Are you going to get up anytime today?"

"Not if I can help it." I was trying to remember going to bed the night before.

Landon pinched my rear. "I'll make it worth your while."

I pushed sleepy clouds from my mind. "What time did you get in last night?"

"It was after midnight."

"Why didn't you wake me up?"

"You looked so cute, all curled up with your Kindle in your fuzzy pajamas," Landon said. "I didn't want to ruin the moment."

"What did you guys do yesterday?"

"The usual stuff. Mall. A few antique stores. We went to an Irish pub for dinner and drinks afterward. What did you do?"

I told him about my visits with Mrs. Little, Edith and Chief Terry. He was impressed. "You had a busy day."

"Yeah. We still don't know what's really going on, though," I said.

"We have more information," Landon said. "That's always a good thing."

"I guess."

"Wait a second … Chief Terry wasn't sure I was good enough for you?"

"He says you're a good man now; that's all that matters," I replied.

"I am a good man," he agreed, pulling me closer. "I'm the best man. I was thinking you could let me prove that to you."

"Oh, yeah? What did you have in mind? Because breakfast in bed sounds great," I teased.

"You wound me."

"Sorry."

"What about Aunt Tillie? Did she drink the truth potion?"

"No," I grumbled. "She did everything but. She hid in her pot field all afternoon."

"I told you not to mention the pot field," Landon growled.

I hadn't meant to mention the pot field. I'm not on top of my game in the morning. "Sorry. I forgot your oath thing."

"What oath?"

"To protect and serve."

"That's cops."

"Do no harm?"

"That's doctors."

"Be prepared?"

"That's boy scouts."

"I give up."

"Well, other than your investigation yesterday, did you have a nice day?"

"It was great being away from your mother and Blanche." Wait. Did I just say that out loud? That's one of those things you keep to yourself.

Landon stiffened. "I know she's been difficult … ."

"I don't know why I said that."

"You're still half asleep," Landon said, climbing out of bed. "I'll give you a pass."

He was angry. I scrambled out of bed, grabbing his arm before he could open the bedroom door. "I'm really sorry. That was a horrible thing to say."

Landon sighed. "It's okay. It's not like she's been nice to you." He brushed his lips against my forehead. "Let's get some coffee into you."

I followed him out into the living room, finding Thistle and Marcus snuggling on the couch.

"Hey, Marcus," I said. "We haven't seen much of you this past week."

"The festival has been a nightmare," he admitted. "It's like a nonstop parade of crap that needs to be done – and guess who gets to do it?"

"You?"

"Yup."

"The only good thing about it is that Thistle has missed me, which makes her more ... pliable."

I smirked. "Is that true? Are you more pliable?"

"I went all out last night," Thistle agreed, frowning as the words escaped her mouth. "That's not what I meant."

Landon laughed from behind the kitchen counter, where he was dishing ground coffee into the filter and starting a pot. "I guess Bay isn't the only Winchester woman with a muddled brain this morning."

"Just how much did you miss me?" Marcus teased.

"So much that I put *The Notebook* in the other night just so I could have a good cry," Thistle admitted. Her mouth dropped open in surprise. She would never admit something like that.

What the hell?

Marcus was obviously shocked. "That's really sweet. Well, not the crying part, but the other part."

"That is really sweet," I said. "And so unlike you."

"Oh, really? What did you do last week when Landon's case kept him away for three nights in a row?"

"I pretended my pillow was him so I had something to cuddle with," I answered. Crap.

Thistle dropped her head into her hands. "Oh, no!"

"How did she find out?"

"She's evil. She has her ways."

"What are we talking about?" Landon asked.

"The truth spell," I replied. "Aunt Tillie turned it around on us."

Landon glanced over from the other room. "Wait, are you saying that you've been cursed to tell the truth?"

"Yes."

"Oh, well, this could be fun," he said, sauntering into the living room with a cup of coffee in his hand. He settled into the big armchair at the edge of the rug and fixed me with a hard look. "What's your favorite color?"

"Purple."

"What's your favorite movie?"

"*The Goonies.*"

"How many guys have you slept with?"

"Five."

"You told me three. Why did you say three before?"

"Because I didn't want you to think I was a slut." I sank to the floor. "This is a nightmare."

"I like it."

Marcus decided to play the game with Thistle. "How many guys have you slept with?"

"Eight."

"You said five. Why did you pick five?"

"You always pick a lower number when you're a girl." Thistle shot me a murderous look. "We have to counteract this spell."

"We can't," I said. "You know it lasts for twenty-four hours."

"Then we're going to have to shut ourselves in this house until it passes," Thistle said. "Landon is going to have to go up to the inn and tell them we're sick."

"Aren't you overreacting?" Landon asked.

Thistle furrowed her brow. "We have to answer any question we're asked with the truth," Thistle said. "Do you know how dangerous that is?"

"I'm with the FBI, I like truth."

"Really?"

"Really."

"Bay, what do you think of Landon's mother?" Thistle asked pointedly.

"I think she's mean and she wishes Landon wouldn't have settled for someone like me." Sonofabitch!

Landon glanced over the chair's arm and met my gaze. "I didn't settle for anyone. Stop thinking like that."

I buried my head between my knees miserably. "This is horrible."

Landon reached over and rubbed the top of my head. "What are the odds that anyone will ask you a dangerous question?"

"With your family and my family locked in one room together? What do you think?"

Landon blew out a sigh. "It will be fine."

"It will be fine," Thistle mimicked.

"Is that supposed to sound like me?"

"That's how your voice sounds in my head sometimes," Thistle said. "You're bossy."

Landon leaned forward. "What do you really think about me?"

Thistle frowned, fighting the urge to answer. She wasn't strong enough, though. "I think you make Bay happy and you're really sweet to her so I like you. Dammit!"

Landon smirked. "I knew it."

We all turned when the front door of the guesthouse opened and Clove slipped in, clad in the same clothes she'd worn the day before. "What are you guys doing up so early?"

"Landon woke me up for sex," I admitted.

"Marcus woke me up for sex, too."

Clove frowned. "What's going on?"

"The truth spell backfired," I replied.

"We're the ones who have to tell the truth," Thistle added.

All hints of color washed from Clove's face. "Are you sure?"

"No, we're making it up because we like being miserable," I grumbled.

Clove reopened the door and started to move back in the direction she'd just come from.

"Where are you going?" Thistle asked.

"I can't be around you guys if I have to tell the truth. You'll find out what I've been doing. I have to get out of here." Clove squeaked and slammed the door shut.

Thistle and I exchanged incredulous looks. We were on our feet and racing toward the door in seconds. Clove was already in her car and backing down the driveway before we hit the front porch.

"I knew she was up to something," Thistle complained. "I knew it."

"She's going to hide all day."

"Which means we're going to be on the hot seat," Thistle said. "Alone."

Marcus and Landon were watching Sports Center when we walked back in the room.

"You don't seem upset about this," I said.

"I'm concerned," Landon said. "I don't think it's the end of the world, though. Marcus and I will run interference up at the inn. If anyone asks you a question, we'll interrupt really quickly and ask you another question."

"What if I say something stupid in front of your mother?"

Landon reached over, tumbling me into his lap and wrapping his arms around me. "I'll just tell her you're drunk."

"It's not even nine in the morning yet. She'll think I'm an alcoholic."

"You're right. You're randy when you're drunk," Landon said. "I'll tell her you're high."

"Is that better?"

Landon gave me a quick kiss. "I guess we'll find out."

Will this week ever end?

"I have one more question," Landon said.

"I'm not answering any more questions," I said. "You're taking advantage."

"It's not a bad question," Landon said. "It's about something you said the other day, when you were talking about Kenneth."

"What did I say?"

"You said he had a magic penis."

"So? What does that have to do with anything?"

Landon waggled his eyebrows. "Do I have a magic penis? And, more importantly, do you want to spend quality time with my magic penis before breakfast?"

Crap.

NINETEEN

"We can still go back to the guesthouse," Thistle offered.

We were at the back door of the inn, Marcus and Landon leaning against the wall of the house, watching us. They seemed more amused than anything else.

"Am I the hottest guy you've ever slept with?" Marcus asked Thistle suddenly.

"Ooh, that's a good question," Landon said.

"Yes," Thistle replied through gritted teeth.

Landon opened his mouth, a similar question on his lips, but I cut him off. "Don't you dare!"

Landon opened the door without knocking. He'd been at the inn enough times to know that my mother and aunts would already be in the kitchen. He wasn't expecting to find Aunt Tillie sitting on the couch.

"Don't you knock?"

"I figured you were already at the table," he replied.

"Obviously not."

"Obviously."

Aunt Tillie glanced over her shoulder, eyeing Thistle and me with an evil grin. "And how are you this fine and sunny morning, my dear nieces?"

"Sucky," Thistle said.

"Terrible," I replied.

"Why?"

"Because you're an evil, evil woman," Thistle said. "We know what you did."

"I should hope so," Aunt Tillie said. "It wouldn't be a very effective punishment if you didn't know who did it to you."

"How did you know what we were doing?" I asked.

"I helped raise you," Aunt Tillie said, turning back to the television. "You wouldn't be the nieces I raised if you didn't try something like this."

"Can you take the curse off of us now? We've learned our lesson."

"No."

"Why not?" Thistle whined.

"It's for twenty-four hours. You know that."

"What happens if someone from Landon's family asks a question that puts us in an awkward situation?" I pressed.

"You should've thought of that before you tried to trick me," Aunt Tillie said. "Your mothers are waiting in the kitchen."

Thistle flipped the bird at Aunt Tillie's back before moving toward the kitchen door.

"I saw that."

"Good."

Mom, Marnie and Twila were busy at the stove, and barely glanced at the four of us as we entered.

"What's for breakfast?" I asked.

"Blueberry pancakes, sausage, eggs and fruit," Mom said, glancing up. "Good morning, boys."

"Good morning," they replied in unison.

"Where's Clove?" Marnie asked.

"She snuck in at the crack of dawn and then ran out before we could question her," Thistle replied.

I shot her a dark look. We gave each other a hard time whenever possible – and it was just the three of us. We lied as a unit where our mothers were concerned, though. Thistle had just thrown Clove under the bus, whether she meant to or not.

"Where was she?" Marnie asked.

"I don't know."

"You don't think she was doing anything dangerous, do you?"

"I don't know," Thistle replied. "I have no idea who she was doing or if he was dangerous."

"Thistle," I warned.

Mom smiled tightly. "Boys, why don't you go and get settled in the next room. We'll be out with breakfast in a few minutes."

Landon looked torn. "I think Bay should stay close to me this morning."

"Why?"

"I didn't get to spend any time with her yesterday and I missed her," Landon lied.

Mom smiled widely. "You're so sweet. I think you can go five minutes without her, though."

Landon looked at me, still unsure. "What do you think?"

"I think they're going to grill us about Clove and then find out about the truth spell anyway, so it doesn't really matter."

Ugh!

Mom narrowed her eyes. "What truth spell?"

"We tried to cast a truth spell on Aunt Tillie yesterday so we could find out whether she murdered Floyd, and she found out about it and rebounded it back to us," Thistle answered. "And we hate her for it."

Well, it wasn't a lie.

Mom mimed words but no sound came out of her mouth.

"I don't even know what to say," Twila said.

"I wish I had that problem," Thistle admitted.

"Wait, are you sure?" Marnie moved in front of Thistle. "Who stole my black bra when you guys were in middle school?"

"I did," Thistle said.

"Why?"

"Clove liked Michael Windsor and she didn't think her boobs were big enough," I answered. "We filled it with balloons full of pudding for her. It backfired when he tried to grab one, though, and it exploded. The pudding stained the bra and we burned it."

I felt like crying. Landon's shoulders shook with silent laughter as he rubbed my back.

"Oh, well, this could be useful," Mom said, fixing me with a pointed look. "Where did you really go after the senior prom?"

"I ditched my date and threw a party on the bluff," I replied. "We got drunk and skinny dipped in the pond with the Baker boys."

"Bay!" Thistle's face was beet red.

"The Baker boys?" Marcus wrinkled his nose distastefully. "I went to school with them. I'm so grossed out."

"And did you drug us that night so we would fall asleep?"

"Yes."

"Why?"

"Because we missed our curfew."

"By how much?"

"Eight hours."

Mom smiled. "You're grounded."

"Fine," I grumbled. "Can it start now? Send me to my guesthouse."

"No." Mom shook her head. "Now you have breakfast with our guests."

"And what if they ask us something that we shouldn't answer?"

"Oh," Twila said, realization dawning. "This could be bad."

Marnie chewed her lower lip. "This could be really bad."

"I already have a plan," Landon said. "If anyone asks them a question anyone deems ... dangerous, someone else just ask them a different question really quickly."

Mom looked doubtful. "I don't know."

"Well, my other idea is to say they're high."

"That could work." Twila brightened considerably.

She always did have a weird sense of humor.

"**SO, WHERE** IS CLOVE?" Daryl asked, forking a bite of pancakes into his mouth.

"Thistle, can you hand me the butter?" Marnie asked quickly.

"Yes."

"Clove had things to do at the store," Mom said, filling in the awkward conversation gap.

"Oh, that's too bad," Daryl replied. "I was hoping maybe she could give me a tour of the grounds later."

Landon's eyes narrowed suspiciously. "Why?"

"What do you mean why? I want to see the grounds."

"I'll show you the grounds," Landon said.

"You know the grounds?"

"I've seen quite a bit of them, yes," Landon said.

"Did you give him a tour of the grounds?" Connie turned to me.

"Not really," I said before anyone could ask another question. "Landon snuck on the grounds to spy on us one night and found my mother and aunts dancing naked under the full moon. Then, when we thought Marcus was a murderer, we took him up to the bluff so we could save Thistle before he stabbed her. Oh, and then there was the time Aunt Tillie was plotting to infest the Dragonfly with magical bugs so it couldn't open on time. He got to see some of the woods then, too."

"Magical bugs?" Connie asked.

"Figure of speech," Marnie said.

"They weren't magical," Aunt Tillie replied. "They were regular bugs."

"It sounds like you guys have a lot of … fun out here," Earl said.

"Oh, we do," Mom replied. "Tons and tons of fun."

"I don't understand," Connie said. "You thought Marcus – this boy with the long blond hair here – was a murderer?"

"I didn't," Thistle replied.

"We thought he was acting funny," I said. "It turns out he was just trying to get in Thistle's pants, not kill her."

Landon squeezed my knee under the table. "Maybe if there's food in your mouth, you won't be able to speak?"

I took a big bite of sausage. It couldn't hurt.

"I want to hear about the naked dancing," Denny said, his eyes twinkling.

"She was exaggerating," Mom replied. "We just like to commune with nature from time to time."

"Naked?"

"Sometimes."

"What's that like?"

"It's totally terrifying," I said, partially chewed sausage flying out of my mouth.

"Yeah," Thistle agreed. "Boobs flying this way and that."

"And you saw this, Landon?"

Landon rubbed his forehead. "I did indeed."

"What was it like?" Daryl asked.

"Floppy."

Mom scowled. "Gravity is something every woman fights at a certain time of her life, young man. Bay will be no different."

"Thanks for the biology lesson."

"Oh, don't act like such a prude," Aunt Tillie said. "Everyone knows you two – you two down there at the end of the table, too – are pawing each other every chance you get. I bet you pawed each other this morning. Am I right?"

I wanted to climb in Floyd's hole and die. I wanted to take Aunt Tillie with me. "Yep, we totally did it this morning," I said. "Landon wanted to prove he had a magic penis."

"I didn't do it this morning," Thistle said. "We did it three times last night, though."

Landon was on his feet. "Okay. This has been a great breakfast." He grabbed my arm. "We're going."

"Where are you going?" Connie asked.

"Bay and Thistle need to get some rest," Landon replied. "They're seriously sleep deprived – and talking crazy."

"From all the sex?" Daryl asked, raising his eyebrows suggestively.

"Sure," Landon said, motioning to Marcus before reaching over and grabbing me by the waist. He lifted me up and tossed me over his shoulder. "This has been a great breakfast."

Marcus didn't look certain, but he followed Landon's lead and did the same with Thistle.

Landon paused at the door. "We'll see everyone tomorrow."

"I don't understand; what are you going to be doing all day?" Connie asked.

"I have no idea," Landon admitted. "I'm sure it's going to involve two gags, though."

"Kinky." Daryl winked.

TWENTY

"I'm not going." I tugged the comforter over my head, burrowing beneath it in an attempt to ward off the new day.

"You're going." I couldn't see Landon's face, but I could picture his expression. It wasn't pretty.

"I can't. I can never leave this bed again."

The side of the mattress dipped down as Landon settled. He tugged at the covers, finally wrenching them from my grip. He looked good in the morning. So good it was almost criminal. "It's going to be okay."

"How can you say that? You were there."

Landon's mouth tipped into a smile. "I was there. It wasn't that bad."

"You're such a bad liar."

"It wasn't great," Landon conceded. "It certainly wasn't the end of the world, though. Just think, in a few years, this is going to be a funny story we tell at dinner parties."

"I'm never telling this story."

"I bet you never thought you were going to tell the black-bra story – or the skinny-dipping story either."

It's a good thing he's handsome, because his comforting skills are lacking at the most inopportune times.

"Your mother must think I'm a freak."

Landon leaned back against the pillow, his blue eyes finding mine. "I have a feeling she thinks your whole family is full of freaks."

"Oh, well, that makes things better."

Landon chuckled. "I've come up with a reasonable excuse for what happened yesterday."

I screwed my eyes shut. "No you didn't. There is no reasonable excuse."

"You haven't even heard it yet."

"I don't want to hear it."

"Listen, this is a great idea," Landon said. "I'm going to tell her you're a nymphomaniac and you put on that display yesterday because you were mad I wouldn't spend the day in bed with you and that was your way of blackmailing me into getting what you wanted."

My mouth dropped open, too many words warring in my mind for one to gain the upper hand and escape first.

"I know what you're thinking," Landon said, his eyes twinkling. "This is going to make me look like something of a hero for putting up with you, like I'm some sort of sex god that you can't get enough of. It's a cross I'm willing to bear, though."

"I hate you," I grumbled.

Landon dropped a kiss on my forehead and got up. "If you don't get up and get ready, that's exactly the story I'm telling them."

I tossed one of the bed pillows at his retreating back. "You're the devil!"

AN HOUR LATER, I found myself standing in front of The Overlook waiting for Landon's family to finish breakfast. My stomach was too unsettled to see everyone over a meal, so I'd begged off and busied myself pulling weeds from the front garden to give myself a sense of purpose. I was still trying to figure out a way to get out of the planned excursion.

"Are you hiding out here?"

Ah, good, the evil aunt had found me despite my best efforts to hide. "Are you proud of yourself?"

Aunt Tillie was standing by the side door eyeing me. Her face was hard to read, but she didn't look as victorious as she normally would under similar circumstances.

"I didn't think things would get as bad as they did," Aunt Tillie admitted.

"Oh, just stop," I snapped. "You knew what would happen."

"I didn't know that would happen," Aunt Tillie corrected. "I just thought you'd babble some embarrassing stuff about Landon and that would be it."

"Well, I guess you're not omnipotent after all," I said.

"I never said I was omnipotent."

"You like to pretend, though, don't you?"

"Sometimes," she conceded. "I didn't mean to put you in this position, though. I was just frustrated."

"Well, join the club."

"I'm not apologizing for what I did."

"You never do."

"I am admitting that … perhaps … now wasn't the right time for that particular lesson."

I rolled my eyes. "None of it would've been necessary if you had just told the truth from the beginning."

"There is no truth to tell," she countered.

I snorted. "Well then, I guess we're at an impasse."

"I'm telling you to let this go, Bay."

I held up my hands in surrender. "You got it."

Aunt Tillie narrowed her eyes. "Why don't I believe you?"

"Maybe because I learned how to lie and deflect from you," I suggested.

THE MICHAELS FAMILY wanted to go for a daylong horseback ride – complete with a picnic. When Landon suggested it during the run-up of their visit, I'd thought it was a great idea. That was before verbal diarrhea derailed what was already a bumpy get-to-know-you ride.

"I'm not sure how I feel about horses," Connie said.

"They smell," Blanche interjected. "I bet they bite, too."

"They don't bite," Daryl argued. "The ones they gave us the other day were really gentle and easy to steer."

"How do we know they have enough horses for us?" Connie asked. She'd opted to ignore yesterday's breakfast debacle – and Landon's absence for the rest of the day – but I wasn't sure why. I had a feeling Earl and Landon had something to do with it.

"Marcus reserved them for us," I said. "He's reliable."

"The boy you thought was a murderer is reliable?"

I sighed. "I overreacted on that front."

"It seems you've overreacted about a lot of things, doesn't it?"

"Mom," Landon warned. "We talked about this."

I knew it!

"Why don't I go ahead and see about the horses," I offered, my tone blunted and dull as I fought to keep my temper in check.

"That sounds like a good idea," Landon agreed. "We have a few things to talk about here. Again."

I headed toward the stables, finally managing to suck in an even breath when I got inside. I leaned against the wall, thumping my head against the hard surface. Maybe this is all a dream? Maybe I'll wake up and Landon's family won't even have arrived yet?

"That bad?"

Marcus was brushing a brown mare a few stalls down. I could see his grin from here, though.

"Yup."

"Did Landon tell them the nymphomaniac story?"

"I don't think so." Goddess, I hope not.

"I'm sure it will blow over," Marcus said. "In a couple years you'll probably think it's funny."

"That's what Landon said," I replied. "You two didn't seem to think it was all that funny yesterday."

"I think I always thought it was funnier than Landon did," Marcus said. "It wasn't my family, though."

I decided to change the subject. "How was Thistle this morning?"

"Steaming mad."

"Is that different from any other morning?"

"Not really." Marcus' smile was warm, his eyes bright.

"You're good for her," I said. "You're really good for her."

"She's good for me," Marcus countered. "She makes me laugh."

"She's got a certain … presence," I agreed.

"You all have a presence," Marcus laughed. "I like how she's so different, though. How she doesn't care what other people think."

"I think that's true to an extent," I said. "I think she cares what you think, though."

"I like everything she does," Marcus said, shrugging. "There's nothing about her I don't like."

"You know what, Marcus?"

"What?"

"That's my favorite thing about you."

"What is?"

"Your willingness just to let people be who they are."

"Landon likes you the way you are," Marcus said. "You shouldn't worry about things like that."

"I'm not so sure that's true."

"When you and Thistle locked yourselves in the bedroom yesterday, we spent the whole afternoon watching television and talking," Marcus said.

"You mean you gossiped like school girls," I teased.

"I guess that's fair," Marcus acknowledged. "Anyway, we could hear the two of you in there plotting, and I asked him if he was worried what his mother would think about you after what happened. I would be worried if my mother had been there, so I was kind of curious."

I tried to act nonchalant. "And what did he say?"

"He said he didn't care what his mother thought about you." Marcus' tone was matter of fact. "He said that he only cares what he feels, and he feels like you're worth embarrassing breakfasts and busybody aunts. Those were his words, not mine, just FYI."

I pursed my lips. "You're a good guy, Marcus."

"I know."

"I don't suppose you have our horses ready? If you told me you were one short, I would love you forever, by the way."

"They're all out in the corral," he said. "I have them all saddled up and ready."

"Great."

"You'll be on a horse," Marcus reminded me. "You don't have to ride next to anyone you don't want to."

"Mom sent a picnic lunch," I replied. "I don't see a way of avoiding that little joyous interlude in a few hours."

"I guess not," Marcus said.

"They're out that way?" I asked, pointing to the far end of the stable.

"Yeah. I'll go with you and make sure everyone gets settled."

As we walked toward our destination, a thought occurred to me. "Hey, what time did Clove come in last night? Did you and Landon see her?"

"She didn't come home last night."

My heart stuttered. "She didn't? Do you think something happened to her?"

"I wouldn't worry," Marcus said. "I saw her out on the trail to the Dandridge this morning. I have no idea what she was doing out there, but she was fine a few hours ago."

The Dandridge? Why would she be out there? A sneaking suspicion started boring a hole in my head. Sonofabitch!

TWENTY-ONE

"You seem distracted."

We'd been riding the horses down the Au Sable Trail for more than an hour, Landon and I leading the way while his family followed.

"Marcus told me something," I admitted.

"Hey, when I told him I wished you would shave your legs more than twice a week I was just searching for a safe conversation topic."

"He said Clove never came home last night," I said, opting to ignore his blathering.

"She didn't come home the night before either."

"You don't find that odd?"

"I think Clove is a grown woman," Landon said. "Where she chooses to spend her nights isn't really my business."

"She's obviously seeing someone."

"Does that bother you?"

"That she's seeing someone? No. That she's hiding it? You bet."

Landon sighed. He was used to the Winchester drama. "Who do you think she's seeing?"

Unfortunately, I had an idea. "Sam Cornell."

Landon shifted in his saddle. "Why do you say that?"

"Because Marcus saw her walking down the Dandridge trail this morning."

"Hmm."

"That's all you have to say?"

"I don't know what to say," Landon said.

"You can't think this is a good idea," I pressed.

"I'm not sure if it's a good idea or a bad idea," Landon said. "It's obvious she's lonely, though."

I glanced at him, his words flooding me with guilt. "What makes you think that?"

"Because you're always with me, and Thistle is always with Marcus."

"We still spend time with her," I protested.

"Not as much as you used to."

Crap. He was right. "That still doesn't make hiding her relationship with Sam okay."

"Maybe she didn't think you would take it well."

"Well ... that's just ridiculous," I sputtered. "I'm taking it fine."

"Obviously."

"I hate it when you get like this," I grumbled.

"No, you hate it when I'm right," Landon countered.

That, too. I blew out a sigh. "So, what should I do?"

"I think you should let it go until she's ready to talk to you about it. Let her come to you."

That wasn't likely.

"You won't do that, though," Landon continued. "So I think you should calm yourself for a few hours before you chase her down and attack her."

I rolled my tongue in my mouth, pressing it against my upper front teeth. "I do hate it when you're right."

"I know." He leaned over and gave me a quick kiss. "You should get used to it, though. It happens every day."

He's so full of himself sometimes. I turned my attention to the trail ahead, a hint of movement catching my attention near a clump of bushes about twenty feet in front of us.

"Where do you think we should stop for lunch?"

I kept my eyes trained on the bushes. "What?"

"Are you listening to me?"

"Uh-huh."

"What did I just say?"

"You said that I'm the best thing that ever happened to you."

Landon barked out a laugh. "You have the weirdest sense of humor."

I realized what the movement was. "Landon."

"I love your sense of humor, don't get me wrong," Landon said. "It's weird, though."

The swirl of movement, all white and ethereal, was gathering into a shape. "Landon."

"And I really don't care if you only want to shave your legs twice a week," he said. "It's scratchy, but cute."

The poltergeist was here. Floyd was here. He was moving this way. "Landon!"

"What?"

"I ... ."

The poltergeist moved quickly, faster than the wind, splitting the rows of horses and spooking them in different directions as they scattered to get away from the malevolence they could feel but not see.

Seven horses bolted in seven different directions. My white steed broke into a run, galloping headlong into the thick trees and leaving the Michaels family yelling behind me. I gripped the reins tightly, squeezing my thighs into the horse's flank as I tried to calm him. "Whoa, Ghost. Whoa!"

Ghost didn't heed my calls, instead galloping into a heavily-wooded expanse in an effort to put as much distance between him and the poltergeist as possible. I did the only thing I could: I held on.

I leaned over, pressing my body flat against Ghost's strong neck. I had to make myself as small as possible, because if a tree branch hit me at this speed I could be seriously hurt.

A sudden noise to my right made me start. I glanced over to find the poltergeist zipping along next to us. The white shadow was without defined form, but the swirling clouds almost looked as though they were reflecting a ghostly face. We were moving too fast for me to be sure, though.

I was watching the poltergeist so I didn't see the danger ahead. That's probably why, when the tree limb hit me, I didn't have a chance to fully grasp what was happening.

I was airborne, sailing through a sea of nothingness. Then I was falling, the ground rushing up at me. I hit. Hard. And then everything went dark.

EVERYTHING WAS GRAY. Was it night? Was it almost night? No, that wasn't right. It wasn't even noon yet. How long was I unconscious? Had I lost an entire day?

I struggled to a sitting position, glancing around to get my bearings. I didn't recognize my surroundings. Hey, trees look like trees. In Ghost's panic, I'd lost track of where he was headed. I had no idea where I was.

Seriously, why is it so gray?

"Where are you?"

I straightened. I didn't recognize the voice. Maybe Landon had organized a search party when he couldn't find me. "I'm over here."

I waited. No one appeared, though. This wasn't a great rescue. I put my hands to the ground and pushed up, gaining my footing. I expected pain, but I didn't feel any. I didn't know whether that was a good or bad sign. On one hand, no pain meant I wasn't seriously hurt. On the other, I could be in shock and bleeding internally. I could be dying and not even know it. What? I'm a glass-half-empty girl.

"Don't make me come looking for you!"

What kind of a search party doesn't want to search? I probably got the lazy crew. Typical.

I followed the voice, pushing through some shrubs and hoping to find a familiar face on the other side. Instead, a ramshackle building came into view. Where the heck am I? I've never seen this place before in my life.

I sighed. Maybe the owners have a phone? Landon was probably worried. Dark was obviously approaching. I had no idea whether the rest of his family was even safe. I mentally cursed myself for leaving my phone in my saddlebag. It would've come in handy right about now.

The front door of the cabin was ajar. I peered inside, praying to see someone I recognized. The small living room was empty, though. Great. I knocked on the door lightly. "Hello."

Nothing.

I knocked again, louder this time. "I'm sorry to bother you," I said. "I got thrown by a horse and … well … I'm not even sure where I am. I was hoping to use your phone."

Still nothing.

There were voices in the other room. I couldn't make out what they were saying, but it wasn't as though I had a lot of options. I walked through the living room and pushed the swinging door.

What I found was … peculiar. A woman who looked to be in her mid-twenties – although the creases around her eyes hinted at a few more years – was cowering behind a ragged kitchen island.

A man, his eyes blazing and the stink of whiskey wafting from his pores, stood a few feet away.

"Um, I'm sorry to interrupt … ."

"I feel fine," he said. "I feel fabulous."

"I'm glad," the woman said, obviously terrified.

What the hell is going on here? "Listen, this looks like a really bad time," I said. "I need a little help, though."

Neither one of them looked in my direction. That's when I realized what was happening. "I'm not really here, am I?"

I watched as the man walked to the stove and tipped the pot over, spilling its contents onto the rusted surface. "Well, I felt fabulous until I came home and found you cooking this slop again."

"I'm sorry. What would you like me to cook?"

What an ass.

"I don't want anything you're going to cook. You're a terrible cook

– and a terrible wife. My mother told me you would be, but I didn't listen to her. I should've listened to her."

"Then why don't you cook your own dinner," I suggested. "Why should she have to cook anything for your ungrateful ass?"

The woman was saying something, but it was hard to hear. Her voice was barely a whisper.

"Don't tell me what to do!"

Why am I here? Am I dead? Is this hell? No, I shook my head. This was something else. There was a flash of ... something. What was it? Where had I seen this before?

"What are you saying? Are you saying I don't pull my weight around here? That I'm lazy?" The man was enraged.

Realization washed over me. "Floyd?"

"You're a good provider," the woman said, shrinking as she pressed against the counter behind her.

"Oh, Mrs. Gunderson," I breathed. "You should've told someone."

"I am," Floyd said. "You're an awful wife, though."

"What you are is a dick," I complained. "I can't believe you got two women to fight over you."

"Please. Please don't hurt me." Her voice was piteous.

"I'm not going to hurt you. I'm just going to teach you a lesson. You obviously need one."

"Don't you touch her!" I realized this was a memory, one that didn't even belong to me. I wanted to change the outcome, though. I needed to change the outcome.

"Floyd, please, I'm begging you."

"Don't beg, Ginny. It just makes me hate you more."

Floyd reached over, grabbing Mrs. Gunderson by her collar so he could hold her still as he struck her.

Mrs. Gunderson grabbed the side of her face, crying out in pain.

"Shut up!"

I tried to grab him. I tried to stop him. I wasn't really there, though. My hands passed through him, finding no flesh, no blood, no life to hold or strike.

"Floyd, please!"

"Just shut up," he growled. "You have no idea how much I hate the sound of your voice."

Floyd reared back and hit her again. I closed my eyes, but could still hear the horror. When I opened them again, Mrs. Gunderson was on the floor, her body curled into a small ball. She wasn't even trying to fight off his fists.

"I hate you!"

Another punch.

"Stop. Please!"

"You're worthless!"

Another punch.

"Ugh."

"You're nothing!"

He lashed out with his foot, making contact with her ribs.

"Floyd!"

My blood ran cold. I recognized the new voice. When I turned, I saw her. Aunt Tillie. She was fifty years younger, but just as terrifying. She'd entered the kitchen through the swinging door as the beating progressed.

Floyd straightened, moving his attention from Mrs. Gunderson's prone body. "What do you think you're doing here?"

"You step away from her," Aunt Tillie warned.

"Don't tell me what to do! No bitch is going to tell me what to do!"

"You're a piece of shit, Floyd," Aunt Tillie said, her voice chilling. "You've always been a piece of shit."

"You obviously need a lesson, too," Floyd said. "I'll be glad to teach you."

"Don't you touch her," I yelled, shivering as Floyd moved through my body in Aunt Tillie's direction. "Don't you touch her!"

I didn't see what happened next. The memory was gone. I jerked to a sitting position, my body screaming in protest.

It was dark and I was alone. I was in the woods. Alone.

"Crap."

TWENTY-TWO

I ran my hands over my body, checking for signs of breaks and profuse bleeding. I was sore. No, I was in pain. Real, hardcore pain. Still, I couldn't find any broken bones. That was a good sign. Right?

I looked up, searching through the budding leaves in the tree canopy. The sun was high in the sky, but it was creeping toward the downward horizon. I'd lost most of the day.

Crap.

I raised my hand to my forehead, cringing when my fingers detected the pronounced bump near my hairline. Great. I probably had brain damage. That would be just my luck. Too bad this hadn't happened the day before. I could've blamed my truthful pronouncements on brain damage.

Dammit!

I blew out a breath and planted my hands on the ground, splaying my fingers to improve my balance. I had to get up. Even if people were looking, there was no guarantee they would find me. It's a big area. I didn't have a phone, so I couldn't be tracked. I couldn't rely on anyone else. I had to help myself.

I gained my footing, swaying a few times and almost going down again, but my equilibrium slowly returned. Once erect, I saw what my eyes missed on first glance: The ruins of a house. No, the ruins of a shack. The Gunderson shack.

The house was barely standing in the memory, a strong storm risking its ultimate destruction. Fifty years had almost wiped it from existence, only a brick foundation and weathered boards standing witness to a lost life of horror.

I glanced around. I still wasn't sure where I was. I could make an educated guess, though.

I pointed my body toward the east – the opposite direction of the setting sun – and started to walk.

Every step made me want to scream, my muscles protesting the trek, my head throbbing as it demanded rest. I pushed forward, one step in front of the other.

I needed to distract myself, so I focused on the memory. Floyd's memory. What did it mean?

Well, Floyd was obviously an ass. A drunken ass, to be exact. A wife-beating ass. Why would Mrs. Little have an affair with him? I understood the pathology of a battered woman. They convince themselves they don't deserve better, so they settle for less than nothing. Mrs. Little, though, she was a different story.

Why was Aunt Tillie there? Did she know what was going to happen? Was she trying to stop it? Had she killed Floyd to stop it?

What if she had? Floyd could've killed his wife. Aunt Tillie was protecting her. Why would they hide that?

Something else was going on here.

I caught a shadow in the distance. I stilled, sighing in relief when I realized it was the Dandridge. Help wasn't too far away.

It took me fifteen minutes to get there. Sam Cornell was the last person I wanted to see – especially now – but beggars can't be choosers and I didn't have another option.

I knocked on the door, trying to decide what I should tell him when he opened it. One look at his surprised face, though, and my mind went blank.

"Bay."

"I got thrown from a horse," I blurted out.

Sam's brow furrowed as he ran a hand through his dark hair. "Are you okay?"

"I probably have internal bleeding and I'm going to die."

"Are you being serious?"

My body was almost numb now, so I wasn't sure. "Possibly."

Sam looked over his shoulder, clearly unsure about what to do. "Well ... come in."

I stumbled into the Dandridge, looking around curiously. I hadn't been inside for almost a month, and Sam had obviously been busy. The furniture in the main room was covered with tarps – new drywall hanging and ready to be painted. "You've been busy."

"It's a work in progress."

I heard a voice in the other room. "Who was at the door?"

Clove. I freaking knew it!

Clove froze when she saw me, stunned worry on her face and a damp dishtowel in her hand. She looked so ... domestic. "Bay. What are you doing here? Are you following me?"

"She was thrown from a horse," Sam said, moving between the two of us.

Clove's brown eyes widened, finally seeing the signs she'd missed on first glance. "Oh ... oh ... are you okay?"

"Do I look okay?"

"You look ... bad. You look really bad." Clove took two small steps forward, lifting her hand to the side of my head, but pulling her fingers back before she made contact. "That looks really bad. Is that your only injury?"

"I have no idea," I replied. "My whole body hurts ... and it's numb. I hurt and I'm numb. I'm pretty sure that means I'm dying."

"I'll call an ambulance," Sam said.

"No."

Sam raised his eyebrows, shifting his gaze between Clove and me. "I think you need to go to the hospital. You just said you were dying."

"I've been missing all day," I replied. "I just want to go home."

"What do you mean you've been missing all day," Clove said, her voice shrill. "I think someone would've called me if you'd been missing all day."

"Did someone call you?"

Clove bit her lower lip. "Thistle has tried to call my phone five times today."

"I'm guessing she was trying to tell you." My tone was cool, clipped. Clove was nervous and I was taking perverse pleasure in keeping her that way. I had no idea why.

Clove paced to her purse, pulled her phone out and looked at the screen. I kept my face devoid of emotion as I watched her press a button and hold the phone to her ear so she could listen to her voicemail. Her face drained of color as the messages revealed a full-on Winchester meltdown. "Oh." She started flapping her hands. "Oh."

I rolled my eyes. Leave it to Clove to have a panic attack when I was the one thrown from a freaking horse.

Sam wrapped his arm around Clove's shoulder in an effort to offer her support. "Are you okay?"

"She's fine."

"She doesn't look fine," Sam countered.

"She's dramatic."

"Aren't you all?"

"Point taken," I said, holding my hand out. "Hand me her phone. She can be dramatic without her phone."

"I can call someone for you," Sam offered, never moving from Clove's side.

I waved my hand again.

Sam sighed, taking the phone from Clove and handing it over. I hit the keypad and started to punch in a number. That's when I realized I didn't know Landon's number. It was programmed into my phone but not my mind. Ugh! I hate technology. I typed in Thistle's number instead.

She picked up on the first ring. "I've been calling you all day! I know you're being all self-absorbed and hiding something – and I don't really care what … okay, I care, but we have bigger worries right now. Bay is missing!"

"It's me."

"Bay?"

"Yeah."

"Have you been with Clove all day? Half the town is out searching for you. I'm going to kill you."

"I was thrown from a horse."

"Are you all right?"

"I was thrown from a horse," I repeated. "I was thrown from a horse and I woke up in … hell. I woke up in hell."

"Are we talking literally or figuratively?"

"Both."

"How did you end up with Clove?"

"Well, when I woke up, I started walking. I found myself at the Dandridge."

"I still don't understand what that has to do with Clove."

"Think about it," I replied through gritted teeth.

"Oh, you've got to be kidding me."

"Send Landon to come get me."

"She's been sleeping with Sam?"

I glanced over at Clove, watching as Sam rubbed her back and whispered something in her ear. "That would be my guess. I haven't gotten to see the actual show, though."

"What's her excuse?"

"Did I mention I got thrown from a horse?"

"Yeah. I heard you the first time … and the second."

"Send Landon to come get me."

"He's not here," Thistle said. "He's out looking for you. Everyone is out looking for you. He went with Marcus because Marcus thought they could cover more ground on horseback. He's a mess, by the way."

"Then you come and get me."

"I'm supposed to stay here in case anyone calls with an update," Thistle said.

"I'm calling with an update," I snapped. "Come out here and get me."

Thistle quieted on the other end of the phone for a moment. "Are you all right?"

"Come and get me now."

"Bay ... ."

"Now!"

THISTLE ARRIVED FIFTEEN MINUTES LATER, greeting Clove with a chilly glare before focusing on me. "You look terrible. I think I should take you to the hospital."

"Take me home."

"Are you sure? What if you have internal bleeding?"

"Then I'll die at home."

"You seem ... off," Thistle said. "Has she been like this since she got here?"

"You mean bitchy? Yeah, she's been like that since she got here," Sam said. "She's been nothing but mean to Clove."

"Maybe that's because Clove deserves it," Thistle said.

"Why? Because she's been seeing me?" Sam was spoiling for a fight.

"I'm not thrilled she's dating you," Thistle admitted. "You're ... a tool, quite frankly, but that's not why I'm angry."

"I think that's exactly why you're angry," Sam countered.

"You don't know what you're talking about."

"Then why are you mad?"

"Because she's a big, fat liar," Thistle said. "She's a big, fat liar and hider and I'm really, really ticked off about it."

"I got thrown by a horse," I muttered.

No one bothered looking in my direction.

"Maybe she wanted some privacy," Sam suggested.

"Maybe I don't care," Thistle replied. "When I wanted privacy she and Bay stalked Marcus behind my back."

"We thought he was a murderer," Clove protested.

"Well, maybe I think Sam is a murderer."

"I'm not a murderer," Sam said.

"He's not a murderer," Clove whined.

"I don't care what he is," Thistle said. "I care that she lied. If she's lying, that means she knows something is wrong with you. That's what I care about."

"There's nothing wrong with me."

"There's nothing wrong with him," Clove echoed.

That was it. I couldn't take it one more second. "I. GOT. THROWN. FROM. A. HORSE!"

Thistle jerked, focusing on me. "Stop being so dramatic and get in the car. I'm done here anyway."

I started shuffling toward the door, fighting the urge to throttle both Thistle and Clove.

"Does everything have to be about you?" Thistle grumbled.

TWENTY-THREE

"Can you believe her?"

Thistle hadn't stopped complaining about Clove since we left the Dandridge. I was sick of hearing about it, but I would be raring to go on the topic after ten solid hours of sleep.

"You called Landon, right?"

Thistle's face sobered. "Yeah. I told him I found you."

"You didn't find me."

"Hey, possession is nine-tenths of the law," Thistle countered, the set of her jaw grim. "You're in my possession. I get the glory."

I leaned my head back against the seat. "You know how I told you that yesterday was the worst day of my life?"

"When did you tell me that?"

"When we were locked in my bedroom hiding from Marcus and Landon so we wouldn't blurt out any more unsavory truths and make ourselves look like total idiots," I reminded her. "It was in between bouts of plotting against Aunt Tillie."

"Oh, yeah," Thistle said, nodding. "I remember plotting against Aunt Tillie."

"I was wrong."

Thistle's eyes filled with sympathy – and even a few unshed tears. "Today was worse?"

"Today was so much worse," I said. "And I spent the bulk of it unconscious and reliving one of Floyd's memories. He was a total dick, by the way."

Thistle frowned. "What do you mean you relived one of his memories?"

"It was him, the poltergeist him, anyway, who spooked the horses," I said. "I woke up twice. The first time was in his memory."

"Why didn't you tell me that before?"

"I didn't want to say anything in front of Sam," I replied.

"I knew he was a tool."

I leaned my head against the cool glass of the window. "He's the least of our worries right now."

"Are you sure?"

"Not really."

"Well, we can only focus on one catastrophe at a time," Thistle said. "Getting you home is all I can handle right now."

"Right."

"After that, though? I'm going to beat the crap out of Clove."

"That sounds like fun. I'll help."

Thistle wrinkled her nose. "Honey, if you're this sore right now you're not going to be able to walk tomorrow."

I considered her words. "Well, on the plus side, that means I won't have to go on another uncomfortable outing with Landon's family."

Thistle giggled. "When did you turn into a glass-half-full girl?"

"Sometime in Floyd's wretched and horrible memory I guess."

"Oh, yeah, what did you see?"

I told her, recounting everything to the best of my ability. When I was done, Thistle looked more confused than when I started. "I don't understand."

"Join the club."

"It sounds like Aunt Tillie was protecting Mrs. Gunderson."

"It does."

"Why would they hide that? That's a noble thing."

I shrugged. "The only thing I can think of is that, back then, the police didn't always believe women when they said they were being abused by their spouses. They didn't get involved in domestic disputes."

"Still."

"I don't know."

Thistle navigated her car onto The Overlook's long and winding driveway. "Are you going to ask her about it?"

"Yes."

"Tonight?"

"I don't know. It depends on what kind of mayhem we walk into when we get back to the inn."

"You seem a little … beat up," Thistle said. "I'm still not sure the hospital isn't the best way to go."

"I don't want to go to the hospital. I'm hurt, but I'm going to be fine."

"I know, but … ."

Thistle's headlights lighted up the front porch of The Overlook, flashing on Landon's tense form as he paced. The passenger door was opening before Thistle killed the engine. Landon knelt down, fixing his soulful eyes on me. "Are you okay?"

"I've been worse," I admitted, instantly feeling better when I saw the concern etched on his face. I reached over and disengaged the seatbelt, letting Landon pull me to my feet and into his arms. My body resisted the movement, causing me to groan.

Landon held me tight for a second and then pulled away, keeping his hands on my arms so he could look me over. "What happened to you?"

"You wouldn't believe me if I told you."

Landon pursed his lips. "Do you have any idea how worried I've been?"

"Not really. I was unconscious for a while. What happened?"

"The horses all spooked all at the same time," Landon said, biting his lower lip. "I didn't go after you … I thought you would be okay. You're used to horses."

He looked guilty, but that seemed inappropriate. He wasn't the one who spooked the horses.

"I went after my mom and Aunt Blanche," Landon said. "They were fine, though. The horses settled down pretty quickly. Everyone was fine – a little rattled, but fine. I had no idea where you were."

"Don't feel bad. I had no idea where I was either."

"I figured you would go back to the stables," Landon continued, his eyes roaming my body. "I kept everyone on the trail. I figured you would either catch up to us or go directly back to the stables."

I'd never seen him so pale. His skin was standing in stark contrast to the darkening sky.

"You weren't at the stables," he said. "Marcus said not to worry. He said you knew what you were doing. He said you'd been riding horses since you were a little kid."

I reached my hand to cup the side of his face. "I'm fine." That was the truth. Mostly.

"I waited. I waited for an hour. I waited too long."

"Landon … ."

"The horse showed up," he said, ignoring my attempts to soothe him. "The horse showed up without you. That's when Marcus started to panic – which made me panic."

"I'm fine," I repeated, trying to ignore how lame the words sounded.

"I'm a trained professional," Landon said. "I'm not supposed to panic. I panicked, though."

Crap. He was losing it. I glanced at Thistle for help, but she seemed as lost as I was.

I tried to keep my voice light. "It wasn't a big deal. The horse threw me and I lost consciousness for a little while. When I came to, I walked to the Dandridge and called Thistle for help."

Landon's hands tightened on my arms. "Why didn't you call me?"

I shifted my lips to the side ruefully. "Honestly? I don't know your phone number."

Landon's face was unreadable, but his shoulders were unnaturally stiff. "You call me all the time."

"Because your number is programmed in my phone," I said. "My phone was with Ghost."

"Ghost?"

"The horse."

Landon laughed, the sound raspy and harsh. "I would yell at you for not memorizing my phone number if I wasn't so relieved to see you."

"Well, then it's a bonus for both of us." I pasted a smile on my face, even though attempting any expression – smile or frown – caused small pains to shoot to the lump on my forehead.

Landon lifted his hand to the knot, touching it lightly. "This looks bad."

"It's fine."

"You said you lost consciousness. I think I should take you to the hospital."

"I'm not going to the hospital," I argued. "I don't want to."

"Maybe I don't care what you want."

"I was thrown from a horse," I reminded him. "I think it's a rule that whenever you get thrown by a horse you get your own way for a full twenty-four hours. I'm invoking the rule."

Landon's face was stern, but I didn't miss the smile tugging at the corner of his mouth. "Is that so?"

"Yup."

He looked at the bump one more time before blowing out a frustrated sigh. "I've decided I'm not going to argue with you."

"Really?" This was new.

He slung his arm around my shoulders and started leading me toward the inn. "Really."

"How long is this going to last?"

Landon pushed open the door and ushered me inside. "I'm guessing it's going to last for about thirty seconds."

I narrowed my eyes. Was this a trick? "Why?"

"Bay!"

Landon moved to the side as Mom, Marnie and Twila enveloped me with worried hugs and cries of concern.

Of course. He didn't want to be the bad guy. He had no problem letting them do it for him, though.

TWENTY-FOUR

"Sit down."

"I'm fine," I protested. They'd led me into the dining room, where Landon's family was gathered around the table eating, but just the idea of sitting seemed like too much work. Plus, I couldn't be sure that if I sat down my body would let me stand back up.

"Sit down!" Mom's tone was the same no-nonsense one she used when she accused me of sneaking off with Aunt Tillie's wine when I was in high school.

I slipped into my usual chair without comment, glancing to my left to find Aunt Tillie watching me. "Hey."

Aunt Tillie's face was hard to read. "We were worried," she said finally.

I glanced at the spread on the table. Meatloaf. Mashed potatoes and gravy. Roasted Brussels sprouts. "It doesn't look like you were worried."

"We didn't serve dinner until we got the call from Landon that Thistle found you," Marnie said.

Aunt Tillie's brown eyes were focused on me. "Look again."

I rolled my eyes. "I've seen dinner before."

"Look again."

I did. That's when I realized that the table wasn't filled with just food; no, it was filled with my favorite dishes. Twila had baked fresh rolls. My mother had baked my favorite dessert: blueberry pie. Someone had even brought out a jug of tomato juice for good measure. This was all for me.

"I'm fine, you guys," I said, my tone gruffer than I intended.

Mom slipped a plate – heaped with more food than I could eat in a week – in front of me. "Eat your dinner."

I didn't think I was hungry. The growling in my stomach told me differently. I felt Landon settle next to me, a similar cornucopia of food magically appearing in front of him within seconds.

I did what I always did and scooped the mashed potatoes on top of the meat loaf, mashing them together into a pile of yummy goodness, and then took a huge bite. I groaned appreciatively, causing Landon to chuckle. "I was hungrier than I thought," I admitted.

"You didn't get your lunch," he said, rubbing the back of my neck. "You didn't eat breakfast either."

I focused on my dinner. It wasn't easy. Mom and Marnie were busy trying to clean the knot on my head, and Twila was rolling up my sleeves to get a better look at the abrasions on my arms.

"She's got some scratches on her arms but nothing serious," Twila announced. "This shirt isn't going to survive, though."

"I don't like this bump," Marnie said. "I don't think she has a concussion, though. Her pupils are even and not dilated. We should watch her."

"When did you become a doctor?" I grumbled.

Marnie ignored me. "What else hurts?"

"Does my pride count?"

"No."

I glanced over at Landon. "Are you going to help me?"

He shook his head as he shoveled another forkful into his mouth. "No. I think you should go to the hospital. If you're not going to do that, then I'm going to let them go nuts."

"What happened to me getting my own way?"

"If you're good, I'll let you have your way tomorrow."

Thistle raised her eyebrows suggestively. "That sounds like fun. Will you make him do what I want, too?"

Marnie straightened suddenly, glancing around. "Where is Clove?"

Thistle and I exchanged a look.

"Where is Clove?" Marnie repeated.

Landon fixed me with a quizzical look. "Do you know where Clove is?"

I rolled my lower lip into my mouth so I could think of an appropriate lie. Unfortunately, my mind wasn't firing on all thrusters.

"She's out at the Dandridge," Thistle answered.

"Way to go, tattletale," I muttered.

"Why would she be out at the Dandridge?" Twila asked.

I couldn't help but risk a glance in the direction of Landon's family. They'd been silent since my arrival. They all sat in front of empty plates – or partially-empty plates in the case of Connie and Blanche – watching the scene play out in front of them. I had no idea what they were thinking.

I was surprised to see that Connie looked unsettled. If I hadn't spent the last few days in the company of this woman, I would have thought she looked worried. I couldn't decide whether it was my health or the fact that I hadn't died that had her so concerned, though.

"Bay," Marnie said, interrupting my thoughts. "Why would Clove be out at the Dandridge?"

I shrugged. "I have a head wound. My mind isn't working correctly."

"You baby," Thistle admonished. "Clove has been sleeping with Sam Cornell."

Landon's eyebrows shot so high they practically disappeared in his hairline. "You were right about that?"

"You knew about that?" Thistle exploded.

"Calm down," I said. "I didn't find out until this morning. Marcus said he saw her walking along the trail from the Dandridge. He didn't tell me until we were there to get the horses."

"Why didn't you tell me?"

"I got thrown by a horse!"

"Stop using that as an excuse," Thistle shot back. "It's getting old."

Aunt Tillie extended her index finger in Thistle's direction. "You need to calm down."

"Who says I'm not calm?"

"I think everyone at the table can testify to that matter," Aunt Tillie replied. "You're all … freaked out … and I don't like it. Sit there and eat your dinner."

"I don't even like meatloaf," Thistle argued.

"Then eat the potatoes."

"Fine."

Landon rubbed his hand over his forehead, his shoulders sagging slightly as the weight of the day caught up with him. "Leave Thistle alone."

Aunt Tillie scowled. "Don't tell me what to do."

"She's upset," Landon said. "She's not really upset with Clove. She was upset that Bay was missing and, because she's Thistle, she can't admit what she's really upset about so she has to bitch about everything else in the world to feel better. Right now, just in this moment, I get it. So leave her alone."

Aunt Tillie's face softened, an expression that jumbled my already confused world. What the hell? "I don't give you the credit you deserve sometimes. You're smarter than you look."

Landon narrowed his eyes. "I'm not going to take any of your crap right now, so don't play me."

"I'm not playing you."

"Forgive me if I have my doubts."

"You've probably earned that right," Aunt Tillie said.

Landon shifted a dubious gaze in my direction. I shrugged, cringing as my aching back protested. Landon's jaw stiffened. "Eat your dinner. You need the fuel. Then I'm taking you home and putting you to bed."

"Maybe she should stay here tonight," Mom suggested. "You know, just so she's close."

Landon considered the offer. "I'll agree on one condition."

"What condition?" Twila asked.

"We're staying in the same room."

Mom worried her lower lip. "I could stay in the same room with her."

Yup, that sounded like a great way to end a horrible day. "I'll just go down to the guesthouse."

"I'm staying with her," Landon said, shaking his head for emphasis. "No, don't even bother arguing. I'm staying with her."

Mom wrinkled her nose and looked at Marnie for support. "Fine. You can stay together."

"So, wait," Thistle interjected. "If you get thrown from a horse you get to sleep with your boyfriend in the main house? This is good to know."

"Eat your dinner," Aunt Tillie barked.

Landon relaxed, moving his hand back to my neck. "Everyone eat their dinner. I'm tired. She's exhausted. You people are exhausting under normal circumstances. There's only so much she can take."

"Her or you?" Thistle challenged.

"Eat your dinner, Thistle."

A HALF HOUR later I found myself in the kitchen, resting my weight against the counter and fighting the urge to curl up in a ball on the floor and sleep. Landon and Mom were upstairs arguing about what sheets – and sleeping potions – were appropriate. His family had retired to their rooms right after dinner, his mother stopping next to my chair to tell me she was glad I wasn't seriously hurt before disappearing with the rest of her family.

I was still marveling over that little miracle.

"I thought you'd be asleep already," Aunt Tillie said, shuffling into the kitchen.

"I can't go up there until Mom leaves," I admitted. "Climbing into bed with a guy when she's watching is too weird to deal with."

"You're in your twenties," Aunt Tillie drawled. "In fact, you're closer to thirty than twenty. Grow up."

"Thanks. I'm glad my near-death experience hasn't affected you in the least."

Aunt Tillie rolled her eyes. "You're obviously not dead."

I glanced around, making sure we were alone, and then focused on Aunt Tillie's tiny but terrifying frame. "Something happened today."

"You fell off a horse."

"The horses scattered because of Floyd."

Aunt Tillie froze, her hand midway to the counter to steal a roll. "Are you sure?"

"I saw him ... it. I saw it right before it happened."

Aunt Tillie tapped her foot on the floor and crossed her arms over her chest. "Well this is just ... undignified. What kind of asshole spooks horses?"

Yeah, that's the appropriate word for what we were facing -- undignified. "I woke up in his memory. Floyd's, I mean."

Aunt Tillie rolled her head to the side. "I see."

"You see? You don't want to know what I saw?"

"Not really."

"Well, I'm going to tell you anyway," I said. "I saw Floyd. I saw Floyd terrorizing his wife. I saw him beating her. I saw him drunk as a skunk and threatening to kill that woman."

"Floyd had issues."

Issues? "I saw you there, too."

Aunt Tillie raised her eyebrows briefly. "No, you didn't."

"Yes, I did."

"No, you didn't."

I slammed my hand on the counter angrily. "Stop telling me what I saw!"

Thistle pushed through the swinging door, not looking surprised in the least to see us arguing. "Did she tell you anything?"

"She says I didn't see her in the memory."

"Of course she did."

"Listen, missy," Aunt Tillie said. "I know you've had a rough day – we've all had a rough day – but there's only so much I can take."

"Try being me for a day," Thistle challenged.

"Oh, you're such a ... kvetch."

"What's a kvetch?"

"Look it up in the dictionary," Aunt Tillie said. "You'll see your photo."

This wasn't how I envisioned this conversation going. I tried to get it back on track. "Did you kill Floyd to protect Mrs. Gunderson?"

"No."

"If you did, I'd understand. He was horrible. I mean horrible. Chief Terry will understand."

"I didn't kill Floyd."

"You were there."

"You don't know what you saw," Aunt Tillie countered. "You're delusional."

The sound of a throat clearing at the door caused us all to swivel in unison. Landon stood there, his arms crossed over his chest, his face teeming with anger. "Why are you arguing?"

"It's a long story," I said.

"Well, you're not telling it tonight."

I opened my mouth to argue, but Landon was already wagging his finger. "No."

"You don't even know what we're talking about."

"I don't want to know," Landon said. "I want to put you to bed. I want to climb in next to you. I want to wake up tomorrow and deal with this all then. That is what I want – and that is what I'm damn well going to get."

"You said you didn't want me to lie," I protested.

"I'm not asking you to lie," he said. "I want you to rest."

"I'm fine."

"Do you have ... do you have any idea what I thought today?" Landon's face was a tortured tableau of guilt and anger. "Do you have any idea what pictures were going through my head? I thought you were lying hurt at the bottom of a ravine. I thought you were bleeding out, dying slowly on the ground in a place no one would ever find you. Even worse, I thought you were already dead. I was out there looking for you and I was worried you were already dead."

Aunt Tillie, Thistle and I were flabbergasted. We'd never seen him this worked up. "I'm sorry."

"I'm sorry, too," Thistle said.

Aunt Tillie shifted her gaze to the left. "I'm not."

Landon was about to blow. "You know what?"

"What?" Aunt Tillie asked, shaking her head sarcastically in an effort to mock him.

"You are horrible. You are mean. You are crass. You are … you are just a terrible person. I've made excuses for you. I've told myself you're just old and set in your ways. I figured you couldn't really be that bad. I mean, Bay loves you. There has to be a reason. There has to be something about you that isn't horrible."

"Who are you calling old?" Aunt Tillie growled.

Landon ran his hand up to his forehead, gripping a handful of hair in an attempt to regain some little bit of control. "Stop talking."

"Don't you tell me what to do."

"Stop it!"

Aunt Tillie jumped back in surprise, the seriousness of his tone finally hitting home. Thistle's eyes widened, exchanging a stunned look with me. He'd actually rendered her speechless.

Landon drew a deep breath. "This is what you're going to do."

Aunt Tillie waited.

"You're going to give your niece a hug," Landon said. "Yes, a hug. You're going to tell her how happy you are she didn't die and break every heart in this damn inn. Then? Then you're going to go to bed and not even think about causing any type of trouble for at least twenty-four hours."

Aunt Tillie didn't look sure, but didn't argue.

"Then, just when you're ready to cause some trouble, you're going to check with me and make sure it's okay. Have you got that?"

I expected Aunt Tillie to freak out. I expected her to rant and rave. I expected her to curse us all into weeks of unspeakable horror. She didn't, though. For a second, I swear, I thought pride – and even more impressively, respect – flitted across her face. Instead of arguing, she squared her shoulders and marched over to me, wrapping her arms around my waist.

I stiffened at the inexplicable show of capitulation.

"I'm glad you didn't die," Aunt Tillie said.

With those words, she let me go and left the room. She didn't look back.

"Omigod, she's possessed," Thistle said, dissolving into mad giggles.

I fixed my eyes on Landon incredulously. "How did you do that?"

"You're going to shut up, too," Landon said. "I'm tired. I'm so tired I can't think straight."

I thought about arguing with him, the firm set of his jaw told me that would be a terrible idea. I merely nodded in response.

Landon moved over to me and swooped me up in his arms. "Now, I'm carrying you upstairs. Don't even bother arguing. You can barely walk. There's no way you can climb those stairs. Then? Then I'm putting you into bed. No one is going to say another word." He shot Thistle a warning look. "Not one more word."

I was asleep before my head hit the pillow, his body draped over mine, not even an inch of space separating us, to make sure nothing attacked me in my sleep.

The day had definitely turned out better than it had started.

TWENTY-FIVE

I was drifting in an ocean of blue when consciousness finally claimed me. Landon's eyes were wide and alert when I focused on him. He was lying next to me, watching me sleep. I had no idea how long he'd been awake.

"Morning," I mumbled.

"Morning."

He lowered his lips to mine and pressed a sweet kiss to my lips.

"How did you sleep?" I asked when he finally pulled away.

"Good," he said. "I woke up a few times, a strange place and all. You didn't move even once, though."

"Yeah, I was out."

"Whatever that potion your mother gave you was, I guess I'm a fan. I thought you would have nightmares."

"I don't think I even dreamed," I said.

Landon twirled his fingers in my hair. "How are you feeling?"

"I'm not sure," I admitted. "I'm scared to move."

Landon rested his head against mine on the pillow. "Then don't move."

"I don't think that's going to be an option forever," I said.

"It's an option for the next five minutes."

"You make a good point."

"You need to stop acting so surprised when that happens," he said, reaching over to entwine the fingers of his free hand with mine. "You need to realize I always make good points."

"I'll keep that in mind."

"Good."

I closed my eyes, wondering briefly if I could slip back into sleep. After a few minutes I realized that even trying was fruitless. "What time is it?"

"It's almost nine."

I did the math in my head. "That means I slept for almost eleven hours."

"Obviously you needed it."

"Did you need it, too?"

"Yes."

"Are you angry with me?"

Landon pulled back slightly to meet my gaze. "Why would you ask that?"

"You were angry last night," I pointed out.

"I wasn't angry with you."

"No," I agreed. "You were just angry."

"I wasn't angry," Landon said. "I was ... I was just overwhelmed."

I didn't know how to respond.

"I'm sorry I yelled at Thistle and Aunt Tillie," he offered.

Was he worried I was angry? "I'm not. It was the highlight of my day. Well, you carrying me up the stairs like a romance-novel hero was the real highlight of my day. That was a close second, though."

Landon laughed, the sound warming my heart. "I'm glad your sense of humor is intact."

"I'm glad you're ... here." I swallowed hard, fighting the burn climbing my cheeks.

"I wouldn't be anywhere else."

I closed my eyes again, happy to have a few minutes to enjoy the warmth of his body next to mine without interruption.

"Bay, I need you to know something."

"What?"

"If you ever die on me, I'm going to be really upset."

I laughed, my back aching with the sudden movement. "Good to know."

A knock on the door caused us both to jump. I wasn't surprised to see Mom and Marnie standing in the archway when the door swung open.

"Is everyone decent?" Mom asked pointedly.

Landon sighed, shifting into a sitting position. "Yes."

Mom marched into the room, a breakfast tray in her hands. "I thought you'd want some breakfast."

Marnie was right behind her, carrying a twin tray. Landon moved to get up, but Marnie motioned for him to stay in the bed. "We thought you two would like a quiet breakfast – just the two of you."

Suspicion washed over me. "Is this a trick?"

Mom ignored me. "Look. I made your favorite. Eggs, hash browns, ham, toast and tomato juice. You need to get some food into you."

"I haven't moved since the last pile of food you put in front of me," I said, shifting to sit up. "Oh … ow … ow."

Landon reached over to help me. "What hurts?"

"What doesn't hurt?"

"That's it. I'm taking you to the hospital."

"It's not that kind of hurt," I said. "It's more of an … ache."

"That's what happens when you fall off a horse," Mom said.

"Good to know."

Mom made sure I had everything I needed and then dropped a kiss on my head. "Don't ever do what you did yesterday again."

She was at the door before I found my voice. "Mom?"

"What?"

"Thanks."

"For what? It's just breakfast."

"For everything."

Mom smiled. "When you're done, come downstairs. Terry is waiting."

"You're not being mean to him, are you?"

"He's eating breakfast."

"You left him alone with Twila? That doesn't sound like you."

Marnie and Mom exchanged a look. "Well, we should get back downstairs. Enjoy your breakfast."

I held off my laugh until the door closed and we were alone. "This is just ... surreal."

"Enjoy it," Landon said, moving his glass of tomato juice to my tray. "It won't last long."

I knew he was right.

"I'M MOVING OUT!"

"You're not moving out."

"Don't tell me what I'm going to do."

"You're not moving out!"

"Fine. Then you're moving out."

Landon and I took our time rejoining the Overlook's special brand of mayhem. When we did, we found everyone enjoying tea and coffee in the dining room – as Mom and Aunt Tillie launched the first verbal missiles of World War III.

"What's going on?" Landon asked.

Aunt Tillie jumped when she heard his voice. "Nothing."

"It doesn't sound like nothing," Landon prodded.

"It's nothing."

Mom furrowed her brow, confused. "I thought ... ."

"I wasn't doing anything," Aunt Tillie said. "We were just talking."

Landon pulled out a dining room chair and helped me settle into it. He greeted his family with a friendly smile.

"You look better," Connie said.

"I slept," Landon said.

"I wasn't talking to you."

Landon pulled up short. "You weren't?"

"Were you thrown off a horse and left for dead in the woods all day?"

"No."

"Then I wasn't talking to you," Connie said. "How are you feeling, dear?"

I was stunned. "I think the best word to describe how I'm feeling is 'stiff.'"

"I bet," Connie clucked. "Did the horse buck you off? Did you see it coming? That actually makes it worse, when you know it's coming, I mean."

Actually I was looking at a poltergeist when a branch hit me in the head. "No, a branch knocked me off. Ghost was terrified."

"Yeah, that was so weird," Denny said. "I wonder what happened."

Thistle and I traded wary looks. "It was probably a snake. They come out more in the spring and the horses hate them."

Landon raised an eyebrow and smirked. I'd told him my story over breakfast – and a joint shower. He said he needed time to process, but the memory was clearly changing his opinion on the possible crime.

"That's horrible," Connie said. "Your mother said you were unconscious for hours. You must've been so scared when you woke up."

"More confused than anything else," I hedged. "It was ... disorienting."

"Well, you should know, your family ... your whole family was amazing. I've never seen people jump into action like they did. And Landon, well, Landon was just beside himself. I've never seen him so ... worried." Connie's face was pinched. "It was really sweet."

"I didn't mean to worry anyone."

"Of course you didn't, dear," Connie said. "It was just a horrible situation. I can't believe how well you're handling it. If it had been me, well, I think I would have just crawled into a hole and died."

I wanted to believe she was sincere, but life with Aunt Tillie made me leery.

"I don't think that's true," I said. "I think you're stronger than that."

Chief Terry walked into the dining room from the kitchen, his dark eyes filled with worry as he searched the room. When they found me, he strode over and dropped a kiss on my head. "There's my girl."

"She's my girl," Landon said, his voice teasing and pleasant.

"I've known her longer," Chief Terry argued, moving away from me and settling into an open chair across the table. "She'll always be my girl."

"I'm ready to fight for her if it comes to it," Landon said.

"Son, until you've spent four hours searching for the mood ring she lost in a pile of leaves, you're not even in the running."

Landon arched an eyebrow. "A mood ring?"

"Hey, I loved that thing."

"And who found it?" Chief Terry asked.

Mom patted Chief Terry on the shoulder as she passed, all animosity from Aunt Tillie's questioning seemingly forgotten. "If I remember right, you kept searching three hours after her bedtime."

Chief Terry blushed. "She wouldn't stop crying."

"Bay always was your favorite," Mom said. "I think it's because she's my daughter."

Marnie scowled. "Or because he liked you least and thought he should make up for that lack of emotion by coddling Bay."

Oh, good, the competition for Chief Terry's affection was back on.

"He didn't coddle Bay," Mom countered. "And he likes me best. Tell her that, Terry."

Chief Terry shifted uncomfortably. Luckily for him, his spot on the hot seat was quickly forgotten when Kenneth breezed into the room. He was carrying a vase full of flowers – one so big he was dwarfed behind its girth – and heading toward Aunt Tillie. When did he get here?

"Tillie, my love, I've come to beg your forgiveness."

Aunt Tillie made a sound in her throat. It was halfway between a gag and growl. "Go home, Kenneth."

"Not until you forgive me."

"I'm not forgiving you."

"Hi, Kenneth," Blanche greeted him with a saucy wink. "Those flowers are beautiful. Some people just don't appreciate the beauty of flora."

Kenneth look confused. "I don't think there are any floras in here. They're roses. Really expensive roses, actually."

"I love roses," Blanche said.

"I hate roses," Aunt Tillie announced. "I hate all things with thorns."

"You have thorns," Landon pointed out.

"Watch yourself," Aunt Tillie warned. "I took pity on you last night, but that won't last for very long."

Landon rolled his eyes.

"They're beautiful flowers, Aunt Tillie," I said. "You should thank him."

"You don't push it either."

"Don't threaten her," Landon warned, going into protective mode.

"I'm not threatening her."

"It sounded like a threat to me."

"Who doesn't like roses?" Blanche said. "Only someone of limited breeding would turn their nose up at roses. Well, look who I'm talking to."

"Blanche," Connie chided, "stop being rude."

"Did she just call me low class?" Aunt Tillie was on her feet. Mom moved in behind her, putting a hand on her shoulder. "Don't you have some gardening to do?"

Mom must be desperate if she was sending Aunt Tillie to her pot field.

"No," Aunt Tillie said. "I have an ass to kick."

"No, I recall you saying you had a full day of … planting to do."

Landon narrowed his eyes. "You know what? I would love to see that crop. How about I go with you?"

"Oh, right, like I'm going to take a narc … planting," Aunt Tillie scoffed.

"What kind of garden are we talking about?" Blanche asked. "I'm a master pruner."

She did remind me of prunes for some reason.

"My balls are shrinking to the size of prunes right now," Kenneth announced. "It's because I've lost my love."

Clove picked that moment to return to the fray. Every eye in the room turned to her as she walked into the room. Clove's eyes clouded in confusion. "What did I miss?"

TWENTY-SIX

"Well, the prodigal daughter returns."

One glance at Marnie's drawn face told me that Clove was in for a world of Winchester complaints, something she obviously wasn't ready to face.

"I'm sorry," Clove said. "I've been busy with work."

Thistle opened her mouth, ready to unleash a torrent of angry recriminations, but she stopped when she saw me shake my head. Now wasn't the time.

"Are you hungry?" Mom asked.

"I already ate," Clove said.

"I bet you did," Aunt Tillie said.

"What is that supposed to mean?" Clove was defensive. I didn't blame her.

"Is something going on?" Connie asked.

"No," I replied, grimacing as I shook my head and several pains shot through my back. "It's just … family stuff."

Connie nodded, glancing at Landon. "I understand. Family is important."

She really didn't.

I shifted my gaze to Landon. "What do you guys have planned for the day?"

"I'm sticking with you," Landon replied. "Don't even try arguing."

"We're going to go up to Mackinaw," Connie said. "We've already discussed it."

"That's like a two-hour drive," I said. "Are you sure?"

"We're sure."

"Are you sure you don't want to go with them?" I asked Landon.

"I've seen the fort," Landon said. "I'm happy here."

I sucked my lower lip into my mouth for a second. "Well, I'm not going to complain about spending the day with you. Why don't you have tea with your family and meet me down at the guesthouse in about an hour or so?"

Landon balked. "Why can't I go with you now?"

"Because I think Thistle, Clove and I need a little … bonding time."

Landon hunched his shoulders, clearly battling an inner demon as he tried to rein in his true emotions. "Okay."

"Okay?"

"You get whatever you want today. Wasn't that the agreement?"

It was. I had no idea he would follow through, though.

Landon fixed his eyes on Thistle. "If she has trouble walking down to the guesthouse, I'm counting on you to call me for help."

Thistle was already on her feet. "I got it."

"I'm not kidding."

"I got it."

Landon nodded. "I'll be down there in an hour. No one better be screaming or pulling anyone's hair, when I get there."

"We'll be civil," I promised.

"No wrestling in the dirt either."

"I got it."

THE WALK to the guesthouse was excruciating. I had no idea why my thighs hurt; they hadn't during the walk to the Dandridge the previous afternoon, but now every muscle in my body ached.

We made the trip to the guesthouse in silence; no one speaking, no one yelling, no one looking at each other.

Thistle unlocked the door and waited until everyone was safely inside before unleashing her vitriol. "I don't know why you're acting like the victim."

Clove jerked back as though she'd been punched. Clearly Thistle was going for the jugular. "I'm not acting like a victim."

I settled in the armchair and watched the two of them. I figured my opinion wasn't necessary unless things really got out of hand.

"You always act like the victim," Thistle said. "That's your thing."

"Oh, yeah," Clove challenged. "What's your thing?"

"Anger."

"Well, at least you admit it."

"I am so mad at you," Thistle yelled.

"Why? Because I tried to grab a little bit of happiness for myself?"

"Is that what you're calling it?"

This was getting out of hand already. "Sit down," I ordered.

Clove and Thistle did as they were told, positioning themselves at opposite ends of the couch, and occasionally shooting hateful looks in each other's direction.

"We're going to fight," I said. "We're going to do it in an orderly fashion, though."

Clove and Thistle waited.

"Let's start with Clove," I said. "Why don't you tell us how you and Sam hooked up?"

"I don't think Thistle wants to hear about it," Clove said, pouting.

"Well, I do. I'm in pain, so you're going to humor me." I was taking a page from Landon's book, hoping it would work for me as well as it worked for him. "How did you hook up?"

"We ran into each other when I was walking one day," Clove replied. "I'm trying to get in better shape. I told you that. I was walking the Au Sable trail and I ran into him. It was innocent."

"I'm not saying it wasn't," I replied. "When did this happen?"

"Ten days ago."

"Ten days?" Thistle was incredulous. "You've been hiding this for ten days?"

I shot her a silencing look and waited.

"We just walked and talked that day," Clove said. "He has a lot on his mind. After that, we decided to walk together. Just to talk. I like listening to him. Like I said, he's got a lot on his mind."

"Like what?" I prodded.

"He knows what we are," Clove said. "He's always known. That's why he came to town in the first place."

"And that doesn't tip you off that he's up to no good?" Thistle snapped.

"He's a good man," Clove protested. "He was born into this world, just as we were. He knows what we are and he doesn't judge."

Well, that was interesting. "What do you know about his family?"

"His mother is a witch," Clove said. "He knows about the craft."

"Okay," I said. "His mother is a witch. What is he? A warlock?"

"He's a solo practitioner," Clove replied. "He's Wiccan, nothing else."

"What are his powers?"

"He doesn't really have any," Clove said. "That doesn't mean he's not enthusiastic."

"That's what I'm worried about," Thistle grumbled.

I ran my hand over my forehead, making sure to keep away from the sore area by my right temple. "Clove, how did he find out about us?"

"He did research."

"What research?"

"The history of this area is pretty well known," Clove said. "If you know what you're looking for, it's easy to ascertain who the real witches are."

"That's fair," I said, rolling my eyes when Thistle leaned forward to argue. "That still doesn't explain why he came here."

"He just wanted to see us," Clove said. "He just wanted to see what we could do. He wanted to see who we are. He wanted to be a part of something. He wanted to be a part of us."

"He's been lying to us," I reminded her. "He came to the paper under the guise of being an investor. That means he's a liar."

"That's only because he wasn't sure how else to approach us," Clove said. "Would you have trusted him if he came up to you and called you a witch and said he wanted to hang out?"

"No ... but ... ."

"We lie to people about who we are every day," Clove pressed.

"That's different."

"Is it?"

"I don't know."

"I'm not saying he's perfect," Clove said. "He's a man. He's a flawed man, but so are Marcus and Landon, and you don't have a problem with them."

"We don't know anything about him," I said.

"We didn't know anything about Landon," Clove said. "Look how that turned out. And the risks with Landon were so much greater than the risks with Sam."

I pursed my lips, glancing over at Thistle. "I want you to be happy."

"Then give Sam a chance."

"I'm not sure I trust him, Clove. He's been so ... sneaky."

"Landon was undercover with meth dealers and you trusted him," Clove pointed out.

"Even when he was undercover, he went out of his way to protect me," I countered. "He was always good ... even when he was pretending to be bad. Sam, though, Sam has been hiding and plotting since he came to town. He pretended to be good and then ambushed me."

"I'm not asking you to love him," Clove said. "I don't. Not yet, anyway. I just want to get to know him better. I want you to get to know him better."

"Why Sam?" Thistle asked.

"It's not just about Sam," Clove admitted.

"Then what is it about?" I asked.

"Loneliness."

Her words chilled me. Landon had been right. "We didn't mean to exclude you."

"You didn't exclude me," Clove replied. "If anything, you went out of your way to include me. You kept inviting me out with the four of you, making sure I was the fifth person at dinner or the fifth person at the town dance. You both made Marcus and Landon dance with me. Do you have any idea how that made me feel?"

I swallowed hard. "We weren't trying to ... single you out."

"I know. I know that you did what you did out of the goodness of your heart. The truth is, though, I want what you have. What both of you have. I need to find it for myself, though."

"We weren't trying to treat you any differently," Thistle said, her voice low.

"I know."

"I don't want you to be lonely," I said. "I just don't know that Sam is the right guy for you."

"I don't either," Clove said. "What I know is that I'm interested enough to find out. Don't I deserve that? Don't I deserve the chance to find whether Sam is the one for me?"

Thistle and I remained silent.

"Sam and I barely know each other," Clove said. "What we know is that we like each other. We're comfortable with each other. We want to get to know each other better. I think you guys owe me the leeway to let me find out whether there's something here."

Crap. If she was going to be reasonable, Thistle and I had absolutely no reason to argue.

"I think we have to set up ground rules," Thistle said.

Oh, this should be interesting.

"What ground rules?" Clove asked.

"I'm willing to go on triple dates," Thistle said. "The six of us at dinner? I'm totally willing to do that."

"That sounds okay," Clove said. "I guess."

"Until everyone agrees, though," Thistle plowed on. "I don't think he should be here. I don't think he should be at the inn."

Clove looked undecided. "We didn't have those rules for Marcus and Landon."

"We didn't," I conceded. "I think we should all vote now, though, about who is allowed here and who isn't."

"Oh, like I'm going to vote against Marcus and Landon," Clove said. "That's not even fair."

"I'm not ready for him to be here, Clove," I said. "I … we … need time."

"I agree," Thistle said.

"I'll agree to those terms under one condition," Clove said.

"Which is?"

"I want to revisit this in three months."

"Why three months?" Thistle asked.

"Because that will give me time to get to know him better and the two of you more time to get to know him better, too."

Thistle and I exchanged unspoken consent.

"We agree," I said. "No more lying, though."

"No more hiding," Thistle added.

"Agreed."

All was right in our small world again. For now.

TWENTY-SEVEN

"Where's Landon?"

Clove, Thistle and I sat on the couch watching a marathon of *The Walking Dead*. It was a few hours after our big "confrontation," and everyone was trying to pretend it was a normal day.

It wasn't going well.

"He mentioned going up to the inn to get us lunch," I said. "I think he just wanted to get away from all of our drama."

"I doubt that," Thistle said. "You should've seen him yesterday. He was a madman."

"I saw him with Aunt Tillie in the kitchen last night," I replied. "That was bad enough."

"What happened with Aunt Tillie?" Clove asked.

"Landon unloaded on her," Thistle said. "He told her she was mean and nasty and then he made her hug Bay. It was hilarious."

Clove looked horrified. "She hugged you? What was that like?"

"Weird," I admitted.

"It was the highlight of my day," Thistle said.

"I miss all the good stuff," Clove muttered.

"That's what happens when … ." I shook my head in warning, and Thistle wisely left the sentence unfinished.

I decided to change the subject. "Did you notice that Landon's mother was actually nice to me last night?"

"And this morning," Thistle said. "I think everyone was so worried that you've got a two-day pass to be as obnoxious as you want to be."

"I don't want to be obnoxious," I countered.

"I would," Thistle said. "Hell, you got our moms to agree to let you spend the night in the same bed as Landon in the inn last night. That's got to be some form of divine intervention or something."

"No way," Clove said, her mouth dropping open.

"They brought them breakfast in bed this morning, too," Thistle said. "It was like, 'Here, you need sustenance for your sexathon.' It totally freaked me out."

"It's not like anything happened," I scoffed. "I was pretty much asleep before I got to the bedroom."

"Still," Thistle said. "Landon was so bossy last night that everyone was afraid of taking him on."

"He did seem a little … manic," I admitted, chewing on my bottom lip.

"He was worried," Thistle said. "We all were. It turns out we had a reason to be worried – and that was before we found out you woke up in the memory of a poltergeist."

Clove shifted forward. "What do you mean she woke up in the memory of a poltergeist? She didn't tell me that."

Thistle winced. "I forgot you didn't know," she said. "We obviously couldn't tell everyone what happened in front of Landon's family," Thistle said. "And you weren't here when she got home last night."

"I was there when she turned up at the Dandridge," Clove shot back. "She could've told me then."

I focused on the television. "I'm really glad the Governor is dead. He was a real asshat."

Thistle immediately caught on to what I was doing. "Yeah. Too bad he had to take Hershel with him beforehand, though."

Clove wasn't fooled. "What am I missing?"

"Who do you think will die first in the new season?" Thistle asked.

"I'm worried about Glenn," I replied smoothly.

Clove reached over and pinched Thistle. "What am I missing?"

Thistle batted her hand away irritably. "Don't pinch me. You know I don't like that."

"Then tell me what's going on," Clove insisted.

"It's nothing," I lied.

"Bay didn't tell you because she doesn't trust Sam," Thistle said.

"We've gone over this," Clove sighed.

"We have," Thistle agreed. "You can date him all you want. What happens in this family, though, is off limits to him right now."

Clove pinched the bridge of her nose. "Fine."

"Good."

"Great."

The door to the guesthouse opened as Landon let himself inside. He was carrying a basket of food. He glanced between the three of us. "Have you been fighting again?"

"No," Thistle said. "What did they send?"

"Sandwiches and soup," Landon said. "Roast beef for the sandwiches and cream of broccoli for the soup."

"More of Bay's favorites," Thistle grumbled. "When am I going to get my favorite foods?"

"When you get thrown from a horse," Landon replied pointedly. "Now either shut up and eat – or just shut up."

Thistle stuck her tongue out in response, wisely snapping her mouth shut when Landon fixed her with a challenging glare.

Once everyone had a plate in front of them, and Landon was settled in the armchair with his own lunch, conversation slowly picked up again.

"Maybe I should put a request in for dinner," I mused.

"You might as well take advantage of it while you can," Clove said. "It won't last."

"I think they've already decided on Polish for dinner," Landon interjected. "They were up there stuffing cabbage rolls when I left, and Marnie was rolling out dough for pierogi."

Thistle made a face. "I hate Polish food."

"Bay loves it, though," Clove said, giggling.

Landon kept his gaze fixed on the television. "I think there's going to be a bigger crowd for dinner tonight."

"Let me guess, Kenneth has invited himself?" Thistle asked.

"And Chief Terry," I added.

"I believe they'll both be there," Landon said, still avoiding eye contact. "I think there will be three more guests, though."

I straightened, suspicion rolling over me. "Who?"

"I'm glad the Governor is dead," Landon said.

"Who?" I repeated.

Landon cocked his head and rolled his eyes until they settled on me. "Your fathers."

"What? Why?"

"Because my mom made mention to your mom that she would like to meet your father," Landon said. "Your mom thought that was a great idea."

"No, she didn't," I grumbled. "She just wanted to be the perky hostess, like usual."

Thistle's face reflected the emotional turmoil gathering in my gut. "I think that's a terrible idea."

"They'd already invited them," Landon said. "What did you expect me to do?"

"Tell them to uninvite them," Thistle said. "Any time our mothers are in the same room with our fathers things get … ugly."

"Maybe this time will be different," Landon suggested.

"And maybe Aunt Tillie will suddenly sprout wings and a halo and start channeling an angel," Thistle replied.

"Don't get snotty."

"I'm not trying to be snotty," Thistle said. "You seem to forget that our mothers and our fathers don't get along under the best of circumstances. You want to throw your family, Aunt Tillie, Kenneth and Chief Terry into that mix and you somehow think this is going to end well?"

"My family will be out of here in a few days," Landon said. "I can't exactly explain why dinner with your fathers is such a bad idea."

"You could if you tried," Thistle said. "I'll help you."

"I think it's a good idea," Clove said.

Thistle rolled her eyes. "No, you don't."

"Yes, I do."

"No, you don't."

"Don't tell me what I think," Clove said.

"Someone needs to."

This could go on forever. "Why don't you think it's a bad idea?" I asked.

"Because, it's new people for Landon's family to focus on," Clove pointed out. "Our dads like to avoid all talk of witchcraft as it is, so that's not going to be a big distraction. It might be a good thing."

She had a point. Still, though ... .

"And what happens when they find out Bay was missing all day yesterday and we never called them?" Thistle asked.

Uh-oh. I hadn't even thought of that. "You guys didn't call them?"

"Why would we?" Thistle asked. She was still bitter about the divide between our mothers and fathers. "We knew you weren't over there."

Family interactions in the Winchester clan are always dicey situations. "We've been really bad about spending time with them lately."

"We've been busy," Thistle said. "Besides, we thought Clove was going out there and spending time with them."

I reached over and pinched her.

"Ow!"

"Stop doing that," I ordered. "We agreed to give Clove some ... leeway in this," I said. "You constantly bringing it up and berating her is not leeway."

"Thank you," Clove said.

"She's not wrong, though," I added. "We've been ... inattentive."

Thistle snorted. "You mean self-absorbed."

That, too. "We need to make a better effort."

Thistle bristled. "You say 'we' but what I'm really hearing is 'you.'"

"Hey! I've been dealing with Landon's family. What's your excuse?"

"You've been dealing with Landon's family for less than a week," Thistle reminded me. "We haven't seen them in almost three weeks."

"I had to plan for Landon's family," I countered.

"Whatever."

I glanced over at Landon. "What do you think about all this?"

Landon shrugged. "I don't know them well enough to offer an opinion."

"That's never stopped you before," Thistle said.

"Eat your lunch, Thistle," he grunted.

"Why is everyone so food-obsessed these days?" Thistle grumbled.

"Maybe we just want you to have something in your mouth so you'll shut up?" Landon retorted.

Thistle narrowed her eyes so that only a narrow swath of color was visible through the slits. "You're really starting to bug me."

"Right back at you."

TWENTY-EIGHT

Aunt Tillie met Landon and me at the back door of the inn a few hours later. "I want you to know that I told them this was a horrible idea," she announced. "No one ever listens to me, though."

I didn't doubt that. She was at war with our fathers – that is when she wasn't covering up a murder and lying about a dead body – and I knew she hadn't forgotten about their grand opening in a few weeks. "I know."

She glanced at Landon, but his face was unreadable. She reached into her pocket and held out a potion. "Here. Take this."

"What is it?" I asked suspiciously.

"It will make you less achy," Aunt Tillie replied. "I take it for my arthritis, but I figured it will help with your sore muscles."

Taking a potion from Aunt Tillie usually had disaster written all over it. I was unsure. I didn't know how to voice my concerns without insulting her, though. I needn't have worried; Landon was up to the task.

"Is that what this really is?"

"Of course."

"Are there going to be any funny side effects?"

"No."

"Is she going to be forced to tell the truth for twenty-four hours?"

"I already admitted the timing of that was ... bad."

"Are her pants going to fit tomorrow morning?"

"It depends on how much she eats tonight," Aunt Tillie sneered.

Landon sighed. "Is she going to smell like bacon? Because I wouldn't mind that one back."

Aunt Tillie grinned. "Maybe for Christmas."

"I'm going to hold you to that," Landon replied before focusing on me. "I think you should take it."

"You do?"

"I can't stand seeing how much pain you're in," he said. "If she can help, then you should let her help."

"I'm not really in pain," I countered.

"You groan like an old woman whenever you move," Landon said. "You're also favoring your right side. I know you like to be tough and brave, but there's no shame in taking something to make yourself feel better."

I took the potion from Aunt Tillie. "Can I drink this with wine? Because I have a feeling I'm going to need a whole bottle of wine to get through this dinner."

"I drink it with wine all the time," she replied.

That wasn't necessarily the response I was looking for. What the hell? How bad could things really get? I uncorked the potion and downed it in one gulp.

Landon watched me. "How do you feel?"

"Let's eat."

"THIS LOOKS AMAZING," Earl said, glancing at the impressive spread on the dining room table. "I love Polish food. Is this all homemade?"

My father and uncles had arrived about ten minutes earlier, and Twila had made nervous introductions in the foyer. The minute he saw me, Dad was striding across the room. "What happened to you?"

"I got thrown from a horse," I replied, accepting his worried hug without complaint. "I'm fine."

"You don't look fine. Has she been to the hospital?"

"She's fine, Jack," Mom warned. "Don't smother her."

Dad didn't look convinced, but he'd let Mom lead him into the dining room anyway. Now, here we were, a full table of multiple families and muddied pasts colliding.

"I've always loved it when you guys make Polish food," Uncle Teddy said. He was sitting next to Thistle, which kept him away from Twila. I noticed that Uncle Warren had been similarly situated away from Marnie.

"It's one of Bay's favorites," Mom said. "After yesterday, I figured she should get whatever she wants for a day."

If that were true I certainly wouldn't be here.

"I'm kind of curious why Bay was missing for a day and no one called me," Dad said. He was seated on my right, with Landon being shifted to my left so he could handle Aunt Tillie if she got out of hand.

"We didn't think to call you," Mom said, scooping food onto Chief Terry's plate. She'd made sure he was sitting next to her, which I had no doubt was for my father's benefit.

"Well, when someone's daughter goes missing, I think one of the first calls should be to her father," he said, glancing at me pointedly.

"Don't look at me," I said. "I was unconscious."

Dad patted my hand. "I'm not blaming you."

"No, he's blaming me," Mom said.

"No one is blaming anyone," Chief Terry interjected. "We're all lucky that Bay was found and she's okay. Let's leave it at that."

"That's easy for you to say," Dad challenged. "I'm sure you were the first one called."

"I'm the chief of police," Chief Terry replied. "Of course I was called."

"Well, I don't think it's too much to ask that I be called next time," Dad countered.

"There's not going to be a next time," Landon said, rubbing his forehead and then reaching for a bottle of wine. He filled his glass and then, after a look at my face, filled mine as well. "Let's talk about something else."

"I want to talk about how beautiful Tillie looks," Kenneth said. He'd been placed between Daryl and Denny at the far end of the table. Blanche kept shooting flirtatious glances in his direction – which wasn't lost on Aunt Tillie – but either Kenneth was pretending not to notice or he really was all about my persnickety great aunt.

"She looks great," I agreed.

"So, Bay tells us that the three of you are opening your own inn," Connie said, turning to Uncle Warren. "That's got to be exciting."

"It's a lot of work," Warren replied. "We're hoping that it will be all worth it."

"I wouldn't count on it," Aunt Tillie muttered under her breath.

Landon sent her a pointed look, which she ignored.

"Did you say something, Tillie?" Dad asked. He was clearly ready for a fight tonight.

"I asked for more wine," she lied.

Landon obediently filled her glass.

"I don't think that's what she said," Blanche interjected from the far end of the table.

"You can't hear when someone is right next to you," Landon said. "You definitely can't hear all the way down here."

"My hearing is fine," Blanche sniffed.

I took a drink of wine and then cut into my stuffed cabbage, glancing at the wall clock for confirmation that we'd only been seated for five minutes.

"What's the name of the inn?" Connie asked.

"The Dragonfly," Uncle Teddy replied.

"That's a good name," Daryl said.

"We thought it was whimsical," Teddy agreed. "We thought it fit in with the rebranding and would be a good draw."

"Will you do your own cooking?" Connie asked, clearly interested in the process.

"Warren and I have been taking classes," Teddy said. "We think we're going to be good. For the opening weekend, though, we've contracted to bring two cooks in from the culinary arts school over in Traverse City. We're keeping our options open in case we need to keep doing it."

"That sounds smart," Connie said. "It sounds like you know what you're doing."

"Well, we had a leg up," Teddy admitted. "We watched Winnie, Twila and Marnie run this inn for years – so we weren't going in blind."

"Does Hemlock Cove get enough tourist traffic to support another inn?" Denny asked.

"More than enough," Warren said. "A lot of people have to stay in neighboring towns. This shouldn't affect anyone's business."

Denny looked to Mom for confirmation.

"Our reservations are full for the entire season," Mom replied, although her voice sounded stiff. "It should be fine."

Aunt Tillie snorted. "Oh, it will definitely be fine."

"So, Tillie," Dad said, leaning back in his chair. "I hear a body was found out here. That must be … upsetting for you."

"Not particularly."

"The town gossip mill says the body has been out here for fifty years," Dad pressed. "You must know who it is."

Uh-oh. He was playing with fire now.

"The body has been identified," Landon said. "It was a local man named Floyd Gunderson. He had a reputation for being a drunk. We still don't have a cause of death."

Dad eyed Landon. "I wasn't aware you were involved in this case."

"I'm not," Landon said. "I was here when the bones were discovered, though, and Chief Terry has kept me updated."

"You're here a lot," Dad said.

Landon shifted so he could meet my father's gaze over my shoulder. "So?"

"It's just that you seem to be spending a lot of time with my daughter," Dad said.

"That's what happens when you're dating someone," Landon replied, taking a sip of wine. "Last time I checked, that wasn't a crime."

"I didn't say it was a crime," Dad said. "I was just saying that you're here a lot."

"Meaning?"

"I think he's asking what your intentions are," Aunt Tillie said, laughing. "That's just ... rich."

"Excuse me?" Dad raised his eyebrows.

"You didn't care who she was dating when she needed fatherly intervention," Aunt Tillie said. "When she was a teenager you should've seen the riffraff that she brought in and out of here. Actually, all three of them brought riffraff in here – and I didn't see any of you then."

Dad swallowed. "If you expect me to make excuses for that you're going to be disappointed," he said. "Mistakes were made by everyone. We're trying to fix that now."

"I didn't make any mistakes," Aunt Tillie said. "I was here when they were teenagers – and let me tell you, I deserve a medal for putting up with their shenanigans."

Landon reached over and ran his hand down the back of my head to calm me, a gesture that wasn't lost on Dad.

"Just how serious are you about my daughter?" he asked. Landon ignored the question, which didn't sit well with Dad. "Hey, I asked you a question."

"And I don't feel the need to quantify my feelings to you," Landon said easily. "She's an adult. I have enough to deal with where the women in this family are concerned."

"That's not an answer."

"Don't you go after my son," Connie warned. "He obviously cares about Bay enough to introduce everyone."

"Although I'm sure he's regretting that about now," Earl said.

"I don't think I'm out of line to ask these questions," Dad said.

"Oh, criminy Jack," Aunt Tillie scoffed. "They spend every night they can together and they fawn all over each other whenever they get the chance. Is that what you wanted to hear?"

One look at the grim set of Dad's jaw told me that was not what he wanted to hear. He cleared his throat uncomfortably. "Tillie, I don't think this conversation has anything to do with you."

"Like hell," Aunt Tillie said. "I like the boy. He's bossy and he doesn't back down. He's not the type to run. That already makes him a better man than you."

Crap. This dinner was quickly deteriorating. "Stop it," I said. "We're done talking about this."

"I agree," Landon said.

"I want to know what your problem with my son is," Connie interjected.

"I don't have a problem with your son that I know of," Dad replied. "All I know about him is that he works for the FBI and he always seems to be around."

"And that's bad how?" Connie pressed.

"I didn't say it was bad."

"Listen Jack, I had my reservations about Landon when I first met him, too," Chief Terry said. "He's a good man, though. He's earned my respect and, more importantly, my trust. He's good with Bay."

"You have nothing to say in this conversation," Dad said. "You're not her father."

Chief Terry sat up straighter. "And yet I spent more time with her for a number of years than you did."

I rubbed my eye in an effort to fight off the incessant twitching that was starting.

"I never asked you to be a stand-in for my daughter," Dad challenged.

"No one asked him," Mom replied. "He just did it. That's the kind of man he is."

"I'm done," Kenneth announced. "Tillie, I don't suppose you'd like to go for a walk with me?"

"No," Aunt Tillie said.

"I think that's a good idea," Landon said. "A few less people in this room can only make things better at this point."

"No one asked you," Aunt Tillie growled. "Just because I stood up for you, that doesn't mean I'm going to let you order me around."

"It was just a suggestion."

"I'll go for a walk with you," Blanche offered.

"No," Landon said. "You're going to eat your dinner and stay right there."

"Why can't she go for a walk?" Warren asked.

Clove leaned in and whispered something in his ear, realization washing over his face as the situation cleared in his mind. "Oh."

"What did she say?" Aunt Tillie asked.

"Nothing."

"Whatever she said is a lie," Aunt Tillie warned.

"I got it."

"You know what? I think Landon and I should go for a walk and get to know one another," Dad said. "That should fix everything."

Uh-oh.

"If you want to get to know me, then we'll do it in a few days," Landon said. "Right now, my family is here for a visit and I'm sticking close to Bay. There's not a lot of room on my plate for much else."

"So, you're scared? Is that what you're saying?"

Landon gripped his fork and glanced over at me. "I really should've listened to you."

"I'll have that engraved on your tombstone."

Things were tense, but that didn't stop both of us from bursting out laughing. There was really nothing else we could do.

TWENTY-NINE

"It's only two more days."

I rolled over in bed, fixing Landon with a sleepy look. We'd been awake about ten minutes, but neither of us had made a move to get up.

Dinner had gone from bad to worse the previous night, with Dad insisting on walking me back to the guesthouse to make sure I got there safely. He'd tried to wait Landon out – as though Landon was suddenly going to leave – but when Landon stripped out of his shirt and headed toward my bedroom that was enough to propel Dad into a pouty goodbye.

"Your family is only here for two more days," I corrected. "My family is here forever."

Landon smirked. "I still don't know what got into your dad last night."

I had an idea. "If it's any consolation, I don't think it was you."

"It sure seemed to be me."

"I think it was Chief Terry," I said. "He couldn't really attack Chief Terry, so he went after you."

"Why would he be upset about Terry? Because of your mom?"

I shrugged, relieved to find my muscles much less sore today. "Maybe."

"You think it's something else," Landon said, reaching over and massaging the back of my neck. "Do you think it's because Terry is so close with you?"

I groaned appreciatively as his fingers kneaded my back. "That feels really good."

"Roll over," he instructed, positioning himself on my waist so he could get better access to my back. "How do you feel today?"

"A lot better now," I murmured.

Landon chuckled. "Other than the world-class massage I'm about to give you, how do you feel?"

"Better," I admitted. "Still a little sore, but nothing like yesterday."

"That's good," Landon said. "Your face looks better, too."

"I'm not sure how to take that."

"I mean the bump on your head looks better," Landon corrected, immediately recognizing his mistake. "It's still a little bruised, but the swelling is almost gone."

"That's something, I guess."

Landon pressed his fingers into my back, going as deep as he could manage, eliciting another groan from me. "I guess I know how to bribe you from now on," he teased.

I didn't answer.

"So, you didn't say," Landon pressed. "Do you think your dad got so worked up because of Terry's relationship with you?"

"I don't know," I admitted. "Chief Terry went to school with my mom and dad. Maybe they didn't like each other."

"Terry never told you?"

"Chief Terry would never say anything about my dad," I said. "It's not his way."

"I guess not," Landon mused. "Your dad was all riled up, though. It was almost funny."

"Personally, I loved the look on his face when you started stripping."

"You should've seen the look on Thistle's face," Landon said. "I thought she was going to keel over she was laughing so hard."

"It was a surreal situation."

"It was."

Landon rubbed my back for another ten minutes, leaving me practically boneless when he finally rolled off of me. "What are your plans today?"

"I'm going to stop in at the paper," I said.

"I thought you were off this week?"

"I am," I said. "I just want to make sure everything is ready to go to press."

"We're not very good at taking vacations," Landon said.

"I think this situation has knocked us both off our game." I rolled over so I could look at him. "You look better, too."

"I always look good," Landon countered.

"You seemed a little … worried yesterday," I said. "Worried and tired."

"Your family makes me tired," Landon said. "My family doesn't help."

"We're both from long lines of crazy people," I agreed. "What are you going to do today?"

"I promised my mom I would spend the day with them," Landon said. "The week is almost up. She's doing that mother-guilt thing, so I don't have a lot of choice in the matter."

"Hmm."

"You could meet us for lunch in town," Landon suggested.

"I was thinking about stopping and seeing Mrs. Little again," I admitted.

"Why?"

"Because, I have more information now," I said.

"Like the baby?"

"And the memory."

Landon stilled. "She wasn't in the memory, though, was she?"

"No. But I didn't see what happened after Aunt Tillie showed up."

Landon rubbed his stubbled jaw thoughtfully. "I don't understand.

SOMETHING TO WITCH ABOUT

From what you told me, if Tillie did interrupt and she did kill Floyd to keep him off his wife, why would they hide that? She was doing a public service for the town."

"I don't think I'm seeing the whole picture yet."

"I don't understand why everyone is lying," Landon said.

"You and me both."

"Well, since we're going to be apart for the day, why don't we spend a little time together in the shower?" Landon said, lifting an eyebrow suggestively.

"Okay," I agreed. "You have to do all the work, though. I'm still sore."

"I can live with that."

AN HOUR LATER, we strolled into the living room more relaxed than we'd been in days. The feeling didn't last long.

"What are you doing here?"

Sam was sitting on the couch, flipping through a magazine. When he saw us enter the room he seemed surprised. "I didn't realize you were here."

"What are you doing here?" I repeated.

"Clove is getting ready," Sam said. "We're going to spend the morning together and then have lunch. She has to work the afternoon shift today."

So much for Clove adhering to the newly established rules of the guesthouse. "That sounds fun," I said, moving to the kitchen to grab a mug of coffee.

"Agent Michaels," Sam greeted Landon.

"Mr. Cornell."

I brought a mug to Landon, settling on the arm of the chair he sat in. "How are things going at the Dandridge?"

I didn't particularly want to talk to Sam, but I'd promised Clove I wouldn't be overtly mean to him.

"It's a work in progress," Sam said. "The structure is sound. It needs a lot of updates, though."

"How is living out there while the construction is going on?"

"It's not easy. I'm managing, though. Clove has been a godsend."

I may puke.

"How has Clove been helping?" Landon asked.

"She's been cooking meals and helping with some of the cleaning," Sam said. "She loves the building."

"She didn't love it when we went out there a few weeks ago," I said. "She's convinced Bigfoot lives out there."

"Yeah, I want to thank Thistle for telling her that, by the way," Sam said. "She still won't go outside alone after dark."

Landon's smirk was hard to miss. "Clove believes in Bigfoot?"

"Well, in a town full of witches, that's not much of a stretch, is it?" Sam asked.

Landon shifted in the chair, running his hand up my back as he fixed Sam with a hard stare. "I wouldn't know."

"You don't know about witches?" Sam pressed.

"I guess it depends on what way you're using the word," Landon said. "I've met a lot of witches in my life."

"I'm talking about the magical ones." Sam wasn't pulling his punches.

"I've met a lot of magical people, too," Landon said, his tone even. "Bay is a magical person and I tend to like her."

"You're full of charm this morning," I teased.

"Twenty hours of sleep in two nights will do that to me," he replied. "I haven't been this well rested in years."

"I'm glad to see you're doing better after your fall," Sam said. "You looked a little rough that first night."

"She's fine," Landon said.

Clove's bedroom door opened. Her eyes were wide when she saw us all sitting together in the living room. "I thought you'd left already."

"Obviously."

"He was just here for a few minutes while I got ready."

Sam eyed me curiously. "Is there a reason I'm not supposed to be here?"

It was time put all of our cards on the table. "I'm not sure what

Clove has told you, Sam, but we had a long talk yesterday about her ... relationship with you."

"That sounds ominous," Sam said.

"Just wait," Landon said.

"We want Clove to be happy," I continued. "If that's with you? Great. Until we're sure of your intentions, though – and by we, I mean Thistle and I – you're not welcome here."

Clove balked. "Don't be rude, Bay."

Sam pursed his lips. "And what if Clove doesn't agree?"

"Clove has already agreed," I said.

"And yet I'm here."

He was a little too smug for my liking. "That's why I'm making you aware of the rules."

"I guess that's fair," Sam said after a beat. "Trust has to be earned."

"And you're nowhere near that," I said.

I reached over and plucked Landon's mug out of his hand, taking it to the sink. After washing our mugs and putting them on the rack to dry, I returned to Landon. "Walk me out?"

"You got it."

Neither one of us bothered to glance back at Sam. I wondered, for a second, what was going through Clove's mind, but I pushed the thought out of my head. Everyone knew where they stood now.

THIRTY

I stopped in at Hypnotic before heading to Mrs. Little's shop so I could fill Thistle in on my morning.

"He was at the house?" Thistle looked incensed. "We just told her yesterday that we didn't want him at the house. Is she trying to make me kill her?"

"That's why I told him directly we didn't want him there."

"How did he take it?"

"He was ... smarmy."

"Smarmy?"

"He's odd to be around," I said. "I don't know how else to describe his attitude."

"What is the matter with her?"

I shrugged. Clove was acting weird – there was no denying it – but I had no way of knowing what was going through her mind. "I thought we got everything out on the table yesterday."

"I don't understand her."

"I think part of it is loneliness," I said. "Landon said something to me the other day about it. I was planning to confront her once his family was gone. We have so much else going on, though, I don't even know where to prioritize her stuff."

"People first," Thistle said.

"What?"

"We prioritize people first."

I waited.

"We have a poltergeist to deal with," Thistle said. "He's been dead fifty years. His issues can wait. A couple more days aren't going to hurt the situation."

"You weren't the one thrown from the horse."

"Point taken. Still, whatever is going on with Clove is ... messed up."

"I think we've been neglecting her," I admitted.

"She's an adult. You can't neglect an adult."

"Just listen to me a second," I said, holding up a hand to ward off Thistle's furious argument. "I've been busy with Landon. You have Marcus. Our moms are caught up in their own little world. Aunt Tillie is always a time suck. That's left Clove on her own for weeks."

"That doesn't explain Sam."

"Clove has always been the one in love with the idea of being in love," I reminded her. "You and I were always okay being on our own. Somehow, though, we've left her behind and forgotten about her."

"And we're not on our own now," Thistle mused, "which has inadvertently left her on her own."

"Yeah."

"So what do you think we should do?"

That was the question. "I think we should let her do what she wants to do," I said finally. "We can't protect her, and we can't bully her."

"Speak for yourself."

"If we try to bully her it's going to blow up in our faces," I said.

"That's never stopped us before."

"I know. Maybe we should try growing as people, though."

"Meaning?"

"If Clove is making a mistake, and I'm not sure she is, then she's got to make it on her own," I said. "She's got to live with her decisions."

"And what if Sam is dangerous?"

"Then we'll send Aunt Tillie after him," I replied. "He's been warned, and yet he's still sticking around. I would like to believe that means he has real feelings for Clove. If he doesn't, then Aunt Tillie can bury him next to Floyd."

Thistle smirked. "That sounds like fun."

MRS. LITTLE was standing behind the counter when I entered her store. If she was surprised to see me, she didn't let on.

"Twice in one week, Bay, this must be some sort of record."

"Maybe I just like pewter unicorns?"

"We just got a new shipment in," she replied. "They're on that shelf over there."

I moved to the shelf, perusing the new selection as I gathered my thoughts. "I wanted to ask you a few more questions."

"I told you everything I know."

"You didn't tell me about the baby." I glanced over my shoulder, finding Mrs. Little's small frame had gone still.

"How did you find out about that?"

Telling her about Edith wasn't an option. "I looked through some old newspaper articles," I lied. "I was looking for anything on Floyd. I found an expectant mother announcement for you instead."

"I forgot about that."

"You said you couldn't have children," I said.

"No, I said I had trouble conceiving," Mrs. Little corrected. "I never said I couldn't – or didn't."

"The baby was stillborn?"

She nodded.

"I'm sorry. That must have been terrible."

"The Lord gives us trials."

"Do you know who the father was?"

"Bob was the father," Mrs. Little said. "He was my husband. He was the father."

That sounded like wishful thinking. "You weren't sure, were you?"

Mrs. Little bit her lower lip. "No."

"Did Mr. Little know about Floyd?"

"Of course not." Mrs. Little looked scandalized.

"This is a small town," I argued. "Everyone knows everything. No matter how hard you try to keep a secret, everyone always finds out here."

"He didn't know."

I rolled my neck. "Did you know Floyd was beating his wife?"

"Like you said, it's a small town," Mrs. Little said. "There were some rumors that suggested that."

"And yet you had an affair with him anyway?"

"Floyd was never anything but gentle and loving with me."

My mind drifted to the Floyd from the memory. "That man hit and kicked his wife," I said. "When she was down on the floor, curled into a ball to protect herself, screaming for him to stop, he still kicked and hit her. I have trouble believing he was one way with you and another way with her."

"How can you know what he did to her?"

"Let's just say I have ... inside information."

"Speaking of town secrets," Mrs. Little shot back.

I ignored the jab. "If you knew Floyd was beating his wife, why would you be with him?"

"You don't always do the right thing in life, Bay," Mrs. Little said. "I know I haven't always done the right thing. I'm guessing you haven't always done the right thing either. If I could go back in time ... if I could change things ... I would. That's not possible, though."

"That's not really an answer."

"Maybe I don't have one for you?"

"The truth about what happened to Floyd is going to come out," I said. "If you know something ... ."

"I think you're the one who knows something, Bay," Mrs. Little said. "I think you're spending all your time trying to prove Tillie didn't do this when you know in your heart she did."

"I don't know that," I countered.

"Really? Well then, let me ask you this: If Tillie didn't do it, how did Floyd end up on your family's property?"

"That's what I'm trying to find out."

"No, that's what you're trying to cover up," Mrs. Little said. "You're so desperate to keep your aunt out of trouble you don't care who you're hurting in the process of protecting her. Now, if you don't mind, I have things to do."

"Mrs. Little ... ."

"I'm done, Bay," she said, her voice serious. "Don't come back here again. The past should stay in the past. Let it stay buried."

THIRTY-ONE

Was Mrs. Little right? Was I digging into this so hard because I knew Aunt Tillie was a murderer? She was in that house. She saw what Floyd was doing to his wife. She would've killed Floyd to stop him.

I was missing something.

It was time to go to the source. Again.

She wasn't at The Overlook when I got there. I found my mother and aunts in the kitchen gossiping.

"What are you doing here?" Mom asked.

"Looking for Aunt Tillie."

"I think she's down in her field," Mom replied. "I'm just glad she's not pouting around here."

"Why is she pouting?"

"Kenneth," Twila supplied. "She's mad about the whole Blanche thing."

"She says she doesn't like him."

"She's full of crap, pardon my French," Twila said.

"That's not French," I pointed out.

"You know what I mean."

"If she likes Kenneth, why doesn't she just tell him that?" I pressed.

"Because of Calvin," Mom said simply.

"Uncle Calvin has been dead for almost three decades," I said. "I think he'd be okay with it."

"He would," Mom agreed. "That doesn't mean she's okay with it."

The women in my family give me a headache sometimes.

Mom sighed. "Aunt Tillie married for life. Uncle Calvin was her life. She doesn't want a new one."

"It doesn't have to be a new one," I said. "It can be the same life, just with enhancements."

"That's what she's figuring out," Marnie said. "She's got to figure it out on her own, though. We can't make her figure it out."

Well, great.

"I'm going to go find her," I said.

"Why?" Mom glanced up from the dough she was kneading. "What's going on?"

"I need to talk to her about Floyd," I said. "Landon's family is gone for the afternoon. I won't get a better chance in the next few days."

"Why are you so caught up in this Floyd business?"

Was she serious? "Because his body was found on our property."

"He's been dead a long time," Marnie said.

"And yet his poltergeist is knocking me off horses," I grumbled.

"That is problematic," Mom agreed. "Hopefully, in time, he'll just dissipate."

"And if he doesn't?"

"Then we'll have to deal with him," Mom said. "We can't do anything until Landon's family leaves, though. Can you imagine what they would think if they caught us performing a ritual? They already think we're halfway crazy."

Halfway was being generous.

"I'm going to talk to her."

Mom wiped her hands on her towel. "You have to do what you have to do," she said. "Keep in mind, Aunt Tillie has to do what she has to do, too. Neither one of you is going to win here."

"It's not about winning. It's about knowing."

"In this instance, I think they're one and the same."

I FOUND Aunt Tillie sitting on a fallen log next to her field. She wasn't alone. Marcus was there, running the rototiller through the ground to make it easier for her to plant a crop in the next few weeks. He was so busy he hadn't noticed my arrival. I still wasn't sure how Aunt Tillie had coerced him into helping. I had a feeling threats were involved.

Aunt Tillie looked up when she caught sight of me. "What are you doing here?"

"Looking for you."

"Why? Do you need another potion?"

"No, I'm feeling much better. Thank you."

Aunt Tillie nodded, grunting in acknowledgement. "Why aren't you with Landon?"

"He's with his family in town," I replied.

"I'm surprised he let you off on your own today," Aunt Tillie said. "He's been your shadow for days now."

"He's been a little protective," I agreed, sitting down on the log next to her. "He's better today."

"You were smart to let him be," Aunt Tillie said. "When a man gets like that it's never wise to start a fight with them. It's better to just let them work those things out on their own."

"Did Uncle Calvin get like that?"

"From time to time." Aunt Tillie had a small smile on her face. "He learned pretty quickly that I couldn't take being smothered, though. He adjusted his attitude accordingly after that."

"Landon wasn't smothering me," I said. "He was just really … present."

"That's not a bad thing."

"No."

"I like him better now, in fact."

"You always liked him," I argued.

"He makes me laugh," Aunt Tillie admitted. "He reminds me of your Uncle Calvin in some ways – although he's a lot feistier. He can't be bullied as easily either, and in our family that's probably a good thing."

"No, he can't be bullied."

"He's a good match for you, no matter what your father thinks."

"I don't think Dad was really upset about Landon," I said. "I think he was really upset about Chief Terry being there."

"You're smarter than you look."

"I'll take that as a compliment."

"It was meant as one."

We lapsed into a comfortable silence, Aunt Tillie finally turning to give me a long look. "Why are you out here? Really?"

"I talked to Mrs. Little today," I said. "I wanted to ask her about the baby."

"That was a tragedy," Aunt Tillie said. "You shouldn't have brought it up."

"I needed answers."

"Did you find any?"

"No."

"Then it was a wasted effort," Aunt Tillie said.

"Mrs. Little says I'm so worried about proving you're not a murderer I don't care who else I accuse during the process."

Aunt Tillie scowled. "She always was an idiot."

"I'm worried she's right."

"She's not."

"You know, if you killed Floyd to save Mrs. Gunderson, that makes you a hero, not a murderer."

"And if I killed Floyd I would admit it and take credit for it," Aunt Tillie said. "The world is a better place without Floyd Gunderson in it."

I could believe that.

"If Mrs. Gunderson killed Floyd because of what he was doing to her, Chief Terry would understand," I offered.

"I know that."

"Does she know that?"

"You'll have to ask her."

This was like pulling teeth.

"Are you going to tell me what happened?"

"No."

"Why not?"

"Because the truth will come out when it's time," Aunt Tillie said.

"And it's not time now?"

"No."

"Then when?"

"When it's time."

She is so frustrating sometimes. I decided to try a different tactic. "What are you going to do about Kenneth?"

"What is that supposed to mean?"

"You obviously like him," I said.

"I do not."

I rolled my eyes. "He's a nice guy."

"He's an idiot."

"Maybe he should date Mrs. Little," I suggested.

"Don't try to be funny. It doesn't work for you."

"I'll keep that in mind."

Aunt Tillie got to her feet. "I should get back to work."

I watched her go. "I'll be here when you're ready to tell the truth."

Aunt Tillie didn't bother looking back. "When the truth comes, I won't be the one telling it to you."

What was that supposed to mean?

THIRTY-TWO

"Did you find her?" Mom and my aunts were still in the kitchen when I returned to the inn. "I found her."

"What is she doing?"

"Watching Marcus till her field," I said. "Does anyone know how she got Marcus involved in all of this?"

"I'm guessing the same way she gets anyone to do what she wants," Marnie said.

"Threats?"

"Pretty much."

"I'm surprised Thistle doesn't put up a fight about it," I said.

"I think that Thistle is just happy they get along," Mom said. "If Aunt Tillie didn't like Marcus, there would be a whole other batch of problems to deal with."

"You mean besides illegally growing pot?"

Mom shrugged. "It's not like she's hurting anyone. Watch the news. People like pot now."

I didn't think Landon would see it that way. I ambled over to the counter to see what they were working on now. "What's that?"

"We're making some homemade salsa," Mom said. "We plan on

having Mexican night once a week over the spring and summer. We're making all the salsa now, before we get really busy."

"That sounds like a good idea."

"All my ideas are good," Mom sniffed.

That's the problem with this family. Everyone thinks their ideas are the best. "Well, I guess I'm going to go back down to the guesthouse to get some work done."

"I thought you were off this week?"

"I am. With Landon and his family gone for the afternoon, though, it will give me a chance to get ahead for next week."

"I suppose that's smart," Mom said. "Before you go, though, there's someone waiting for you in the dining room."

Uh-oh. This sounded like a trick. "Who?"

Mom shrugged, avoiding my pointed gaze. "You'll have to see for yourself."

"Yeah, I'm not twelve anymore," I said. "That's not going to work. The last time you tried pulling this was right after I first moved back home and you tried to set me up with Connor Ridgeway."

"Connor was a perfectly nice boy," Mom said. "There was no need to smack him the way you did."

"He collects snakes."

"Everyone needs a hobby."

"He asked me if I wanted to see his trouser snake," I said, catching Marnie's small smile behind my mom's back.

"It's a weird hobby," Mom said. "You could've looked at his snake."

I bit my lip to keep from laughing. "Do you know what a trouser snake is?"

"No. I'm sure it wasn't poisonous, though."

"Yeah, I want you to think on that one after I've gone," I said. "If you still don't get it in an hour, Marnie can explain it to you. I'm leaving out the back, by the way."

"Oh no you're not," Mom said, dropping her knife on the counter and grabbing my shoulders. "You're going out into the dining room. Your guest has been waiting for you for thirty minutes."

"No."

"Yes."

"No." I started to struggle against Mom's hands. She's stronger than she looks. It took her two minutes, but with a little help from her sisters she finally managed to wrestle me into the dining room.

Connie was sitting at the table, sipping from an antique teacup, watching me with unreadable eyes as I stumbled through the door. Crap. This was worse than Connor Ridgeway and his trouser snake. "Mrs. Michaels, I didn't realize you were in here."

"Then why were you fighting so hard to stay in there?"

I didn't think explaining about the trouser snake was going to help this situation. "My mom has a bad track record when it comes to setting me up for surprise afternoon teas."

"I see." She took another sip, never moving her eyes from me. "Don't you want to sit down and join me?"

I'd rather help Marcus till an illegal garden. "Sure."

Once I was settled across from her, my own cup of tea steaming in front of me, I had no choice but to meet her gaze. "I thought you were off with Landon for the afternoon."

"I was," Connie said. "Then, I realized, the only thing I haven't done since coming to Hemlock Cove is spend any time with you."

"That's not true," I protested. "We've sat through more uncomfortable meals than I can even count."

Connie laughed. It was small, but it was still a laugh. "I guess that's true." Connie sipped again. "When Landon first told us he wanted us to come for a visit, I wasn't sure."

I remained silent. I'd been waiting for this since our first introduction. She was about to tell me why I was a bad match for Landon. I steeled myself for the inevitable.

"Landon hasn't shown real interest in anyone for quite a while," Connie continued. "I figured you had to be something special."

Ah, so this was disappointment – not outright dislike – fueling her mood. "I'm sorry I'm not what you wanted for Landon."

"I didn't say that," Connie cautioned. "You definitely weren't what I expected, though. My son has always had … peculiar tastes. Still, the women we've met – which haven't been many, mind you – have all been superficial lookers with absolutely no substance."

Huh. That definitely wasn't me.

"I think he did it on purpose," Connie said. "He wanted to bring home someone he thought I would like but who he couldn't possibly see a future with. I knew there was something different about you before I even met you."

"How so?"

"The first time he brought you up I didn't know what to think," Connie said. "I could tell there was something different about this situation right away."

"What did he say?"

"He said you were loud, immature and completely oblivious to the feelings of others." Her tone was matter-of-fact, but there was a twinkle in her eye.

"Really?" I wasn't sure how to respond.

"He said you didn't listen, you didn't do what you were told and you made him want to pull his hair out and beat his head against the wall," Connie said.

I could see that. "Well, I did get him shot."

Connie tilted her head. "I'm sorry I said that to you. I had no idea that he'd been hurt. I was ... thrown. Landon has explained things, and I'm thankful you were there to save him."

He explained things? It sounded like he'd gussied things up, not explained them. "I think everyone saved each other that night."

"Perhaps," Connie said, sipping her tea again. "The more I see of you, though, I think you're stronger than you look. You would have to be, of course, growing up in this family. They would expect nothing less."

"The Winchesters definitely have big personalities."

"They do indeed," Connie said. "They're also loyal and ... odd."

I don't think any family that claims Aunt Blanche should be using the word "odd" in anything other than an ironic way. "Aunt Tillie prefers the term eccentric."

"Your family is what it is," Connie said. "They're warm and funny ... and hiding something."

Uh-oh. I sipped my tea to give myself a second to form a response. "We don't really hide things," I said. "We put everything out there and then handle the fallout." That was mostly true.

"So, you're saying nothing else has been going on this week?"

"Well, the bones being discovered on the property did screw everything up," I admitted. "I really wish we could've put that off for the week. That wasn't the first impression I was hoping to make."

Connie pursed her lips, considering. "Were you worried about making a good first impression?"

"Of course," I said. "Landon's family is important to him. He's important to me. I wanted you to like me."

"You're very important to Landon," Connie said. "I think ... I think I didn't want to like you because you were so important to him."

"I'm not sure I understand."

"No one wants to admit their child is an adult who can make his own decisions," Connie said. "Even when your child works for the FBI and is in danger constantly, you still like to believe that he finds comfort with his mother. I wanted to think I was still the most important woman in his life."

"I can see that," I hedged.

"He doesn't find comfort with his family now, though," Connie said. "He finds it with you and your family and, more importantly, he wants to give you comfort."

"I don't think he wants to comfort Aunt Tillie," I said, going for levity.

"And yet, when you were missing, he was the one sitting with Aunt Tillie while she threw an absolute fit," Connie replied. "He took her out back and talked to her. I couldn't hear what they said but whatever your Aunt Tillie had planned had her so worked up that she could barely speak. He sat out there with her for twenty minutes, even though I'm sure he wanted to be out looking for you. If that's not comfort, I don't know what is."

Huh. No one had told me about that little interlude. "He's a good man."

"He is," Connie agreed. "He seems to have found a good match in you."

I definitely wasn't expecting that. "Forgive me for saying this, but I can't help but think you don't like me."

"I don't dislike you," Connie said. "You worry me – or at least you did at first."

"How so?"

"If you look at things from my point of view, the first thing I saw was a woman hiding in the kitchen because she didn't want to meet her boyfriend's family," Connie said.

"I wasn't hiding."

"You were hiding. I don't really blame you. Then, minutes later, there was a body found on the property and Landon wanted you to go out there with him," Connie said. "That seemed odd to me."

"I'm generally the most rational under pressure," I said. It's true -- kind of.

"Then something obviously happened out there, because you two disappeared for a while, and when you came back you were white as a sheet and Landon was hovering around you like a worried mother hen."

"We fell in the hole." It was a lame response, but it's not as though I could tell her the truth.

"Then I noticed you and Thistle were constantly hiding in corners and whispering about something," Connie continued. "You were trying to talk to Aunt Tillie about something and she was putting you off. Landon has been hiding something, too."

"I just think he was upset about the bones."

Connie brushed off my explanation. "At first, I thought Landon was trying to hide something from us, something he didn't want us to know about. Then I realized he wasn't hiding anything. He was protecting you … well, your family to be more precise."

This conversation was veering into the uncomfortable far too quickly. "I think he just didn't want you to think badly of Aunt Tillie."

"Maybe," Connie said. "I think he's trying to help you figure something out, though. Whether it's that your aunt is a murderer – which I don't believe, for the record – or that there's some big secret here, I'm not sure."

"If you want to know the truth, I don't know what to say about Aunt Tillie right now," I said. "It's a mess. I don't know when it will get sorted out. I'm only sorry you've had to bear witness to our … family stuff."

"I'm not," Connie said. "It's given me a chance to see how your family operates. Sure, it's been from afar, but I've still gotten a glimpse of all of you as a whole."

"Let me guess; you want to kidnap Landon and get him far away from us?" It was a joke, but I had a feeling it was also the truth.

"All parents want their children to be happy," Connie said. "While I wasn't sure about you at first, I am now. You make him happy. You make him want to hit something a lot of the time, but that's where true happiness comes from. You challenge him. And that, my dear, is why I like you."

All of the air whooshed out of my lungs. "You like me?"

"You have ghosts," Connie said. "Everyone does. Your family certainly does. At least you confront your ghosts together. There's nothing to dislike about that."

My cheeks were burning under her praise. "Thank you."

"You just need to lighten up," Connie said, reaching across the table to pat me on the hand. "Sometimes life is hard, and sometimes it is funny. You need to roll with the punches and not take life so seriously. You'll learn, though. I have faith in you."

Okay, this was definitely a better interlude than Connor Ridgeway and his trouser snake.

THIRTY-THREE

"I think we should conduct a séance."

I was back at the guesthouse and my conversation with Connie – all her talk of confronting ghosts together – had given me an idea.

Thistle glanced up from the couch. "Yeah, because that always works out well for us."

"I thought you didn't want to do a séance until Landon's family left," Clove said. "What if they see?"

"We can do it out in the clearing after midnight tonight," I said. "They've been going to bed early. It's not like they're going to be wandering around the property in the middle of the night. Who does that?"

"We always do that," Clove complained. "And I always hate it when we do it."

"You hated the property by the Dandridge because you thought it was filled with sasquatches, too," Thistle pointed out. "You seemed to have gotten over that."

Clove flipped her off – a gesture Thistle had no problem reciprocating.

"We're stuck," I said, ignoring their silent finger conversation. "We need answers."

"I thought you were going to talk to Aunt Tillie," Thistle said. "Why don't we do that first?"

"I did talk to her," I replied. "She said that when the truth comes out, she won't be the one telling it."

"And you took that as an invitation to sit in the dark and talk to an angry poltergeist?" Thistle asked. "And people say our family is crazy. I just don't get it."

"Are you going to go with me or not?"

"Of course I'm going with you," Thistle said. "I'm bored. It sounds like fun."

"I want it known that I said this was a bad idea first," Clove said, "just for the record."

"That's always on the record," Thistle scoffed.

"**I THINK** we should wait until tomorrow," Clove said.

We were in the clearing, setting up candles. It was almost midnight and Landon was still at the inn with his brothers in the game room. I'd left him a note, but I hadn't told him what we had planned. I was hoping we would be able to beat him back to the guesthouse. He hated it when we did stuff like this.

"We're already down here now," I said.

"Yes, but it seems like a much worse idea when we're stuck in the dark," Clove said. "Why can't we ever do these things in the middle of the day?"

"Because that would break every horror movie trope," Thistle replied, blandly. "And we don't like to stray from the mainstream. We're followers."

I glared at Thistle. "You're really sarcastic today."

Thistle shrugged. "I have to get my kicks where I can," she said. "It's been a stifling week, what with having to behave myself because Landon's family is in town."

"You behaved yourself?" I raised an eyebrow in challenge.

"I could've been worse."

Unfortunately, I knew she was telling the truth. "Let's just get this over with."

"Let's not even start it," Clove interjected.

I ignored her. "Light the candles. The sooner we start, the sooner we'll be done."

Clove and Thistle did as instructed, and each of us joined hands to form a triangle. We closed our eyes and began to chant, our voices starting in unison and then overlapping as everyone's tonal pace shifted.

"We call to thee."

"Let us see."

"Join us now."

"So mote it be."

We said the words over and over until it was impossible to ascertain where one chant began and another ended. The candle flames shot higher in the sky as the spell grew, casting an eerie pall on the clearing.

All at once – and in unison – we straightened and lifted our heads to the sky, never letting go of one another.

Floyd was here.

Clove gasped when she caught sight of the misty form. "He doesn't look like a ghost."

"That's because he's a poltergeist," Thistle said.

"He doesn't look like a poltergeist either."

"When have you ever seen a poltergeist? Other than the movie, I mean."

"You don't have to be mean."

We separated hands and stepped back, forming a line, shoulders touching. "Floyd."

He watched us, his features nothing more than a blur of white with the occasional glimpse of red where his eyes should be.

"We want to know what happened to you, Floyd," I tried again. "We want to understand."

Floyd pointed at me.

"Maybe he can't talk," Thistle suggested.

"Then how is he supposed to answer our questions?" Clove asked.

Thistle shrugged. "Mime?"

"That's not funny."

"It's kind of funny."

The poltergeist moved toward me. Crap. Not again. He was on me before I could even contemplate moving. The last thing I heard was Clove scream, and then everything went black. Again.

This time Floyd showed me everything.

"**GET OFF** OF HER, ASSHOLE!"

Things came into focus – although the real world was just as much of a jumble as the memory Floyd had just yanked me into. When had Aunt Tillie gotten here?

I struggled to a sitting position, Thistle and Clove flanking me to lend their support.

"Are you all right?" Clove asked.

"I feel a little sick to my stomach."

"Well, join the club," Thistle said. "We thought you were dead."

"We couldn't get him off you," Clove explained. "We tried every spell we could think off."

"Clove was going to try to beat him off with a stick," Thistle said. "Once I explained that he wasn't corporeal and she would actually be hitting you with a stick she let that one go."

"I'm not good under pressure," Clove complained.

"I noticed."

I pushed their argument out of my mind. I was focused on Aunt Tillie, who, for her part, didn't seem rattled in the slightest. She stood two feet in front of us, facing off with Floyd.

"You always were the sort of deadbeat who attacked women, Floyd," Aunt Tillie said. "I guess death hasn't mellowed you any."

Floyd zipped back and forth angrily, but he didn't cross the invisible line Aunt Tillie had drawn in the dirt.

"Move on, Floyd," Aunt Tillie commanded. "There's nothing here for you. This whole world would've been better if you'd never been born."

Floyd still wasn't talking, but he was now emitting a high-pitched keening. It wasn't words, but the emotion behind the sound was clear: He was pissed.

"What the hell is going on here?" Landon barreled into the clearing, his face a mask of concern and anger. He glanced down at the three of us on the ground and then back at Aunt Tillie. "Seriously. What have you guys done now?"

"Holy crap!" I realized he wasn't alone. Daryl and Denny were close on his heels – and they were fascinated with the tableau playing out in front of them.

"What are you doing down here?"

Landon walked over to me, reached under my arms and hoisted me up. "We heard someone scream. I tried to get them to stay behind but they wouldn't. I didn't have time to argue."

"That was Clove," Thistle said. "She always screams. She's such a baby."

"What is that?" Daryl asked.

"It's a bastion of hell," Denny said.

"It's Floyd," I said, rubbing the dirt off of my elbow.

"Dead Floyd?" Daryl asked.

"He's a poltergeist," Thistle said.

"A ghost?"

"A pissed-off ghost," Thistle replied. "Ghosts are generally easy to get along with. Floyd here, well, Floyd is just a dick."

"How do you know so much about this?" Denny asked.

"We watch a lot of movies," Thistle lied.

Landon shook his head and turned back to me. "What were you guys doing?"

"We were just taking a walk," I said, avoiding his gaze.

"With candles?"

"We like ambiance when we make out in the woods," Thistle deadpanned. "Oh, what? Don't give me that look. You know exactly what we were doing. Why even ask the question?"

"You and I are going to have a talk later," Landon warned.

"I can't wait."

Landon glanced back at Aunt Tillie. "Does she have that thing under control?"

I shrugged. I had no idea.

"Floyd isn't a danger right now," Aunt Tillie said. "I think he got what he wanted when he attacked Bay."

Landon's eyebrows nearly shot off his forehead. "You got attacked? Again? Are you trying to kill me?"

"Oh, it's all about you," Thistle muttered.

If Landon's face was any indication, visions of strangling Thistle ran wild through his head.

"What did he show you?" Clove asked.

"He showed me the truth," I replied grimly.

"Which was?"

"We have to get rid of Floyd first," I said, taking a step toward Aunt Tillie. "Can you banish him or something?"

"Not with the supplies we have here," Aunt Tillie said. "This is what happens when you dabble with magic instead of doing it right. Why are you three always dabblers?"

"Why didn't you help us from the beginning?" I shot back. "If you had told us the truth when we asked for it then none of this would've been necessary."

"The only thing I can do is temporarily transport him out of here," Aunt Tillie said, ignoring my reprimand.

"Well, do it."

Aunt Tillie muttered something under her breath and then clapped her hands. Floyd winked out of existence almost immediately.

I turned to find Daryl and Denny standing behind us, mouths agape.

"Wow," Daryl said. "That was awesome."

Denny looked a little more shaken. "I think everyone here has some explaining to do."

Uh-oh.

THIRTY-FOUR

"What did your brothers say?"

It was the next morning and Landon had woken up in a bad mood. I couldn't really blame him. Still, I thought he was being overdramatic.

He was sitting at the edge of the bed, looking everywhere but at me. "Do you mean before or after I had to explain what you were doing in the woods in the middle of the night?"

I waited. He was going to unload. All the signs were there.

"I told them the truth."

My heart skipped a beat. "You told them we were witches?"

Landon shifted his body, finally meeting my gaze. "What did you expect me to tell them?"

"I don't know," I admitted. "What did they say?"

"Daryl thought it was cool," Landon said.

"And Denny?"

"He thinks you're evil."

I ran a hand through my tangled morning hair and sighed. "And just when your mother was starting to like me."

"What?"

"Your mother had tea with me yesterday. She said she didn't dislike me. That's not the same as liking me, I know. It's better than hating me, though. This is going to change that."

Landon let out a long-suffering sigh. "I asked them to keep what they saw to themselves."

I met his eyes, not liking the angry set of his jaw. "Do you think they will?"

"For me? Probably."

I rubbed the back of my neck, shifting to test my muscles. Thankfully, it didn't seem another hard tumble left me with too many more aches and bruises. This really hadn't been my week. "Well, that's something at least."

"Do you think I'm angry with you because my brothers found out what you are? Do you think I even care about that?"

"I would understand if you were," I admitted. "Your brother is a minister."

Landon stood up. "I don't care that you're a witch. That doesn't bother me at all. I'm used to it. I even find it amusing sometimes. I've found it helpful sometimes, too. I don't care if my brothers know. I wanted to tell them from the beginning, but it wasn't my secret to tell."

I watched Landon pace in front of the bed worriedly.

"I am not angry with you because the secret is out," Landon continued. "I am angry with you because you snuck out with your cousins in the middle of the night. Again. I am angry because you didn't tell me what you were doing. Again. I am angry because you put yourself in danger. Again."

"We didn't think it was dangerous," I said. "We just wanted answers."

"So, why didn't you tell me?"

"You were at the inn with your brothers."

"And you thought that meant I didn't want to know?"

"I don't know."

Landon extended his index finger at me. "Don't do that. You knew I would want to know. You just hoped you would be done and back to the guesthouse before I found out. Again."

He had a point. This was all starting to feel very familiar.

Landon ran his hand through his hair, his frustration evident. "You promised to tell me the truth."

"It wasn't a lie," I protested.

"I can't keep you safe if you don't tell me the truth," Landon argued.

"Did you ever consider that I was trying to keep you safe?"

Landon stilled. "What?"

"Maybe I didn't want you there so you wouldn't get hurt," I said.

"I'm sorry. You didn't invite me to the séance because you didn't want me to get hurt? How does that work?"

"Floyd has gone after me three times now," I said. "If you were there and he tried it again you would try to get in the way, and I couldn't stand it if you got hurt because of me. You've already been hurt because of me. I won't let it happen again."

"Stop that! I wasn't hurt because of you. I was hurt because of my job. I am not going to keep having this argument with you." Landon strode toward the bedroom door, pausing with his hand on the knob. "You need to decide whether we're in this together. If we are, then we're in it together all the way – not just when you and your cousins can't handle the situation. Make a decision."

I WAS GRUMPY. And guilty. That didn't make for a pleasant afternoon.

Landon hadn't spoken to me since this morning – not even a "pass me the milk" at breakfast. He'd left with his father and brothers so they could go off-roading with Marcus not long after.

Connie and Blanche stayed at the inn, and my mother assured me they would be well taken care of – and entertained – while I handled the Floyd situation.

I hadn't gotten a chance to tell Landon what I saw in the memory, but it really didn't matter. Punishing someone for this crime was out of his hands.

Confronting Mrs. Little was another story.

She was sitting in her rocking chair, staring off into space, when I entered the store. She glanced up when she heard the bell, frowning when she saw me. "I thought I told you not to come back."

"I don't really care what you want," I said, settling in the open chair next to her. "I care about the truth."

"And what truth are you interested in today? Because you're certainly not interested in the actual truth," she countered.

"You'd be surprised."

"What is that supposed to mean?"

"I saw Floyd last night," I announced, not caring at all how ridiculous I sounded.

"Floyd is dead."

"Part of him is dead," I corrected. "Part of him, that angry little bit of him he called a soul, well that's still running around Hemlock Cove."

Mrs. Little straightened. "What do you mean?"

"When his body was discovered his soul escaped," I said.

"His soul? You mean his ghost?"

"He's not a ghost," I said. "He's a poltergeist. A really angry poltergeist."

"I don't believe in stuff like that," Mrs. Little replied.

"I don't care if you believe it or not," I said. "Floyd has been … showing me things."

"What things?"

"The past. His memories. What really happened to him."

"I see. And what has he shown you?"

"He showed me what Mrs. Gunderson had to put up with," I said. "How he beat her and terrorized her. He showed me Aunt Tillie interrupting one of those beatings."

"So, he showed you Tillie killing him?"

"No. That wasn't the whole memory. He showed me that last night."

Mrs. Little waited, watching me carefully.

"You see, Aunt Tillie did interrupt him. She beat him with a rolling pin. She beat the crap out of him. She called him every name in the book – and then she kicked him a few times for good measure. She probably would've killed him," I said. "Uncle Calvin showed up and stopped her, though. He carried Mrs. Gunderson out of that house and made Aunt Tillie leave with them. Floyd was still alive when they left."

"He probably succumbed to his injuries afterward," Mrs. Little said. "They left him there to die alone."

I shook my head. "No. They only thought that's what happened."

"I think you're mistaken," Mrs. Little said, pressing her lips together so tightly they'd gone white.

"Someone came to the house after they left," I said.

"It wasn't me!"

"I didn't say it was you," I replied. "It was Mr. Little."

"No … ." Mrs. Little faltered. "I told you, Bob didn't know."

"Bob knew. He found Floyd unconscious on the floor."

"That doesn't mean he did anything," Mrs. Little argued.

I remained quiet.

Mrs. Little whimpered. "What did he do?"

I kept my tone even. "He knelt down and checked his pulse. Then he got back up, picked up the phone, and then he put it back down. I thought he was going to call the police or an ambulance, but he didn't. Instead, he picked up a towel from the counter and knelt back down."

"No. Don't."

"He pressed that towel to Floyd's face, covering his nose and mouth, and then he just waited. Floyd's legs kicked a couple of times, but he never regained consciousness. Then, when it was over, Mr. Little got up and left."

"Did he say anything?"

Part of me wanted to ask why Mrs. Little wasn't questioning the validity of my story. The other part of me, though – the bigger part of me – knew. "He said that you were his wife and it was going to stay that way."

"Oh, Bob."

"You knew all of this, though, didn't you?"

Mrs. Little refused to meet my gaze.

"Because Mr. Little told you before he died," I continued. "I'm not sure when he told you, but he told you."

"Does it matter now? Floyd is gone. Bob is gone. Let it be. Don't you dare tarnish my husband's good name."

"You were willing to tarnish Aunt Tillie's name," I pointed out.

"Tillie has done some terrible things over the years," Mrs. Little countered. "Floyd could've died on that floor and she wouldn't have cared. She left him there to die!"

"He deserved to die! Do you have any idea what he was doing to his wife?"

"Maybe she deserved it," Mrs. Little replied. "Maybe she asked for it. Maybe she made it so he had no choice but to do it to her."

I felt inexplicably sad for her. "No one asks for that," I said, getting to my feet.

"Where are you going?"

"To talk to Chief Terry."

"And you think he's going to believe your little vision?"

I knew he would. "It doesn't matter. I'm still telling him the truth."

Mrs. Little jumped to her feet. "Your family is terrible. You are terrible. If you do this, I'll never forgive you."

"Mrs. Little, I don't want you to forgive me. Knowing what you know, you were willing to pin all of the blame on Aunt Tillie. That makes you a coward. You also knew what Floyd was doing to his wife. Instead of admitting what you did was wrong and trying to help her you blamed her. That makes you the worst kind of woman."

"Oh, really? What kind of woman is that?"

"The kind who makes excuses for wife beaters and abusers," I said. I opened the door, pausing before walking through it. "It's probably good you weren't a mother," I said. "Passing on morals like yours would've made for one really messed-up kid."

I could hear Mrs. Little sobbing as I left, but I didn't turn around. I was done with her. She was worse than her husband in my book.

THIRTY-FIVE

When I got back to the inn, I found Landon sitting on the front porch swing. He glanced at me as I approached, but his mood was hard to gauge.

I sat down on the swing, making sure not to touch him, and then joined in with his gentle swinging rhythm.

"Where were you?"

"I went to see Mrs. Little to tell her what I saw last night," I said. "Then I went and told Chief Terry."

"We never got around to that," Landon said. "What did you see?"

I told him, laying the whole thing out. When I was done, I waited for his reaction.

"Well, I guess we know why Aunt Tillie buried the body," he said. "She thought she had killed him."

"I still don't understand why she didn't call the police," I said. "She was protecting Mrs. Gunderson. The cops would've understood."

"If you can explain the inner workings of Aunt Tillie's mind to me that would be some sort of miracle."

I risked a glance at Landon, but his attention was focused on the landscaping. "I thought about what you said this morning."

"I should hope so."

"You're right."

Landon let out a shaky sigh.

"You're wrong, too."

"How am I wrong?"

"I didn't tell you about the séance for two reasons," I explained. "The first was because I didn't want you to be hurt. I didn't want me to get hurt either," I added hurriedly. "I didn't expect anything bad to happen."

"You had an idea it could, though," Landon said. "That's why I'm angry."

"Fine. You have a right to be angry. You've earned it. You've put up with a lot of crap. Most people would've run when faced with all this crap."

"I did run at first," Landon reminded me. "I did walk away."

"You came back, though. You needed time to think. I get that. We're ... difficult." Heck, we idled at difficult. "When you came back, though, you weren't constantly throwing stuff in my face. I appreciate how hard that was for you. I appreciate what a ... sacrifice dating me has been for you."

"What sacrifice?" Landon finally looked at me.

"We're crazy," I said. "We're hard to deal with. Our lives defy definition or order. You don't have to put up with that – and yet you do."

"It's not a sacrifice," Landon growled.

"I know that's not true."

"It's not a sacrifice," Landon said, reaching for my hand and then pulling away before touching me. The gesture hurt more than it should. "You said there were two reasons you didn't tell me. What's the second?"

"I'm afraid," I admitted. "I'm afraid that one too many séance, or one too many ghost, or one too many of Aunt Tillie's curses is going to push you over the edge."

"And what do you think is over the edge?"

I shrugged. "An easier life. A life away from us."

"So you think that, at some point, I'm going to walk away again," Landon said. "I guess I deserve that."

"That's not what I meant," I protested.

"I know, but that's where your fear comes from," Landon said. "Bay, I can't tell you what the future holds. This is all still new – and different. I can tell you, though, that it's not magic and your crazy family that's going to drive me away. It's you not telling me the truth. It's you pushing me away and internalizing everything, which seems to be your default mode when faced with a tough situation."

Tears pricked at my eyes. "Okay."

"Okay what?"

"Okay. I'll tell you the truth – even when I think it's going to drive you bonkers."

Landon laughed, reaching his arm over so he could drape it across my shoulders and pull me closer. He dropped a kiss on my forehead. "That's all I ask."

"Well, since we're telling the truth, I should tell you I have raging PMS and I'm starving."

Landon cringed. "That's an overshare."

"You wanted the truth."

"I guess I did."

"I'm actually feeling bloated."

"Don't push it."

"I also have to talk to Aunt Tillie," I said. "I need to tell her what I saw."

Landon rubbed his thumb over my shoulder. "Well, she's inside with Kenneth – and Aunt Blanche. She's probably ready for some good news."

"What is Kenneth doing here? I thought she was done with him?"

Landon smiled. "It's not so easy to forget a Winchester woman."

He's too cute for his own good.

I FOUND Aunt Tillie in the kitchen, leaving Landon to join his family around the dinner table. I wanted to get this over with.

"We didn't get a chance to talk last night."

"No," Aunt Tillie agreed. "The antics of Daryl and Denny threw us all off our game."

"I saw what happened."

Aunt Tillie sighed. "You saw what I did to Floyd?"

"I saw you beat the crap out of him with a rolling pin," I said. "I saw Uncle Calvin come in and stop you. I saw the two of you leave with Mrs. Gunderson."

"Then you know I lied, that I'm the one who killed Floyd," Aunt Tillie said. "The question is, what are you going to do with that information?"

"I've already been to Chief Terry," I said.

Aunt Tillie stiffened. "What did he say?"

"He said Floyd deserved your beating."

"Well, I guess that's something. Is he going to arrest me?"

"No."

"Are you sure?"

"That's not all there is to the story," I offered softly.

"What?"

"There was more to the memory," I said. "I saw more after the three of you left."

"You saw us come back for the body?"

"No, but I do have a question about that," I said. "How did you manage to bury him alone?"

"I didn't bury him," Aunt Tillie said. "Calvin did. He went back and found the body and then he took care of Floyd. He only told me after the fact."

Realization washed over me. "That's why you didn't know where Floyd was buried," I said. "You wouldn't have let construction on the greenhouse progress if you knew. I never could reconcile that fact. You're too smart for that."

"He never told me," Aunt Tillie said. "I assumed he buried him in the woods. I have no idea why he buried him on the property – and it's too late to ask."

"That probably wasn't the smartest move," I said.

"Your uncle wasn't a criminal mastermind," Aunt Tillie said. "I kind of liked that about him."

"What would you have done?"

"I would have burned the body in a fire pit," Aunt Tillie said. "Then I would've scattered the bones out at the Hollow Creek."

"You've given this some thought, I see."

"Floyd isn't the first body I've thought about disposing of," Aunt Tillie admitted.

I decided to let that one slide. "Anyway, about the rest of the memory … ."

"Do I want to know?"

"I think you need to know."

"All right. Tell me."

"Someone else came in the house after you left," I said.

"Who?"

"Bob Little."

Aunt Tillie shifted her jaw back and forth as she absorbed the news. "What did he do?"

"He smothered Floyd and then left him on the floor."

"So, I didn't kill him."

"No. You should also know that Mrs. Little knew."

"She knew?" Aunt Tillie was incensed.

"I don't know when she found out," I said. "I saw her this afternoon."

"And she admitted she knew? All this time and she knew?"

"She didn't actually admit it," I countered. "She didn't deny it, though. She asked me not to go to Chief Terry."

"But you did."

"I did."

"Good for you."

"There's nothing he can do about it anyway," I said. "Mr. Little is gone. Chief Terry says they can't prove murder. It's going to go in the books as an unexplained death."

"Floyd doesn't deserve anything more," Aunt Tillie said.

"He was still murdered."

"Justifiable homicide."

"I find it interesting that Uncle Calvin was willing to cover up what he thought was a murder you committed," I said.

"The man was always a fool for love."

"It seems to me you must have done something to earn that love."

"I did," Aunt Tillie said. "I picked a good man."

I smiled. "I guess you did."

"You have, too," Aunt Tillie said. "He's a little bossy for my taste, but he's still a good man."

"He is."

"How did you leave things?"

"With Landon? We made up."

"Not with Landon."

I furrowed my brow and then realized who she was talking about. "Mrs. Little said we're terrible people and she would never forgive me."

"Does that upset you?"

"No."

"Why not?"

"Because she said that Mrs. Gunderson probably deserved her beating and drove Floyd to it," I replied. "I don't think I want to be friends with a woman who could believe something like that."

"She's damaged," Aunt Tillie agreed. "She's always been damaged."

"She's lost," I corrected. "I have a certain amount of … pity for her."

"Don't waste your pity on people who don't deserve it, Bay. Lavish it on those who do."

Aunt Tillie shuffled toward the dining room door.

"I have one more question," I said.

Aunt Tillie stilled. "I guess you've earned it."

"Why aren't you friends with Mrs. Gunderson anymore? You would think, after all you've been through together, you would be close."

"There are different kinds of friends in this world," Aunt Tillie said. "After Floyd died, Ginny just wanted to pretend none of it ever happened. That meant distancing herself from me."

"That didn't upset you?"

"I understood it."

"Still."

"That doesn't mean we're not friends, Bay. It just means we're friends from afar."

That didn't make a lot of sense to me, but I let it go. "Let's get something to eat. I'm starving."

"Landon's family leaves tomorrow," Aunt Tillie said. "I guess everything is back to normal after that."

Not everything. "What about Floyd?"

"Once the Michaels family leaves, we'll take care of Floyd." Her tone was ominous – but Floyd had earned nothing less than Aunt Tillie's wrath. May the Goddess have mercy on his horrible soul.

THIRTY-SIX

"Is everything okay?"

Landon's plate was heaped with food, and he'd already started in on it, but he turned his attention to me as I settled into my chair. I glanced at Aunt Tillie. "Everything is fine."

"I can't believe this is our last meal here," Earl said, smiling happily. "I think I've gained ten pounds this week. Seriously, I've never had better food."

"I think it's a little bland," Blanche interjected from the end of the table.

Out of the corner of my eye I saw Thistle grip her fork weapon-like as she eyed Blanche with overt dislike.

"What are you talking about?" Kenneth said. Mom had wisely seated him far from Blanche, instead placing him next to Aunt Tillie. She always was a meddler. "This is the best pot roast ever made."

"I agree," Chief Terry said. "Pot roast is my favorite."

"You know what my favorite is?" Blanche asked.

"No one cares," Connie said. "Eat your dinner."

A glance at the end of the table told me that Daryl was enjoying his meal, but Denny seemed lost in thought. I nudged Landon's knee with mine. "Is he okay?"

"He's having a crisis of faith," Landon said. "He'll be fine."

That didn't sound good. "Maybe I should talk to him."

"He's afraid of you right now."

"He's afraid of me?"

"Well, it's more like he's afraid of Aunt Tillie," Landon said, his voice low. "She banished a ghost with nothing more than two words and a clap of her hands. That's pretty shocking when you're not used to seeing it."

"She didn't banish him," I replied. "She just kind of kicked him in the balls."

Landon barked out a laugh, causing a few heads at the table to shift in our direction. Landon ignored them. "You have a way with words," he whispered.

At least he wasn't still angry.

"I hear the mystery of the bones was solved today," Connie said, focusing on Chief Terry. "That's got to be a relief."

"I don't know if it's been solved," Chief Terry replied, shooting a look in my direction. "More like it's been put to rest."

"What does that mean?" Denny asked, shifting in his chair.

"It means that the coroner can't find a cause of death," Chief Terry replied. "Without a cause of death, we can't prove a murder."

"So the guilty party just gets away with it?"

"We don't know that there was a guilty party," Chief Terry said. "We know that Floyd Gunderson was a real SOB and we know there was any number of people in this town who wouldn't mind seeing him dead.

"We also know that Floyd was a drunk who very well could've drank himself to death," Chief Terry continued. "If he was murdered, for all we know, the killer could already be dead."

"So, that's it?" Connie asked.

"That's it."

"What happens now?" Earl asked.

"Now we release Floyd's remains to Mrs. Gunderson," Chief Terry replied. "She'll probably have some sort of service for him."

"And that's it," Denny mused. "It seems somehow ... anticlimactic."

"It does," Chief Terry agreed. "Sometimes that's just how it goes, though."

I took a bite of pot roast, my stomach urging me to eat faster with a few small rumbles. Landon raised an eyebrow. "Hungry?"

"I haven't eaten today," I admitted.

"I know you didn't eat breakfast, but why didn't you eat lunch?"

"I had a lot on my mind."

Landon patted my knee under the table. "Well, eat up kid. You have PMS, which means I'm going to have get my money's worth tonight."

I looked up in time to see a piece of meat fall out of Connie's mouth. I don't think Landon meant to say that last little bit so loud.

"Landon!"

Landon blushed. "Sorry."

"I know how that goes, son," Earl said, smiling widely.

Chief Terry glowered at Landon. "Don't ever say anything like that again."

"Trust me. I wish I hadn't said it this time."

"I'm not joking," Chief Terry said. "I'll beat you to within an inch of your life."

"I have PMS, too," Clove announced. "I think that's why I'm so hungry."

Thistle kicked her under the table. "Don't tell people that."

"You have it, too," Clove said. "We're all synced up together. It's a girl thing. It's nothing to hide."

Aunt Tillie shook her head. "In my day we didn't talk about things like that."

"I agree," Blanche said.

"I think we should all change the subject," Mom suggested. "What time are you guys heading out tomorrow?"

"We thought we would all have breakfast together, if that's okay with everyone," Connie replied.

"That sounds good," Mom replied. "Any special requests for breakfast?"

Clove's hand shot up in the air. "Can you make chocolate waffles?"

"PMS, party of three, we're making reservations for breakfast," Thistle cackled.

"Stop it," I ordered. Although, to be fair, chocolate waffles sounded divine. "I'm voting for the waffles, too, though."

Landon's shoulders were shaking with silent laughter.

Mom fixed him with a hard stare. "Do you want to request anything, Landon?"

"The waffles are good," he said.

"You've had them?" Connie asked.

"I eat breakfast up here a lot," Landon said, refusing to break his gaze from hers. "I think I've had just about everything up here."

"Well, at least I know you're being well fed."

"Amongst other things," Daryl teased.

"Eat your dinner, Daryl," his mother ordered.

"Yes, ma'am."

"Well, these chocolate waffles must be something special," Earl said. "I'm in."

"You better enjoy all those carbs," Connie said. "You're going to be back to oatmeal and fruit when we get home."

"I'll be here," Kenneth announced. "I wouldn't miss waffles."

"Who invited you?" Aunt Tillie challenged. "I know I didn't."

"Awe, buttercup, you can't still be angry."

Buttercup? Thistle and I exchanged amused smirks.

"I see what you two are doing," Aunt Tillie warned before turning on Kenneth. "Don't call me buttercup."

"What do you want me to call you?"

"I have a few suggestions," Thistle offered. Clearly she wasn't worried about staying on her best behavior – or Aunt Tillie's good side – any longer.

"Listen, sass mouth, you're pushing your luck."

"She's been like this for days," I said.

"It's because Marcus has been so busy with the fair – and tilling your pot field," Clove said. "She's barely seen him. I think she's going through withdrawal."

Everyone at the table froze. Clove realized what she'd said, but it was too late. "Did I say pot? I meant pea. She's planting a pea field."

"You're on my list," Aunt Tillie announced.

Daryl looked interested. "You have a pot field?" He glanced at Landon. "Can't she be arrested for that?"

"I have no idea where this purported pot field is located," Landon replied. "It's not a federal issue."

"I have glaucoma," Aunt Tillie said. "I need it."

"You don't have glaucoma," I scoffed. "You just like it."

"Be careful, missy," Aunt Tillie shot back. "You've had a rough week. That's not going to keep you off my list."

"Yeah, Bay," Thistle teased. "Aunt Tillie is back and she's badder then ever."

"You've been on my list all week," Aunt Tillie said, causing the color to drain from Thistle's face. "I've only held back because we have guests."

"This is an inn," Daryl said. "Don't you always have guests?"

"Not important guests," I said.

Earl looked pleased. "We're important?"

"Eat your dinner," Connie ordered.

A dish crashed to the floor at the end of the table, causing everyone to jump.

"Did you drop something, Blanche?" Mom asked.

"It wasn't me."

I looked under the table and saw one of the smaller plates in pieces by Blanche's chair. "You probably just knocked it over accidentally."

"I didn't touch it," Blanche protested. "It just flew off the table."

I straightened, sharing a worried look with Landon. "Why don't we go into the parlor for dessert?"

"We're not even done with dinner yet," Mom said, pushing back her chair and getting to her feet. "It will just take me a second to clean up the mess. It was just an accident."

"I did not drop that plate!"

I scanned the room, looking for a hint of white mist. I didn't see any sign of Floyd. A quick look at Aunt Tillie told me she was doing the same. "Anything?"

"If he's here, he's hiding."

"Who's hiding?" Connie asked.

"Nothing," I said. "We were just ... um ... it's nothing."

Landon got to his feet. "I like the dessert-in-the-parlor idea. Let's do that."

Thistle's glass suddenly flew through the air, smashing against the wall and shattering into a thousand pieces.

"What was that?" Earl asked.

"It's that thing, isn't it?" Denny wrung his hands, his face drained of all color.

"It's just dinner theater," I said. "It's nothing."

Something grabbed my hair, wrenching my head to the side. "Ow. Sonofabitch. Ow."

Landon reached for me. "What is it?" An invisible form swatted his hand away. "Okay, I felt that."

Chief Terry stood, reaching for his gun. "What's going on?"

"It's Floyd," I said. "He's here – and he's pissed."

"From what I can tell, he's always pissed," Thistle said.

"Isn't Floyd the dead guy?" Earl asked, clearly confused.

I shifted my eyes in his direction, pulling up short when I saw that Connie was the only one still sitting calmly at the table. What's that about?

Aunt Tillie slammed her hands on the table. "That did it! I'm coming for you, Floyd!" She disappeared through the swinging kitchen door. I had no idea where she was going – or what she was doing – but the sound of more breaking glass drew my attention back to the table.

Dishes flew through the air, smashing against the wall at an alarming rate.

I heard Aunt Tillie again, her voice from the back of the house.

"I'm coming for you, Floyd!"

THIRTY-SEVEN

"What is going on?" Earl asked.

"It's a ghost," Connie replied, evenly. "Or a poltergeist. Given the anger in this room, I'm leaning toward poltergeist."

I felt as if I'd been kicked in the gut. "What?"

"Yeah, what?" Landon faced his mother. "How do you know about that?"

Connie rolled her eyes. "I've known about ghosts and poltergeists for years," she said. "I've known about witches for even longer."

I stumbled backward, Landon's arm shooting out to keep me steady. "You know about witches?"

"Witches aren't real," Clove said, ducking as another plate flew over her head. "We have no idea what you're talking about. We're not witches."

"If you're not witches, then you have a lot of explaining to do," Connie replied. "Because being witches is the only thing that explains everything going on at this inn the past week."

"You know about witches?" Landon's blue eyes were wide with wonder.

"I know about a lot of things, honey," Connie replied. "Witches are only one of them."

"We're not witches," Clove repeated. "Witches aren't real. This is just a mass hallucination." Clove glanced around the room for help. We were all too busy dodging dishes to offer any. "I know what happened. Aunt Tillie probably slipped some pot in our food."

Landon scowled. "Mass drugging is actually worse than being witches, Clove."

"Let it go," Thistle agreed. "We can't exactly hide it."

Clove wrung her hands. "I think everyone is just high."

"Clove, get a grip," Mom ordered. "Now isn't the time for you to freak out."

"Well, when should I freak out?"

"I'm coming for you, Floyd!" Aunt Tillie screeched from the back of the house.

I shot Landon a look. "I have to see what she's doing."

"Go."

I pushed through the kitchen door, Thistle close behind me. "What are you doing?"

"I'm not going to miss this."

"Where's Clove?"

"She's still spinning her pot story," Thistle replied. "She'll catch up."

We found Aunt Tillie gearing up for war in the living room of the family living quarters. She tossed hard hats in our direction. "Suit up."

"Why do we need these?"

"So we look cool," Aunt Tillie said. "After the week you've had, the last thing you need is another head injury. Am I right?"

She had a point. I placed the hat on my head. "So, what do we do?"

"We kill him."

"He's already dead."

"Do you think now is the time to play semantics?"

"I guess not."

"Grab those bags," Aunt Tillie instructed, pointing.

"Are we going to do it here?" Thistle asked, collecting the bags.

"It's too messy," Aunt Tillie replied. "We have to go back to the clearing."

Landon strode into the room, everyone from the dining room following in a line behind him. "What are you going to do?"

"What I should've done days ago," Aunt Tillie said, "give Floyd his due."

"Where?"

"The clearing."

Landon glanced around. "Okay. Let's go."

I wanted to argue with him. I wanted to tell him to stay here. I didn't, though. His face told me that wasn't an option.

"How do we get him to follow?" Chief Terry asked, looking over his shoulder at the sound of another dish breaking.

"He'll follow Bay," Aunt Tillie said. "He's been fixated on her from the beginning."

"I don't like this," Landon said. "She's not bait."

"She's all we have," Aunt Tillie said.

"Why is he fixated on her? You're the one he blames," Landon countered.

"Bay released him," Aunt Tillie said. "He's attached himself to her."

"I didn't release him," I argued. "That was the construction crew."

"You're the first one he saw, though," Aunt Tillie said. "He rushed through you. He must've realized you could see his thoughts when he melded with you. That's why he's stuck close."

"He's not always around, though," I pointed out. "He only shows up occasionally."

"That's because he hasn't figured out how to harness his power yet," Aunt Tillie replied. "When he does that, we're in for a world of hurt."

"It gets worse?" Landon asked.

Aunt Tillie ignored him and focused on me. "You have to give us time to get out there and set up. You have to distract him. Keep him here."

"For how long?"

"Give us ten minutes."

"What are you going to do?"

"Set up a circle."

"We don't have enough people," I said. "We need twelve women. Twelve witches."

"We're going to have to make do."

"Even when I get out there, that's only eight," I reminded her.

"I can count," Aunt Tillie snapped.

Connie stepped forward. "I can help."

Landon was flabbergasted. "You're going to get in a circle with them and chant away a poltergeist?"

"I've done it before. Well, not a poltergeist. I have banished a ghost, though."

Aunt Tillie nodded. "Good. We can use you."

Landon shot a dark look at his mother. "When this is over, we have to talk."

Connie patted her son's arm. "I'm looking forward to it."

Landon turned to Chief Terry. "You lead them out there and get them set up."

"What are you going to do?" Chief Terry asked.

"I'm sticking with Bay."

"No," I protested. "You'll be in danger."

Landon laced his fingers through mine. "We'll be in danger."

I reluctantly nodded. "If you die, I'm going to be really pissed."

Landon gave me a hard, fast kiss. "Right back at you."

"SO, HOW do you keep a poltergeist busy?"

Everyone was gone, led away from the danger by an extremely agitated Chief Terry and a completely deranged Aunt Tillie. It was just Landon and me.

"I have no idea," I replied. "We need to try to keep him from touching us, though."

Landon ducked as a vase collided with the wall above his head. "He's going to run out of things to break before long."

"We can fix most of this once he's gone," I replied.

"Like Harry Potter?" Landon teased.

"Kind of."

"You need to give me a book or something so I can catch up," Landon said, rubbing the bridge of his nose. "I'm so lost."

"Honey, what I've got to teach you can't learn from a book." I stood up straight, pooling energy in my gut, and then pushing it out with my mind. "Dark."

The lights in the room winked out. Landon looked impressed, the moonlight shining through the window illuminating his face. "What else do you have?"

I grabbed his hand, pulling him toward the door. "Let's at least get him outside."

Landon followed. Once we were on the back porch, he straightened his lanky frame. "Where is he?"

"Floyd! Hey, Floyd! You woman-beating loser! I'm out here."

"So we're taunting the poltergeist now?"

I glanced to my left when I saw an empty planter shift. I couldn't see Floyd, but he was obviously trying to lift it. He didn't have the strength. Yet. If his anger built, though, it would only be a matter of minutes.

"How long has it been?"

Landon glanced at his watch. "Six minutes. How long will it take us to get to the clearing?"

"About two minutes."

"So we have to stall for two more minutes?"

"Yep."

"Any ideas?"

I frowned. "Just one."

Landon sighed. "I'm not going to like this, am I?"

"Probably not." I closed my eyes, calling for power again. "Reveal." When I opened my eyes, I found Floyd floating in front of me, only a foot separating his anger and my fear. Crap.

I held up my hand. "Floyd, I didn't do anything to you."

"Really? You're trying to talk rationally with the angry ghost?" Landon was nonplussed.

I ignored him. "Aunt Tillie didn't do anything to you either. You need to let it go and move on. There's something out there for you, something better than this." I had no idea whether I was telling him the truth. I just wanted to give him something to think about. "You need to let this go. You need to move on."

Floyd's ghostly hands reached out for me, causing me to take a step back and smack into Landon's chest, tipping the hard hat off of my head. He wrapped his arms around me from behind. "This isn't working."

"Floyd," I tried again. "Nothing can make this right."

Floyd screeched, causing me to raise my hands to cover my ears.

"Can we run now?" Landon asked, his lips close to my ear.

Floyd was moving toward me again. "Yep. Let's go."

Landon gripped my hand and started pulling. I followed him into the darkness, letting instinct lead me to the clearing. I risked a glance over my shoulder during the trek. Floyd was still following. He was at a safe distance, but he wasn't going to be dissuaded. Not now.

Relief washed over me when we tumbled into the clearing and my gaze fell on Aunt Tillie.

"We're ready," she said, motioning to the spot beside her.

Landon reluctantly let go of my hand and joined all of the men at the edge of the clearing.

I stepped into the circle, joining hands with Connie and Aunt Tillie, and then lifted my arms into the sky in unison with the other women in the circle. We were one now.

"I call on the four powers of this land," Aunt Tillie intoned, signifying there was no time to call to each directional power individually as we usually did. "We have might. We have right. We have power."

"Why do I feel like he's the one with power?" Chief Terry asked, clearly nervous. Landon shushed him, never moving his eyes from me.

Floyd advanced on me, paying no heed to the others joined in the circle. I was the one he wanted.

"I call on the four powers of this land," Aunt Tillie said. "Banish Floyd Gunderson to his fate. Make him see the terror he has wrought.

AMANDA M. LEE

All the fear that he caused, all the pain that he inflicted, let him relive it now. So mote it be."

"So mote it be," I echoed, watching in wonderment as Connie repeated the words.

Our joined hands illuminated the night sky, an explosion of bright light engulfing us all. Floyd tried to move – away this time – but the light drew him in. He screamed, an otherworldly sound that would plague my nightmares for weeks to come, and then he was absorbed into the white circle.

The light brightened briefly and then flamed out, leaving nothing but scorched earth where Floyd had been drawn into the circle.

I let out a sigh, letting go of Connie and Aunt Tillie's hands, and wrapping my arms around myself to ward off the sudden cold. Landon's arms were there, too, within a few seconds. "Are you okay?"

"I'm good."

"That was amazing," Daryl announced. "That was awesome."

"I can think of a few other words," Blanche replied.

"My Tillie is badass," Kenneth announced, swooping in for a kiss, which Aunt Tillie easily sidestepped.

"Is he gone?" Denny asked, clearly not as enamored with magic as his brother. "He's gone, right?"

Mom patted his arm reassuringly. "He's gone."

Landon narrowed his eyes as he regarded his mother. "We have to talk."

"Don't be such a baby," Connie said, laughing. "This was fun. I forgot how much fun this was."

I shrugged as Landon searched my face for an answer that would satisfy him. "It was fun."

"So," Chief Terry said. "Who's up for dessert?"

THIRTY-EIGHT

"You were part of a coven in college?" Landon said the words over breakfast the next morning. I still didn't think they were sinking in.

"I think coven is a harsh word," Connie replied. "We were more dabblers."

"I hate dabblers," Aunt Tillie said. I kicked her under the table. "We couldn't have done it without you," she said, rolling her eyes.

I smiled at Connie. "I agree."

Aunt Tillie glared at me. "You're mine in another couple of hours," she warned.

Landon met her gaze. "I think, given all that's happened, you're going to take everyone's name off your list and let this one slide."

"What makes you say that?"

"If you had told everyone the truth from the beginning, we might've been able to stop all of this earlier," he replied.

Aunt Tillie snorted. "If I had told the truth then I would be in jail. We wouldn't know the truth if Floyd hadn't shown it to Bay in that last vision."

Landon wagged his finger. "Don't push me."

"Don't you push me."

AMANDA M. LEE

Landon rolled his eyes and forked another bite of chocolate waffles into his mouth before turning back to his mother. "So you were in a sorority of witches in college? I still can't fathom it."

"It didn't seem strange," Connie said. "It was mostly fun and games. We didn't have a lot of the real life-and-death stuff that everyone seems to be dealing with here on a regular basis."

"I feel like I've been lied to my whole life," Denny announced.

"You'll get over it," Connie said. "Nothing that has happened here changes your life. You need to grow up and suck it up."

"It changes everything." I felt bad for Denny. There's nothing worse than having your religious beliefs challenged. He'd built his life around his faith. This was going to be hard for him.

"No it doesn't," Connie countered. "Good and evil still exist. You've chosen the side of good. This doesn't change that."

"But … witches."

"These witches have chosen the side of good, too," Connie pointed out. "You should like that. They're not evil – well, most of the time."

"I'm never going to be able to wrap my head around this," Landon muttered.

I leaned my head against his shoulder for a moment. "You'll get used to it."

"How can you be sure?"

"You got used to me."

"I don't think that was my choice," Landon argued. "I think that was … ."

"Fate?" Aunt Tillie interjected.

"Maybe," Landon said, brushing a quick kiss against my temple. "I just don't think I had much of a choice in the matter. Once I saw you, I had to have you. Your family was just an added … bonus."

"I like a man who knows when to let the big questions answer themselves," Aunt Tillie said, "even if he's a pain in the ass most of the time."

"Did you know, Dad?" Daryl asked.

Earl chuckled, wrapping an arm around his wife's shoulders. "How do you think she snagged me?"

Everyone at the table laughed. Even Landon. Connie looked pleased with herself, and I couldn't help but look at her in a whole new light.

AN HOUR later everyone gathered in front of the inn to say goodbye.

Landon hugged each member of his family in turn, lingering with his mother. She kissed his cheek when she finally pulled away. "You have a good one here."

Landon shifted a look in my direction. "Most of the time."

"She's a good girl," Connie said. "Be good to her."

"Hey, I'm the angel where this family is concerned," Landon said. "I deserve an award. Or, at least, a special dinner with all of my favorites for a change."

"Tell me what they are," Mom said. "I'll make them tonight."

"Don't tease me," Landon warned.

Mom rolled her eyes. "You're never going to survive around here if you don't just say what you want."

Connie laughed. "He likes tuna noodle casserole and coconut cream pie."

Thistle made a face.

"It's his favorite," Connie said.

Mom smiled as she hugged Connie. "Consider it done. I'll make sure he has it at least once a month."

It was my turn. Connie reached for me, giving me a warm hug. "Take care of my boy."

"I'll try. Luckily my mom does most of the cooking. He'd starve otherwise."

Connie smiled. "Be happy."

"We will. I hope."

"You will," Connie said, winking. "Happy comes in many different forms – even in the form of witches."

Once they were gone, Landon turned to me, his face relaxed and happy. "So, how long do I have?"

"Until what?" I asked, puzzled. "It's going to take them most of the day to make your special dinner. I hate warm tuna by the way. It's fine for a sandwich. Casserole is a whole other thing."

"Screw food. That's not what I'm hungry for," Landon said, poking me in the ribs. "How long do I have?"

I smirked. "Until tomorrow morning."

"Well, that's good then," Landon said. "We can spend the day in bed. Then I can have my special dinner to bulk up on carbs. Then we have the whole night. You better get yourself ready. Drink some fluids."

I started running, his laughter chasing me all the way back to the guesthouse.

Aunt Tillie still had her list, I reminded myself. The Dragonfly would be opening soon and that was a whole other mess to deal with. That was on top of the Clove situation, of course. For now, though, life was good.

Printed in Great Britain
by Amazon